The Stumblebu

Part One – The Beginning.

Michael Elmet

The Stumblebum Chronicles. Part one – The beginning.

Michael Elmet

This book is a work of fiction. All characters herein described exist only in the author's imagination with no relation to any persons bearing the same name, living or dead, known or unknown to the author. All names, characters, places, and incidents are either used fictitiously or are the product of the author's imagination. Any resemblance to any person or persons, living or dead, is purely coincidental and unintended.

Cover art by: Canva

First Edition: 2020

ISBN #: 978-0-244-23529-1

Publisher Mooncat Press

www.stumblebumchronicles.com

Contents:

Chapter One

'Hello dear, how was your journey?' Mystical Maggie greeted her nephew as he put his bag down and gazed around her shop.

'Oh, alright I suppose, a bit tiring though.' He replied as his attention strayed.

Auntie Maggie's little shop, *Magnolia's Magic Memorabilia,* was located in the front of her house, a musty smelling old rambling Tudor building with narrow stairways and with wooden panels on all the walls and with tiny leaded windows. The shop was full of crystals, crystal balls, tarot cards, dream catchers and a range of other strange and exotic stuff. The smell of joss sticks perfumed the shop and a small income came from the sale of these items. She also charged for her mystical advice to her clients, some of whom would attend her séances in the room immediately above the shop.

The lad browsed around the shop's stock looking at the fascinating items on sale. He came across a bookrack with lots of books on magic and spells and became preoccupied with them as his auntie busied herself at the big old fashioned till. He picked up a book entitled *'A beginners guide to magic and sorcery'* which intrigued him and he thumbed through its pages with interest.

'Auntie, do many people in Bilge on Sea buy these books on magic?' he queried.

‘Oh yes dear, there is a long tradition of magic and witchcraft here on this part of the South Coast. In fact there are several witches covens in the town and various groups of people who practice the old religion, a pagan form of magic, as well as the Guild of Wizards and the academy. Some of them are good customers and often come to the shop quite regularly.’ She informed him.

‘Why don’t you take the book up with you to look at in your bedroom before dinner dear, in preparation for your entrance to the academy? It would be a good idea to have some practice before then.’ Auntie Maggie said to him as she observed his interest in the books.

He had been given the bedroom at the top of the house above two narrow wooden flights of stairs. It was furnished with a large four poster bed and had bookshelves either side of a little fireplace and redbrick chimney breast. He went up to his room and eagerly took his book of spells to study at the table in front of his bedroom window which overlooked the seafront with its little harbour and gave a good view of the variety of boats and fishing vessels that bobbed about on the sea beyond. He spent the next few days immersed in his studies and attempted to practice some of the simpler spells in his impatience to get on with the task of becoming a successful and powerful wizard.

His studies, alas, did not at first produce much in the way of any magic or sorcery. He could not quite get the hang of the precise instructions regarding charms, potions and spells. He organised his room to accommodate a variety of artefacts and included some concoctions in bottles and jars. He arranged these items along the bookshelves that covered the panelled wall either side of the old fireplace at the far end of the bedroom beyond his four-poster bed.

Frustrated and annoyed by his lack of progress he laid the blame on the regular disturbances caused by the activity in the room below which Auntie Maggie used for séances. He complained bitterly to her and implored her to cease holding the séances as the chatter of her clients and the loud footsteps on the wooden stairs on these occasions disturbed his concentration. Auntie Maggie pointed out that this was a good part of her income so he would have to adapt. Perhaps he could wear some earplugs?

He sulkily retreated to his room and suffered these indignities in more or less silence over the coming weeks and felt more and more niggled by it all and his temperament became even less tolerant of adults in general, given how selfish and unreasonable they always seemed to be. He looked forward to the time when he would be able to command their respect and awe due to his anticipated fantastic magical powers.

He would sit by his window reading his book of spells with a huge wad of cotton wool thrust into each ear and it was during one of these silent study sessions one evening that a movement caught the corner of his eye. He looked up from his book and turned his head to be startled to see the spectre of a First American chief who appeared to float in the corner by the bookshelves as he stared straight at him and mouthed silent commands. Taken aback somewhat, and rather bewildered, he remembered the cotton wool. After he had removed the earplugs he heard the apparition say '…the clock on the mantelpiece.'

'What clock, what are you talking about?'

The apparition rolled its eyes in exasperation and spoke again in a slow deliberate voice.

'I said that Uncle William says that the money is in an envelope behind the clock on the mantelpiece.'

'Ah, I think you want to be in the séance, it's in the room below this.' the boy pointed to the floor.

The apparition took in this information for a moment, looked somewhat embarrassed and slowly glided into the floor until only the tip of a single feather hovered briefly before it too sank beneath the floorboards.

* * * * * * *

One morning, some days after the incident with the spectre, Auntie Maggie informed her nephew that she had had a visit from an important wizard and a member of the guild of wizards. He had arranged for his admittance the next day to the academy and provided a list of protocols of dress and behaviour which the lad had to observe. Upon his arrival he was to wear his wizard's cape and provide the name with which he wished to use as his wizard's name from then on, a sort of *nom de plume*.

'But Auntie I haven't got a wizards cape to wear and I can't think of a name either.' he whined.

'Well, I am sure that we can come up with a suitable name,' she reassured him

'...and I can easily make you a lovely cape so don't worry about a thing dear.'

Sure enough, the next morning just before breakfast Auntie Maggie presented him with his wizard's cape. She had made it from one of an old pair of purple velvet curtains that used to hang in one of the rooms behind the shop and she had adorned it with a selection of stars and magic symbols from her shop stock and attached a large Scottish sporran pin to serve as a clasp just below the neck.

'Umm, I don't know.' he said as he scrutinised the cape.

'Try it on' Auntie Maggie urged as she held the cape aloft.

'It's a bit long don't you think?' he glanced at the extra foot or so of material which circled his feet.

'Oh that's all right, that's how they wear them. It gives the wizards an air of mystery and importance.' she said,

'...and anyway it will allow for you growing!'

'Mmm, OK then, if you are sure.'

'Oh, and I have good news on the name you wanted to come up with. One of my spirit guides said it would be an honour if you were to take him as your personal spiritual adviser provided you take his name for yours. He came into your room once by mistake. A First American chief, very important. His name is Rumbling Drum, a good, strong name to take as a wizard, what do you think?'

The boy mulled this over, repeating the name to himself a few times to get the feel of it.

'Mmm, yes, I think that will do. Sounds important doesn't it?'

After he had finished breakfast the boy went up to his room to get himself ready for his interview. He put on his favourite blue sweatshirt with a Superman logo emblazoned across the chest as he thought he would look 'cool'. He also wore his baggy three quarter length cargo pants with huge patch pockets in places where one would not expect to find pockets and his favourite trainers to complete his 'cool' look.

'Don't you think you ought to wear something more formal for your first day dear?' Auntie Maggie suggested.

'This looks cool!' he insisted, somewhat hurt by his auntie's implied criticism.

'Well if that's what you really want to wear dear I'm sure it will be all right.'

As he proudly made his way along the winding cobbled street and as he passed the various shops and cafes his cape dragged litter and refuse along which followed with a loud clatter in his wake. This cacophony attracted the attention of a stray alley cat. Mesmerised by the motion of the cape's hem the cat pounced and gripped it with its front claws and kicked vigorously with its back claws as it subjected it to a vicious attack.

As he proceeded to the entrance of the Academy of the Guild of Wizards he tried to ignore this indignity but the frenzied cat dragged itself along, kicking and hissing with each step. When he arrived at the door he shook the accumulated debris from the hem of his cape, aimed a spiteful kick at the cat and rapped on the huge wooden door with its large brass knocker which was below a small hatch. After some time he heard footsteps approach from within before the hatch slid open and a pair of eyes squinted at him for a moment before the hatch again snapped shut.

A few moments after this he heard the sound of heavy bolts being drawn and the loud creak of hinges as the door was opened by a lad about his age who wore a red fez and black cape, which draped down to just below his knees.

‘Oh hello, you must be the new boy.’ The lad scrutinised him from head to toe. His eyes rested on the hem of the cape where the stray cat sat washing its face with its paws.

‘You are not allowed to bring pets in here. Rules!’

After he shooed the cat away the boy followed his guide into the building. The great door slammed shut and the lad with the red fez led him along a corridor into a small room where an old wizard wearing a tall pointed hat was perched on a high stool behind a sort of lectern. He stooped over the lectern as he scribbled into a huge leather bound ledger with a plumed quill, which he frequently had to dip in to a large pot of ink.

Looking up from his work the old wizard peered over his wire-rimmed glasses at the two lads and put his quill down beside the great book. He then picked up a large trumpet shaped goat’s horn and held it to his ear.

‘So you are the new candidate for the academy are you?’ the old man scrutinised the boy with some disdain.

‘Do you have a name for me?’ he picked up the quill and turned the pages of the great book until he came to a long list of names, the guild’s catalogue of all of its wizards, past and present.

‘Yes sir, my name is to be Rumbling Drum.’ The boy announced proudly.’

‘Eh, what’s that, Underdone! What kind of a name is that for a wizard eh?’

‘No, no, not *Underdone*, it’s *Rumbling Drum*.’ he informed the old man, a little put out by this unintended sleight.

‘Well why didn’t you say so in the first place?’ the old wizard scratched with his quill onto the page at the bottom of the list.

‘He’s a bit deaf these days.’ whispered his guide as he led him out of the room and back into the corridor …’and getting deafer by the day.’

‘My name’s Secundus by the way, it’s my wizard name. We are only allowed to use our wizards’ names from now on. The old boy you just saw is the Scribe Grand Magister, very important. He keeps all the archives and records and conducts any ceremonies. Your naming ceremony will be in about an hour in the Great Hall of Wizards after I have taken you to the library to get you kitted out.'

The pair then weaved their way along a labyrinth of corridors and stairways until they arrived at the library. It was a high ceilinged hall, lined with rows of bookshelves creaking under the weight of huge, leather bound tomes and with pigeonholes stuffed with parchment scrolls. Stained glass windows were set high up against the far wall and illustrated with magic symbols and runes, above a massive glass fronted rococo cabinet containing a display of a variety of wizards' headgear. The row of hats sloped in order of height and importance from one side to the other, from the tallest pointed cone shaped hat right down to the smallest, a red fez at the lower end.

Secundus pointed at the fez in the cabinet which was similar to the one he had on his own head and explained that these were for the novice wizards who would, over time, progress through some of the other various taller hats as they gained in proficiency.

'Yours will be awarded to you at the ceremony after the brother wizards have welcomed you into their company.'

The two lads were approached by an official looking wizard wearing a blue square based pyramid shaped hat adorned with runic symbols.

'He's the Academy Scribe, a sort of librarian.' Secundus nodded to the official.

'Here is the latest new boy for you sir. Come to get kitted out before his initiation.'

The Academy Scribe gave the boy the same look of disdain as the Scribe Grand Magister had given, bade the pair to follow him as he strode over to a desk covered in piles of books and an assortment of boxes and caskets. He rummaged amongst this chaos and emerged with a small curved topped casket with a brass handle on top of its lid and a red leather bound book.

The Academy Scribe handed the casket and book to Secundus and instructed him to explain procedures to the newcomer.

Secundus carried the items over to a nearby table and they both sat down beside each other as he unlocked the casket with its key and opened the lid to reveal an odd mixture of items. Amongst them was a pot of ink with a cork firmly wedged into its neck, a few feathered quills and about half a dozen scrolls of parchment rolled up together and secured by a green ribbon which was tied in a neat little bow. There were also a few other items which included some herbs and spices and a short willow twig. Secundus explained that this was his personal magic wand which he had to first charge with magic power.

'It doesn't look very powerful.' The new boy grumbled.

'Oh, it will be but you have to do a little ritual to charge it with magic energy. You can change their shape and size with practice. My wand looks like a conductor's baton. You will find it all in that red book. There are a number of rituals, spells and charms in there as well as other instructions about the academy and its requirements from novice wizards. It is very informative so you must study it thoroughly when you get home. Speaking of rituals, it's about time we got down to the Great Hall of Wizards for your initiation ceremony, I bet you're looking forward to it eh?'

The lads got up and descended the complexity of stairways and corridors until they arrived eventually somewhere in the bowels of the academy building. They approached The Great Hall of Wizards by a short tunnel lit with candles which flickered from sconces set in the crumbled stonework of the walls, dimly lighting the way to a large oak door.

This led into a vaulted chamber also lit by candles set along its walls, which had benches and settles against them at the far end of the hall for the company of wizards to sit on. Just to the side of the door a raised rostrum supported a high table with a large gilded throne behind it upon which was seated the Scribe Grand Magister who busily thumbed through the pages of the huge book which listed the register of wizards.

Secundus took his charge before the Scribe Grand Magister and gave a low bow and elbowed the new novice in the ribs as if to urge him to do likewise, which he did, if not somewhat awkwardly. They heard a shuffling amongst the assembled wizards as they rose to their feet and the boys turned around to face them. The old Scribe Grand Magister got up from his high seat and stood behind the boys and held the great book aloft rather unsteadily.

'Brother Wizards' and members of the Sacred Guild,' he intoned,

'I salute you and welcome you to this most sacred of ceremonies.'

'Hail Scribe Grand Magister!' They all chanted as if with one voice.

'We are here today to welcome our newest novice wizard to our great Academy.'

'Hail to our great Academy!' The voices again rose loudly in unison

The old wizard squinted at the open page of the great book.

'I present to you, the assembled brotherhood of wizards this supplicant. Please welcome - STUMBLEBUM!'

Horrified at the massive error by the deaf old wizard the boy opened his mouth to protest but was drowned out by the raised voices of the assembly.

'Hail Stumblebum! Hail Stumblebum! Hail Stumblebum!' they roared as the offending name echoed around the chamber.

The boy tried to protest again but as his mouth opened to speak he felt something crunch down on his head followed by a soggy sensation as the old Scribe Grand Magister cracked a large goose egg on to his cranium.

'A new wizard is hatched! I anoint this boy 'Stumblebum'. Long may his spells be effective.'

'Hail Stumblebum! Hail Stumblebum! Hail Stumblebum!

The old wizard rammed a novice's fez onto Stumblebum's now sticky head and ended the ceremony as he snapped shut the great book.

The new novice turned to Secundus with a look of sheer anguish on his face.

'He's done it again, the deaf old twonk!' Secundus exclaimed.

'Sorry about that mate but you are stuck with the name now that it's entered into the register of wizards and the ceremony is over. I'm afraid you will just have to get used to it.'

'Stumblebum? Stumblebum? I can't have a name like Stumblebum!' The boy was beside himself.

'Oh, I don't know it's not too bad. You will get used to it. You can always tell people that you have German ancestry and you pronounce it *Shtoom-bell-baum.*'

This did not help. Stumblebum was now lost for words. This day was not turning out the way he had hoped, not at all.

'Don't worry. You're not the only one to end up with a wrong name.' Secundus explained.

'See the youth sitting over there?' he pointed to a striking looking novice with staring blue eyes and long, dark Teddy-boy style sideburns and thick curly black hair which wildly tumbled out from under his fez nearly down to his shoulders.

'That's Morris, only he wanted to be called Boris but the Scribe Grand Magister misheard him and it came out as Morris. It could have been worse, though, the old boy nearly named him 'Doris' so he felt he had got away lightly. A good few of the later enrolees have ended up with misheard names as the Scribe Grand Magister has become deafer. He will not wear a modern hearing aid. Most of the older wizards prefer us to use traditional, antique looking implements. They think it looks more mysterious. That's why we have to use quills and ink, even fountain pens are frowned on here.'

'Then there are those two over there.' Secundus nodded towards a couple of podgy, surly looking novices seated side by side in one corner.

'They are brothers, you wouldn't guess, would you?' he went on.

'I have never come across such sibling rivalry as exists between those two, they absolutely hate each other. They always try to outdo or upstage one another. Anyway, when the time came for their naming ceremony which they had at the same time, the one on the left had decided to be "Moonbeam Light" which the Scribe Grand Magister had misheard as "Mooning Mike" so he is now stuck with it.' Secundus explained with some relish.

'It was even worse for his brother though.' Secundus chuckled fiendishly.

'He tried to surpass his brother's choice of name and arrogantly called himself 'Great Wizard' but the Scribe Grand Magister anointed him as 'Breaks Wind!' To be honest, I think on that occasion the old boy did it on purpose, he hates precocious novices!'

None of this gossip did anything to lift the boy's spirits in any way as he shuffled out of the chamber. Secundus led the way through a few more corridors until they reached a small wooden door which led out into an alleyway at the side of the building.

'You are allowed to have the rest of the day off after your initiation ceremony. From now on you are to use this door to come and go from, it is for wizards use only. There is a key for it on a chord in your casket. Good luck with your studies mate.' Secundus left him in the alleyway and closed the door behind him.

It was with a heavy heart that the crestfallen Stumblebum made his way out of the alley and shuffled his way home. As he passed by the great front door of the Academy of the Guild of Wizards' he hardly noticed the cat sitting on the doorstep patiently awaiting his return.

He also hardly noticed the cats renewed onslaught of his cape's hem as he trudged back to his auntie's shop. She called out to him as he slammed the front door behind him and stomped noisily up the stairs to his bedroom.

'How did it all go on your first day at the academy dear?' she enquired.

'I don't want to talk about it!' he yelled back down the stairs as he slammed the bedroom door and flung himself onto his bed and stared for a long time at the ceiling beyond the bed's overhanging canopy and muttered 'Stumblebum' over and over again to himself.

Chapter Two

The following morning having spent much of the evening before in his bedroom in a massive sulk Stumblebum arose from his bed early and went over to the casket on the table by the window and took from it the inkwell, a quill and a sheet of parchment. He dipped the quill into the ink and scrawled onto the parchment in big letters 'STUMBLEBUM (Pronounced Shtoom-bell-baum)' under which he then wrote 'WIZARD' before he attached it to the outside of his bedroom door with drawing pins. After he had done this he went downstairs for breakfast in a slightly better mood than he had been in for most of the previous day.

When he went in for breakfast he was astonished to find the stray cat from the day before sitting on a high stool in front of the breakfast table beside his auntie and eating a kipper from a little bowl.

'What's that creature doing here?' He demanded, hardly able to believe what he was seeing.

'He followed you in yesterday. I thought the academy must have given him to you or something. He is such a lovely well behaved cat. Have you given him a name yet dear?'

'I'll give him a name, how about 'Get Lost You Mangy Moggy!'

'Oh, he's such a sweetie, we've got to keep him now. He seems to like you and besides, lots of wizards have cats, they sort of help with the spells and things and give the wizards an air of importance.' Auntie Maggie said persuasively.

'I suppose he could stay' Stumblebum begrudgingly agreed as he liked the idea of having an air of importance.

'... so what shall we call him then?'

'How about "Kipper"? He's a sort of kipper colour and he seems to like eating kippers!'

Although Stumblebum could not fault his auntie's logic, nonetheless dismissed the name as unsuitable for the pet of an important wizard.

'Nah, that's a stupid name. He needs a more appropriate kind of name. Something that has a hint of rank and position about it, a name that would go with a successful wizard and have a ring of mystery about it. A bit more romantic than 'Kipper'!

'How about Skipper then? I once had a little dog called Skipper and it had a similar temperament to your cat, really loveable he was, and a skipper is a sea captain so that would be important.'

'Well, that sounds better, I suppose it will do.' He conceded as he sat down for his breakfast with some anticipation, ready to eat something substantial.

'I think I shall have a kipper please Auntie, they smell delicious.'

'Oh, I'm afraid that there are no kippers left. Kipper, or rather Skipper, had the last one, bless him he seemed to be starving hungry, the poor little mite. I can get you some porridge?'

As Auntie Maggie busied herself making a bowl of porridge for Stumblebum, he glared at the cat and already regretted the decision to keep him. The cat looked up as he washed his face and returned the gaze with what seemed to be a look of smug, self-satisfaction on his feline features.

Stumblebum fell into a silent sulk as he ate his porridge then went back upstairs to get ready for his day at the academy. When he returned wearing his cape and egg stained fez the cat sat up and stared at the hem of the cape with a glazed expression and then stood up to accompany the boy.

'You're not coming.' he quickly tried to slam the door shut, but Skipper was too fast for him.

It is a commonly held observation that most cats appear to have the ability to be in two places at the same time. We have all experienced the situation where we get up from our seat to go into the kitchen to make a cup of tea whilst the cat is soundly asleep in front of the fire. A moment or so later we enter the kitchen to find the cat sat waiting by the refrigerator all alert and looking expectantly for some treat. This is always quite a mystery as we never notice the cat pass us by, therefore one can conclude that all cats have the ability to be either invisible or in two places at once. This is one of life's great riddles!

Consequently as soon as Stumblebum had slammed the door in the cat's face he then turned around to find Skipper sat in the street in anticipation for the journey to the academy. The cat seemed to have taken possession of the cape as his own and so as soon as Stumblebum got into his stride Skipper once again attacked the hem as it sashayed along the street.

When he arrived at the alley he shooed Skipper away then let himself in by the little door with the key, which now hung around his neck, and tried to remember his way to the library. When he eventually arrived he found a number of novices seated at tables around the hall as they read or scribbled notes. Secundus read a book at a table close to the door and looked up and smiled as Stumblebum drew up a seat next to him.

'You found your way here alright then?' he said cheerfully.

'I got here with some difficulty but I think I will remember better next time.'

Secundus nodded towards a notice board next to the library door with a number of parchment notices pinned to it. He pointed to one of them in particular.

'There's an interesting talk being given in the lecture hall by Morris this morning, you should attend. I'm going to it. It is a part of his examination for his upgrade to the next stage. It should be a good lecture. Morris is quite a laugh when he gets going. I'll show you the way there if you like'

Stumblebum agreed to go with him as he was still a new boy and felt more comfortable being with Secundus whom he found to be quite a friendly chap.

A little later both lads entered the lecture hall and found a place to sit about halfway up the sloping rows of benches so that they could get a good view of the coming proceedings.

Stumblebum was feeling much better now and a bit exited at being at his first lesson in magic. After more novices came in and found seats for themselves Morris arrived carrying an assortment of sticks of various lengths. He placed these on the table and arranged them in rows then welcomed the audience to his lecture. A senior wizard wearing a tall stovepipe hat and carrying a clipboard had accompanied him into the lecture theatre. He took his place at a chair in one corner behind a small table, produced a pot of ink and a quill and placed them side by side in front of him.

Morris smiled at his audience and after he had rearranged the sticks more to his satisfaction began his address.

'Today's lecture is concerned mainly with magic wands, how to care for them and store them and, most importantly, how to give them their initial charge of magical energy.'

'You will see in front of me here a selection of implements that are often used as personal wands for wizards and also have been in common usage over the ages by other sorcerers and witches.' He picked up some of the samples and held them up for inspection.

'As you can see, a wand can be any size within reason and is a useful instrument in the execution of spells and other magic. It is important that the wand be ritually charged with magic by its owner by way of the prescribed instructions you will find in your handbooks.'

Morris took one of the smaller sticks from the selection of walking sticks, swagger sticks, broom handles, batons and even a large lollipop stick that he had laid out on the table. He placed it on the edge of the table and positioned it closer to him then went on to explain.

'Magic wands were often disguised in past centuries due to persecution, mainly of witches, and so they were disguised so that they did not betray their owners. Witches, for instance, would conceal their wands by tying twigs to them so that they resembled brooms, thereby hiding the magic symbols they had carved on them. Even today, in our more enlightened times, many wizards like to disguise their wands in order to be discrete. My personal favourite is the lollipop stick, though you have to be careful carving it as they have a tendency to break when least expected.'

'I am now going to demonstrate how to levitate your wand and again I give the example of the witches who would perform this magic on their broomsticks so as to use them as transportation from time to time. Our friends in the orient would do the same with their magic carpets using a similar principle. Now pay close attention.'

Morris went over to the stick he had placed in front of him earlier and dramatically extended his arms and held his hands over it. At this moment a flutter of playing cards fell from out of his jacket sleeve. They displayed an ace of spades on each of them which brought a guffaw of laughter from the audience. Morris looked rather put out and hastily scooped them up and put them in his jacket pocket and gave an embarrassed cough as he did so.

Secundus leaned over and whispered to Stumblebum.

'Morris hires himself out as a part time stage magician in order to make some money on the side. He sometimes blurs the boundaries between stage magic tricks and real magic.'

Morris now muttered several incantations as he waved his hands over the stick and, with beads of perspiration on his forehead as he concentrated intensely, slowly drew his hands upwards and away from the stick as it gradually rose from the table. Morris got it to hover just below the ceiling and for good measure had it perform a couple of circuits around the lecture theatre before finally guiding it back to its earlier position on the table.

'You will find the incantations in your little red handbook.' He informed the students as they applauded him enthusiastically.

Morris then went on to explain the ritual needed to charge the wands with magic energy and a few other useful pointers, again advising them to refer to the red book if in doubt.

He decided to conclude his talk with a demonstration of his skill with his own personal wand. He reached under his cape before theatrically whipping out a short black, silver tipped baton with a flourish. The baton immediately turned into a posy of flowers much to Morris's embarrassment. He stared at the bunch of flowers in surprise and then dropped them quickly to the floor before he again fumbled about under his cape and finally produced his real wand. The novices laughed loudly at this blunder as the adjudicator scribbled a good deal of notes on to his clipboard.

Deciding that a demonstration at this point might do more damage to his reputation, Morris speedily brought his lecture to its conclusion, gathered up his sticks and left the theatre with some haste.

For the remainder of that day at the academy Stumblebum could not stop thinking about Morris's demonstration and was impatient to get to work on his own wand. All day his mind kept returning to his wand and the fun he would have with it once he had charged it with magic.

As soon as he got back home he went straight up to his room and found the pages in his little red book concerning wands. He read the relevant section several times over then went down for his teatime meal, after which he intended to make a start on his magic by energising his wand into a powerful tool.

The instructions in the book had recommended that when conducting any rituals, ceremonies etc. it was auspicious to do so in a natural setting such as a wood, a meadow or near to the sea and preferably under the light of a moon in order to harness the energy of these natural phenomena.

Stumblebum put on his cape and fez, took the willow twig out of the casket and secreted it in one of the many patch pockets in his cargo pants and decided to go down to the little pebble beach at the side of the small harbour below his bedroom window. It was not quite dark yet but the moon was clearly in the sky and one or two stars just beginning to flicker with dim light so this was good enough.

He looked around to be certain that no one was about and went down to the water's edge where the sea was gently lapping with small ripple like waves. Here he took out his wand and dipped it into the sea for a moment so as to engage it with the natural power and then held it aloft and pointed it toward the moon. For a few moments he struggled to remember the appropriate incantation so he just remained still as he stood and pointed his stick at the moon for what seemed to be a long time before he remembered the spell. As he uttered the magic words, a small wave broke over his feet and soaked his trainers, soaked his feet and caused him to lose some concentration.

The spell seemed to be working, however, as Stumblebum could feel the wand tingle in his hand, sleight at first but getting stronger until it almost jumped from his grip. He concentrated very hard and attempted to make the stick become larger and change shape, hopefully into something impressive.

As the magic energy surged through the wand a wavy tendril several inches long grew from the end of it. Startled by this he closed his eyes and concentrated with all of his might and then opened his eyes to have a look. The tendril had now grown two little buds on the end which then opened to form a couple of little leaves before the wand gave one last shudder and then ceased to tingle.

Stumblebum remained on the little beach for a long time with soggy feet and holding his wand aloft and staring at it. He was very disappointed. He tried the incantation again several times but to no avail. The wand remained as a small twig with leaves sprouting out of the end.

Eventually his feet got cold in the evening air so he gave up and squelched his way back to the house. He put the wand back into the casket and consoled himself with the thought that at least he had empowered it and would be able to make magic with it now. Perhaps, as he got better at it he could try again and make it into a more impressive wand but right now it would have to suffice.

He wondered if his spirit guide might be able to give advice regarding the wand so he went back downstairs and spoke to Auntie Maggie asking how he could summon the spirit.

'Oh, I meant to tell you dear, I've got some rather bad news on that topic. Rumbling Drum flew into a bit of a hissy fit when he heard that you had failed to take on his name. He was rather insulted so withdrew his offer to be your guide. I did try to persuade some of the other First American spirits to do it, but in an act of solidarity with Rumbling Drum they too refused.' Auntie Maggie informed him.

'There is a bit of good news though,' she went on.

'...another spirit offered to be your guide. Well, he was the only one left really, a gentleman from ancient China. He is a very friendly chap and I am sure you will get on with him. Shall I try to contact him later and get him to visit you in your room?'

'Yes I suppose so,' said Stumblebum moodily as he had been hoping for an important chief as his personal adviser. Still, perhaps a Chinese mandarin would be good. He mulled this over as he went upstairs to do some more reading.

When he got to his bedroom he found Skipper curled up in the middle of his bed fast asleep. He left him there since he had a few hours of studying to attend to before he retired. He then sat by the window at his table and scrutinised the section on wands in his red book again.

As he closed the book some time later, he was about to throw Skipper off his bed when some vapours materialised in the corner by the bookshelf and then they half-solidified into a group of hostile looking First Americans, with Rumbling Drum standing at the front with his arms folded across his chest and a fierce look on his countenance.

Rumbling Drum raised his arm, pointed straight at the bewildered novice and declared, not without some malice,

'Stumblebum! STUMBLEBUM! Pah!'

'Pah!' The other chiefs snarled, before the whole group faded out of sight.

This was quite disconcerting to Stumblebum as he felt that there was no need for that kind of behaviour towards him, after all it wasn't his fault the Scribe Grand Magister had got his name wrong. He felt quite aggrieved and made a mental note to tell his auntie to admonish them the next time she held a séance.

He decided to turn in early and was about to throw Skipper off his bed when the cat stiffened, arched his back and shot his tail into the air and hissed as his hackles stood on end. Stumblebum looked up to see what had troubled Skipper and was startled to see the spirit of a scruffy old Chinese person hovering by his table and giving a wide grin. The rather pot-bellied spectre clasped his hands in front of him and gave a little bow before he straightened up and beamed at the other two occupants of the bedroom.

Skipper continued to hiss so Stumblebum scooped him up and deposited him outside of the bedroom door. He could detect that a faint but pungent, bitter smell permeated the room as he addressed the unkempt visitor.

'Who are you and what are you doing here.' He demanded, forgetting the earlier conversation with Auntie Maggie in his surprise.

'I'm your spirit guide. Your auntie sent me and asked me to help out.'

'You don't look much like a mandarin.' Stumblebum said to him as he observed the stains down the front of his raggedy tunic and his dirty bare feet.

'I'm not, never said I was.' The spectre replied.

'I knew a mandarin though and he often used to speak to me'

'Oh really, and what did he have to say to you then?'

The spectre looked a bit embarrassed at the question.

'Usually something like "Get out of my way you filthy swine!" or "If you don't get those pigs out of my garden sharpish I will have you executed." That sort of thing.' He admitted to the boy.

'Pigs? Pigs? You mean you were a swineherd?'

'Oh no, I wasn't a swineherd. I *worked* for the swineherd. I looked after his shovels and cleaned the pigs out and such. It had its perks. I was allowed to sleep in the pig's shelter. Very warm in winter.'

'So you were a swineherd's labourer then?'

'I suppose you could say that, I preferred to be called a "Porcine Hygiene Mechanic" it has more of a ring to it.'

'So you mainly mucked out the pigs?'

'Yes, if you want to put it that way.'

'OK then, I take it you are here to give me advice when I need it.' He decided he had no choice since the First Americans had all taken off in a huff.

'How do I summon you when I need you then, what do I have to do?' Stumblebum asked.

'Oh, it's quite easy. Just say my name three times and I will get here.' The spirit guide beamed at him.

'What is your name? I don't think you have mentioned it yet.'

'Dung Ho. Just say Dung Ho three times. I will appear.'

'Dung Ho? Is that your name? Dung Ho?'

'What's wrong with it, it's a good Chinese name!' he said, rather indignantly.

'I can't have a spirit guide with a name like Dung Ho!'

'That's rather rich coming from someone called Stumblebum.' Dung Ho retorted.

'Anyway, I'm your only option.' he went on. 'Call me when you need me.' He gradually faded from sight and left the faint odour of what Stumblebum now knew to be pigs manure to linger in the room.

He rolled onto his bed and again stared long and hard at the ceiling as he took stock of his situation. He had a psychotic cat called Skipper. He had been misnamed Stumblebum. His spirit guide was a stinking swineherd's labourer called Dung Ho and his wand had sprouted leaves!

'Out of the three of us, Skipper has got the best name!' he observed, before sticking his pillow over his head and trying to get to sleep.

Chapter Three

During the days following his encounter with his spirit guide Stumblebum got into the habit of rising early in order to do some studying before breakfast and before he went to the academy. If it was not too cool he would sit with the window open as he found the sea air refreshing and would occasionally glance outside to watch the fishing boats as they took to the sea for the day's fishing.

Two old mariners, Salty Sammy and his brother Barnacle Billy, who lived in a little fisherman's cottage a few doors up from Auntie's house, scuttled about most mornings as they dragged their boats from the little pebbled beach just beneath Stumblebum's window to launch them into the sea.

The pair would haul their little skiffs onto the cobbled ramp at the side of a stone walkway that extended outwards, forming the harbour wall. A sloping ledge a couple of feet wide was set into the side of the walkway for the mariners to walk along to drag their boats into the water so that they could then clamber aboard.

Stumblebum found this activity interesting, if not distracting, and often put down his book and watched the two old men go about their business. He could hear them as they grunted and swore whilst they performed their tasks and was amused when they quarrelled with each other, which was often, as they got in each other's way. He was glad that he would not have to do this kind of work when he grew up destined as he was to become an important and powerful wizard if things worked out well for him at the Academy.

One such morning as he was making his way to the Academy a gorgeous young woman stopped him so that she could stroke Skipper. She cooed at the cat and chucked him under his chin which prompted the cat to roll on his back so that she could also tickle his belly. She briefly chatted to Stumblebum about how cute his cat was before going on her way. This encounter had a lasting effect on the boy who was at that age now when he was showing an interest in girls although rather a bit shy when around them.

A day or so later he saw the same girl outside the academy with Morris, who chatted to her with some intensity and charm. Stumblebum felt a pang of jealously at that point as he rather liked the girl himself and although he got on well with Morris he now resented the older boy for muscling in on the object of his desire.

He was distracted throughout that day and hardly took in any of the subjects he studied as his mind kept returning to thoughts of the girl. Secundus came and sat next to him in the library during one of these reveries and noticed how distracted he had become.

'You seem to be in a world of your own today, what's up?' He enquired.

'Oh nothing really' Stumblebum lied.

'Why don't any girls study here?' He asked, vacantly.

'Aha, I see what's bugging you.' Secundus said with a grin.

'I know, it's a bit of a pain not having girls here…' he went on,

'…but there have never been girls at the academy. It has its origins hundreds of years ago when it began as a guild of alchemists, mainly they attempted to make gold from other stuff, but over the years' the alchemists became wizards and did magic spells and things so decided to found the academy. Traditionally they have never admitted girls as students, sadly.' Secundus sighed.

'There have always been lots of witches covens in these parts though, for many century's' he continued.

'…and they used to have male and female witches in their covens, six men and six women and a priestess, but when the local feminist movement became rather militant some years ago they threw out all of the male witches. They put it to the vote and since the priestesses had a casting vote the women outnumbered the men and all the male witches were purged.'

'What happened to the male witches when they left the covens?' Stumblebum asked with interest.

'Oh, well some of them tried to apply to join our academy but most of them were rejected as not suitable. The witches practice an old pagan form of magic whereas we wizards see ourselves more as scientists in the old alchemist tradition and the two are not really compatible. A few were admitted, but not many.' Secundus carried on explaining.

'The remainder either gave up magic and witchcraft or carried on as lone witches. Some also strayed into some very dark and dodgy practices and became very secretive sorcerers. The all women covens' burn effigies of men on the annual bonfire celebrations. It's all meant to be a bit of fun but there is a real animosity seething beneath the surface. Best to steer clear of them if I were you.' He gave stumblebum a curious look.

'Why do you ask? You haven't got involved with a witch have you? You should be careful.'

'No, no' Stumblebum replied, surprised at the question.

'Well, I don't think so. There is a girl that I met recently and I rather like her but I don't know her name though. She's very pretty with lovely blonde hair. I saw Morris trying to chat her up earlier and he seemed to be doing alright.'

'Ah, that sounds like Brigitte, the Bilge on Sea blonde bombshell. Yes she is some beauty, all the lads fancy her. You will be wasting your time though if Morris is closing in on her, all the girls seem to like Morris, I think it's his thick, long black hair they go for. Girls can't seem to resist it.'

Stumblebum ran his fingers through his own wispy, mousy hair and gave a big sigh.

'Are there any magic spells to darken and thicken hair?' He said, absently thinking aloud.

'I should think so but it would be easier to buy a potion from one of the herbalists in the town. There's a Chinese herbalist, Mr Lee in the High Street. He is supposed to be very good for that sort of thing. I would try him first.'

This suggestion stuck in Stumblebum's mind during the rest of the day at the academy and he could not wait to follow this line of action as he liked the idea that he could attract Brigitte's attention and perhaps win her affection. If only he could display a lush head of flowing dark locks the same as Morris. She could find him to be irresistible!

As Stumblebum and Skipper made their way home through the High Street he looked out for the herbalist shop that Secundus had mentioned. Eventually he saw a sign proclaiming *'The Golden Dragon: Chinese Herbs and Remedies'* above a small shop nestled in between a restaurant and a pub. As he entered the shop, which was permeated with a powerful aroma of strong, exotic incense, a little bell tinkled above the door and after a few seconds the shopkeeper, a tall man whom he took to be Mr Lee, appeared from out of a small doorway behind the shop's counter.

Stumblebum discussed the topic of hair treatment remedies with Mr Lee who showed the boy several bottles of potions and a number of packets that contained powders and spices. Unfortunately for Stumblebum, the prices were far in excess of his own limited expenditure so he left the shop empty handed and with something of a heavy heart.

When he returned home a thought occurred to him that his spirit guide, who was after all from China, might perhaps have some knowledge of Chinese herbal remedies so decided to summon him after supper. When he had finished supper and just before he prepared for bed Stumblebum called for Dung Ho in the prescribed manner. Sure enough a faint odour of pigs permeated his bedroom followed by the now familiar swirling of vapours, which then formed into the portly person of Dung Ho, bowing and beaming at the young wizard.

'How may I be of service my friend?' The spirit asked, grinning from ear to ear.

'I was wondering' Stumblebum said, a little embarrassed.

'Do you have any knowledge of any herbal remedies, for instance, say, to thicken and darken hair, for example?'

'Funny you should say that!' Dung Ho replied.

'My family had a long tradition of passing on secret remedies such as you just described from generation to generation. These remedies were jealously guarded secrets passed down from father to son over many years.'

'So do you know of any hair remedies then, like I just mentioned?'

'Of course I do. The mandarin of my district, an important man, asked me for the same advice when he was due to marry the beautiful young daughter of a wealthy merchant by arrangement. As he was middle aged and had started to thin a little on top naturally he wanted to look his best when his new bride first would see him on his wedding day. I told him of how to prepare a potion that had been kept secret in my family for hundreds of years as a remedy for just his problem'

'And do you still remember this remedy? Will you tell me how to make it?' The boy urged.

'Of course, your wish is my command.' He beamed at the boy.

'You must keep it to yourself though and follow my instructions to the letter as it is quite a complicated concoction. You might have trouble getting some of the ingredients.' The spirit guide cautioned.

'Oh, I should think I will manage. I am quite resourceful you know.' the boy answered, rather cockily.

'First you will need a large mortar of about five or six pints capacity with a good strong pestle for mixing the ingredients which must be done in precise measures before being placed in a towel like a poultice and wrapped around your head for no less than five hours. Do you have a pencil? I will give you the list of herbs and spices you will need. Once you have gathered all of these I will return and tell you the secret ingredients, which are vital to the remedy.'

Stumblebum felt a sense of success as he took out a quill and his pot of ink from his casket, along with another square of parchment and scribbled down Dung Ho's instructions. He would be able to borrow one of the large mortar bowls from the academy the next day, and what herbs and spices he did not already have on his shelves he would also probably be able to acquire from the academy.

* * * * * * *

The next morning Stumblebum arose bright and early and sat by the open window as was his habit and watched the seagulls circling as the little fishing boats put out to sea. Dung Ho's hair remedy was preoccupying his thoughts so much that he was unable to concentrate on learning his spells so he placed the little red book back on the table and stared for a long time at the comings and goings outside He chuckled at Salty Sammy and Barnacle Billy as they cursed at each other and mused about how his hair would look after Dung Ho's potion had done its trick.

He was in an unusually cheerful mood as he got ready to go down for breakfast and was just reaching for his cape when he glanced at Skipper who was fast asleep in the middle of the bed and gave a wide, mischievous grin as a cunning thought occurred to him.

Very slowly and with much stealth he carefully lifted the cape from its hook as he kept his gaze on the slumbering Skipper and then quietly opened the bedroom door and silently crept out before he closed the door carefully firmly behind him. He sniggered as he made his way downstairs and was still sniggering as he went in for breakfast.

'You are in a cheerful mood for a change dear, did you have a good night's sleep?' Auntie Maggie enquired as she busied herself with breakfast.

‘Yes thank you Auntie, I have a good feeling about today. Are there any kippers today?’ he replied, still grinning widely.

‘Yes dear, I have done plenty. Speaking of kippers, where is Skipper? He’s usually ready and waiting.’

‘Oh, I left him asleep on my bed. He looked so peaceful I didn’t want to wake him.’ he lied, stifling another sniggering fit.

‘I think he tired himself out yesterday so it’s best to leave him to sleep. I daresay he will come down when he is ready.’ This time he chuckled out loud.

After breakfast he made his short journey to the academy without the embarrassment of Skipper’s frenzied attacks although he still managed to drag a good assortment of tin cans and other refuse along as usual. He arrived at the wizards’ entrance in the alleyway in an upbeat mood and remained upbeat for much of the day.

Everything went without any snags and he enquired about where to borrow equipment and acquire the herbs on Dung Ho’s list. He said that these were for some spell practice at home, which the academy liked to encourage.

He was sent to the academy apothecary, a dark, gloomy storeroom with jars and bottles of all sizes haphazardly displayed on row upon row of dusty, solid wooden shelves and cabinets. He was met by the Keeper of Potions, a small, wiry old man with a long white beard and a large hooked nose protruding like a sharks fin from his wrinkled old face, beneath a tall, conical shaped hat with alternate red and white stripes that spiralled down from the point a bit like an old barbers’ pole. The old man was friendly and cheerful and went to a lot of trouble to be helpful to the young novice wizard and seemed keen to encourage his homework project.

He gathered all of the herbs and stuff from Stumblebum’s list and went into a back room where the sound of loud clatters and clunks accompanied his search for a suitable sized mortar and pestle. He returned with these along with an old piece of parchment with something scribbled on it which turned out to be a chitty to be signed and dated by Stumblebum for the loan of the equipment. The herbs and spices were provided free as they were supposed to be for the purposes of study and practice.

The rest of the day at the academy went smoothly and Stumblebum even made some progress on his magic practice. He successfully performed a few simple tasks in the spells laboratory during practice for the afternoon's lesson. He was feeling very pleased with himself as he made his way home carrying the stuff from the apothecary and anticipating more success with his hair tonic venture.

After struggling a little to open the front door to his auntie's shop as he juggled his mortar and pestle and packages of herbs he made his way up the narrow wooden stairs to his bedroom. As he opened the door Skipper suddenly shot out and flew between Stumblebum's legs before he galloped down the stairs with some haste. This startled Stumblebum and nearly caused him to drop his packages. He had forgotten he had locked the cat in his bedroom. The thought of his prank on Skipper, however, made him start to snigger again as he entered his bedroom but then he abruptly stopped short as the grin at first froze on his face before it transformed into a sickly grimace.

Now he knew the reason behind Skipper's haste in exiting the bedroom! The wretched cat had done an enormous dump right in the middle of the little red book of spells which had been left lying on the table. Stumblebum went pale with disgust, and then red with rage, and then pale again with disgust.

Gagging at the vile smell he gingerly lifted the book by its edges and carefully carried it over to the window which he opened widely before he then flicked the offending deposit in the direction of the little beach. He went straight into the bathroom and spent a long time as he scrubbed the leather cover of the red book with several cleansing solutions that Auntie Maggie kept in the bathroom until he was satisfied that all traces of Skipper's vandalism had been eliminated.

At supper he moaned incessantly to his auntie about what the cat had done but could not get any sympathy from her on the topic.

'Well, if you are going to lock the poor mite in then what do you expect? You have only got yourself to blame. Let this be a lesson to you to be a bit kinder to him in future, it's not his fault at all. You shouldn't play tricks on poor Skipper. I'm sure you must have hurt his feelings!'

'Hurt his feelings! How about my feelings? I'm the one who had to clean the mess up!' He whined, no longer feeling upbeat about the days' events.

'Well, serves you right, that's all I can say.'

Stumblebum retreated to his bedroom in a dark mood and felt thoroughly defeated. Now both Skipper and Auntie Maggie seemed to be ganging up on him. It was all so unfair. He laid on his bed and stared at the ceiling for a very long time before drifting into a troubled sleep.

Chapter 4

Stumblebum awoke in a grumpy mood and sulkily read his notes from the day before at the academy as he sat by the window and occasionally glared at the seagulls as they noisily circled above the little harbour. His mood did not improve much when the two old mariners dragged their fishing boats onto the cobbled ramp. Their loud swearwords and curses, usually a cause for his amusement, now had him tut-tutting as he shook his head in disapproval.

Barnacle Billy dragged his little boat on to the cobbled ramp and eased it into the water as he pulled on the painter, the rope attached to the bow of his vessel, and walked along the sloping ledge. When the boat was afloat he deftly jumped in and pulled on the line that hauled the sail up the mast and sat down with a thump on to the little seat at the stern of the boat all in one graceful flowing movement. The sail unfurled and billowed out in the breeze and propelled the little skiff out of the harbour.

A few moments later Salty Sammy dragged his little skiff into the water and like his brother had just done leapt into the vessel as he grabbed hold of the line for the sail and pulled it up the mast at the same time as he lowered his rump on to the wooden rear seat in another graceful flowing movement. Unlike Billy, however, he did not land with a thump but more of a soggy squelch. This sound was followed by a few moments of absolute silence which was then broken by a blood curdling howl of anguish as Salty Sammy realised what he had just sat in.

At this point Stumblebum renewed his interest in the comings and goings outside, always amused by the misfortunes of others as he was. His spirits rose somewhat as he watched Salty Sammy drag his boat back out of the water before he then slowly walked in a strange crablike bow legged gait back to his cottage and turned the air blue with maritime oaths and curses as he did.

As Stumblebum realized that the cat mess that he had flung towards the beach the day before must have landed in Salty Sammy's boat his mood lightened immensely. He had to close his window swiftly so that the old fisherman did not hear his loud laughter and work out that the lad had something to do with his sorry predicament. Once he had the window firmly closed he flung himself on to his bed and laughed uncontrollably until tears ran down his face. Ah, the joy of seeing others come a cropper!

All of that day, at breakfast, during his walk to the academy and during all of his lessons and study periods, Stumblebum would break out into loud uncontrollable laughter whenever his thoughts took him back to the events of that morning. He was even very sternly admonished to be quiet by the Academy Scribe during one of his laughing fits in the library before being eventually evicted from the library for the day, although this did little to thwart Stumblebum's merriment.

Later that evening, back home in his room, Stumblebum summoned his spirit guide to obtain his secret ingredients to add to the herbs and spices which he had mixed precisely to Dung Ho's instructions and ground them up with the pestle. He was looking forward to getting on with his 'new look' image makeover and attracting all the girls, especially Brigitte, with his flowing dark hair.

Dung Ho materialised in his usual manner, bowing several times to the young wizard, who was impatient to finish the potion and grow a lush head of hair. Dung Ho peered into the mortar and examined the contents until he was satisfied that Stumblebum had mixed them properly. He gave a big smile of approval and again asked the boy to write down the rest of the secret ingredients.

'You will need to mix in to the herbs and spices the following two ingredients, both of which are essential to the success of the treatment. First you will need to mix in two hundred grams of gunpowder, and this is very important, do NOT use the pestle to grind it in to the herbs or you might cause a small explosion! Then you will need to obtain a bucketful of fresh pig manure and again take care when adding it to the rest of the mixture. Fold it in with a wooden spatula until it reaches the brim of the mortar and then put it to one side and let it stand for three days in order to ferment.'

'Pigs manure! You are joking aren't you?'

Stumblebum had had his fill of handling animal excrement recently and was horrified at Dung Ho's suggestion.

'No, no, not joking, it is a vital part of the potion, but if you don't want it to be effective that is up to you. In any case after three days it blends in with the other ingredients and you would never guess as to its origins. But if you don't want a good head of hair that's up to you.' Dung Ho sounded a little peeved at the boy's response.

'Where am I going to get pig's manure from? And gunpowder for goodness sake!'

'You are very resourceful remember. Very clever wizard can get anything.' Dung Ho beamed at Stumblebum as the spirit guide faded from sight leaving him to reflect on the cost of vanity and also how to get his hands on the last two ingredients. So near yet so far away.

Over the next few days Stumblebum tentatively made some enquiries concerning the whereabouts of any pigs in the near vicinity and eventually was told that a man with a plot on the allotments near to the cliff top at the far end of town used to keep a few pigs so he might enquire there.

Armed with one of Auntie Maggie's buckets from her broom cupboard Stumblebum set off to seek out the allotments in the hope that the man with the pigs still kept them. After leaving the shop he turned in the opposite direction from the academy, going eastwards along the High Street until the old town quarter gave way to the older fisherman's cottages and beach, where the buildings became more hap-hazard and nestled beneath the cliffs and where the local beach-launched fishing cobs rested on the pebbled beach.

Near to the boats and opposite the little fish market where an assortment of neighbouring jellied eel stalls and ice cream kiosks plied their trade, *The Captain Barnaby*, a pub in which the fishermen drank cider and beer, led to a steep narrow pathway to the cliff top.

At the side of *The Captain Barnaby* some steep stone steps led on to a winding pathway punctuated with more steps at intervals as it rose behind the pub and surrounding cottages until it emerged at a road end above the buildings. Across the road a second steep pathway wound its way upward toward the cliff top and site of the old beacon.

Stumblebum panted and puffed, a little out of breath by the time that he reached the top of this path. Here he was confronted by a wooden style in the middle of a fence with a strand of barbed wire nailed on to the top bar to discourage the sheep grazing on the cliff top from straying.

Stumblebum paused to get his breath back before he climbed over the style and stopped to get his bearings. He was surprised to find how busy the place was. It teemed with several groups of women dressed in wellington boots and dungarees or jeans. Some of them carried a number of big cardboard boxes as others put the finishing touches to a large wicker man which they hoisted into place in front of the old beacon near to the edge of the cliff top. He surveyed the scene for a few moments and presumed it must be something to do with the annual bonfire celebration due to take place on the fishing beach below. He approached the nearest group in order to ask directions for the whereabouts of the allotment.

Too late he realised his error as one of the women spun around as he got near and shrieked loudly to the other women and pointed accusingly at Stumblebum as she did.

'It's a novice from the academy! Sent to spy on us by the old wizards! Get him girls!'

Before he could protest he found himself surrounded by a mob of very angry women who snarled and sneered at him as they jostled around the frightened young lad. As the penny dropped he realised that he had inadvertently stumbled upon the infamous witches of whom he had heard so much recently, particularly regarding their hatred for wizards.

'I'm not a spy, honest.' He implored as he suddenly felt very vulnerable.

'I only wanted to find the allotments. I was told they were somewhere up here.'

Stumblebum held up the bucket to show to them as if that would verify his excuse.

'A likely story!' one of the women pushed her face close to his with what seemed to be a cross between a sneer and a snarl clouding her features.

The other women began to jostle and shove him as he got rather panicky. One girl shouted from the back of the group.

'I know, let's put him inside the wicker man and sacrifice him with fire tomorrow!'

Now he really did panic as a sinister sniggering swept through the group of witches.

'It's a tempting thought girls but we are not living in the dark ages.' the first woman said, followed by a groan of disappointment from the other women.

She then grabbed Stumblebum by his throat and lifted him until his face was level with hers.

'The allotments that you are looking for are over there behind the cricket pavilion if that's what you really are looking for. If I find out that you have told anyone what you have seen here I will personally find you and you don't want to know what I will do to you then. Just let's say you will never be the same again. Now beat it boy and pronto!'

The witch propelled him towards the cricket pitch with a hefty kick to his rear as he scurried off, pulse racing, in his hurry to get away.

In the opposite direction from the cliff edge where the wicker man teetered precariously secured by ropes to the old beacon there was another style which led to a path behind the pavilion and cricket pitch. Some women still carried their boxes and took them inside the building as he scurried past them. He noticed what was in the boxes which caused him to perk up a little as his mind hatched a plan that might help him resolve another problem.

The further he got from the witches the calmer he became. This calm then turned to indignation and a desire for some kind of revenge. His thoughts turned to visions of imagined torments he would like to inflict on these witches though in reality he was scared almost senseless of the thought of any encounter with them again. Even so, a plan had formed in his mind which might go some small way to redress the outrage.

Stumblebum was deep in thought by the time that he arrived at the allotments. He was confronted by a high pair of wrought iron gates that bore a large sign that proclaimed: *The Bilge on Sea Corporation Allotments* beneath which was a long list of rules. His heart sank as he read the first of these rules: *The keeping of livestock on these allotments is strictly forbidden. By order of the Committee.*

Looking around he noticed several plots where chickens clucked about with small improvised roosting sheds made from wire mesh and old wooden doors and also a number of what could only be pigeon lofts came into his sight as he looked along the gravel pathway beyond the gate. Perhaps the rules were not strictly adhered to he thought as he entered the gateway and made his way along the path.

Before long he came across an old man doing some hoeing on a plot beside the path. After enquiring as to whether anyone kept pigs he was directed to a plot at the end of the gravel path and told to ask for a Mr Closet, the allotments' committee chairman. Stumblebum thanked the man and proceeded down the path.

As Stumblebum made his way along the path a now familiar stench assaulted his nostrils and grew stronger until he arrived at the plot of a Mr Walter Closet who was in evidence as he tended to a huge sow and a litter of piglets behind a fence made up of a patchwork of bits of waste timber. Mr Closet was a wiry little man who wore a tweed flat cap, waistcoat and wellington boots. His brown corduroy trousers, tucked into the wellingtons, were held up by a sturdy pair of braces and an even sturdier leather belt for good measure. The man leant on the fence as he smoked a pipe and vacantly observed his pigs grubbing about the bare soil.

'Excuse me sir, I wonder if there is any pig manure I could have.' Stumblebum addressed the pig fancier and held up his bucket as if to emphasise his request.

Walter Closet looked at Stumblebum through weary, rheumy eyes, then turned his gaze to the bucket with a slight look of disappointment before looking over to the back of his plot where a huge steaming mountain of pig manure mixed with rotting straw loomed menacingly.

'You are welcome to take as much as you like lad.' Walter sighed and nodded towards the enormous stinking pile of manure.

'Er, I was wondering if it would be possible to have some fresh manure please.'

Walter stared at him curiously for a moment then turned and went up to his shed, a small ramshackle homemade affair with his initials painted on the door in large white letters, reached in through the doorway and brought out a large long handled shovel and walked over to the pig sty as he beckoned the boy to follow.

Walter Closet scooped up several shovelfuls of slurry from puddles around the sty and filled Stumblebum's bucket to the brim. A man of few words, he gave the boy a slight nod and handed the bucket over.

'Come back whenever you want any more son,' said the old man, 'as much as you like.'

Before he took his leave Stumblebum asked the old man if there was another way out of the allotments as he was not keen to encounter the witches again if possible. He was directed to another gate at the far end where the allotments sloped down to near the main road out of Bilge on Sea. This was a longer route back to the Old Town but Stumblebum was glad to take it as he did not want any more hostile confrontations with the witches to befall him.

As he made his way home his mind was working out a little plan that he would implement under the cloak of darkness later that evening.

He passed by an old junk shop on his way home and noticed a box with an assortment of old rusty second hand tools outside. He rummaged about in the box until he found what he needed. He left the bucket and its foul contents on the pavement as it was now making his eyes water and he took the rusty crowbar he had found in the box into the shop and bought it at a bargain price, due to its age and condition.

Upon leaving the shop with his purchase he picked up his bucket and set off towards home with a renewed spring in his step. His mind so busily worked on his new plan that he was oblivious to the number of people sat outside the cafes and wine bars who gagged and retched as he walked past. Two very elderly ladies looking in a haberdashery shop window both fainted and a dog slipped its collar and lead and scurried away with some haste and yelped frantically as it did.

When he got home Stumblebum went straight up to his room and placed the bucket in the fireplace on top of the grate in the hope that most of the bad odour from its contents would waft up the chimney. This was only partially successful so he lit a lot of incense sticks and placed them around his bedroom before he flung the window wide open to let some fresh air in. He also burnt some incense on the stairwell so that Auntie Maggie would not detect the other smell and tell him off.

After supper Stumblebum went back up to his room and placed a clothes peg taken from his auntie's kitchen drawer on his nose and studied his little red book whist he waited for it to get dark outside.

As dusk arrived he stealthily slunk down the stairs and closed the door quietly behind him as he entered the High Street. Carrying his newly purchased crowbar he made his way back to *The Captain Barnaby* and back up the winding path to the cliff top.

At the style he paused and carefully scanned the area around the beacon and in the dim light assured himself that no one was about. He scrambled over the style and swiftly made his way to the second style and the cricket pavilion where he carefully prised a side window open with his jemmy and clambered in. Once inside he looked around at the dark shapes of the cardboard boxes and lit a small taper that he had brought with him and held it up so that he could see better.

After helping himself to some of the larger fireworks that the witches had stored there he put out the candle and climbed back out of the window before scurrying back to the steep path carrying a collection of the larger sky rockets and roman candles in his arms. Had he looked back at this point he would have seen a sinister figure who had been lurking behind the wicker man and who watched him with interest step out from his place of concealment.

Slippery Jack watched Stumblebum as he climbed back over the style and disappeared from view in the gloom of the dusk as he descended the pathway carrying his fireworks. The youth stared beyond the style for some time whist he stroked his chin, deep in thought, before he turned on his heel and walked over to the pavilion and also clambered in through the window that he had seen Stumblebum force open earlier. He passed all of the remaining boxes back out of the window before he climbed out and made a number of journeys to carry them over to the wicker man until he had them all stacked by the giant effigy's feet.

The young man very carefully made a slight opening in both of the wicker man's legs and then concealed most of the fireworks inside. He had kept several large sky rockets behind and he placed these in a small pile. When he had arrived earlier, just before Stumblebum had got there, Slippery Jack had been busy loosening the ropes securing the wicker man to the beacon. He had also noticed that the witches had painted a large white circle with a pentagram inside it in front of the wicker man for the purpose of dancing around, as witches often did when performing rituals and observing special events.

After Slippery Jack had watched Stumblebum's burglary and escape armed with his pile of fireworks he had amended his plan somewhat. He now unwrapped the paper on the rocket tubes and carefully poured the contents along the ground between the wicker man and the centre of the pentagram where a small stack of kindling and firewood had been built in readiness for the next evening. He teased the grass over the line of powder to conceal it then stood back and surveyed his work as best as he could in the now descending darkness. Finally, he threw the boxes and empty firework cartridges over the side of the cliff before he made his way back down the steep path that Stumblebum had recently gone down and chuckled devilishly to himself as he did.

* * * * * * *

It was a little before midnight when Slippery Jack made his way along the driveway and up to the front door of Mordecai Manor, the gloomy gothic mansion where he lived and was taught the blackest of magic by his evil mentor, the sorcerer. He lifted the large iron gargoyle shaped knocker and rapped on the front door and waited. After a minute or so the door opened and Slippery Jack entered and then closed the door firmly behind him.

Tiberius Mordecai led his apprentice along the hallway and into his panelled study where a log fire blazed and illuminated the room. Several large candles also flickered on the high mantelpiece and seemed to animate the collection of old human skulls also arrayed along the mantelpiece. Two leather armchairs occupied a space each at either side of the fire and Slippery Jack went over and sat in one of them as the sorcerer poured two goblets of red wine and sat down in the remaining chair, handing one of the goblets to his apprentice as he did.

'Well Slippery, how went your mission? All accomplished I take it?'

'All accomplished, and a chance offered itself to better the original plan.'

Slippery grinned widely as he took a sip from his goblet before he recounted to Mordecai the events that had taken place earlier on the cliff top. This included his observation of the academy novice's robbery and Slippery Jack's own subsequent removal and concealment of the witches' fireworks. Mordecai smiled as he took in the information.

'Excellent, excellent! Well done Slippery, thinking on your feet, I like that.'

'So who do you think this academy novice is, he sounds like he might prove to be useful? Have you encountered him before?' Mordecai questioned his apprentice with interest.

'No, never set eyes on him before so he must be fairly new. I will make some enquiries and see what I can find out.' Slippery finished his wine and got up to refill his goblet.

'The witches will get a real shock when they start their little ritual. It should go off with quite a bang!' Both men laughed sardonically at this and after they had quaffed several more goblets of wine each they retired to their respective rooms for the night.

* * * * * * *

Meanwhile, back at his room, Stumblebum was putting the finishing touches to his hair tonic potion as Dung Ho had instructed. He now had both of the final ingredients and had taken the gunpowder out of some of the fireworks he had stolen from the witches and carefully mixed it in with the herbs and other stuff in his mortar. Next he slowly added some of the pigs manure as he poured from the bucket and stirred it in until the mortar was full to the brim. After he did this he carefully took the mortar and its putrid contents and placed it in the fireplace where the bucket had been kept. He then flung the remaining contents of the bucket out of the open window in the direction of the beach before he rinsed it out in the bathroom and took it back into the bedroom where he placed it upside down over the mortar in the fireplace, which had the effect of containing most of the stench.

A little tired after the day's events but feeling good about making progress with his hair thickening remedy the lad soon fell in to a deep restful sleep. He dreamt pleasant dreams of beautiful girls who flocked around him and fought to take turns to stroke his lovely, lush, long black hair. The next morning, having overslept a little, he was rudely awoken from his dreams by a commotion out in the harbour outside.

Salty Sammy had never known lightening to strike in the same place twice and had therefore not expected there to be the large pile of evil smelling slurry that now covered the seat of his boat and only was made aware of it when he once again found himself sat in something unspeakable. This time what can only be described as an unearthly primal scream emitted from his lips as it pierced the twilight like the shrill cry of a Banshee.

Yet again the old seadog pulled his boat back to the shore. Then he kicked off his wellingtons and removed his trousers altogether and flung them in to the harbour where they slowly drifted out to sea like an abandoned raft. Sammy's skinny legs protruded from below his shirt tail and with a wellington boot in each hand he painfully picked his way over the pebbles to his cottage in his stockings.

Stumblebum looked out of his window and stifled a snigger as he watched Salty Sammy head back to his home, although he was a little worried that the old man would sooner or later work out where the offending effluvium came from and had no wish to be at the receiving end of his foul temper. He must take greater care in future if he ever had to throw stuff out through his window again and be sure to give the little boats a wide berth. He was still very amused at the old man's plight though but was little bit afraid that his actions might find him out.

The boy was in a happy mood as he went in for breakfast where Auntie Maggie was busy giving Skipper his meal. Stumblebum had noted that the cat had not been near his bedroom since he had brought the secret ingredient home in the bucket and was glad of a few days' respite from him, although, reluctant to admit it, he was becoming fond of the annoying creature.

After breakfast Stumblebum laid out his 'coolest' clothes on his bed in preparation for the Guild of Wizards' bonfire and parade that evening where he had arranged to meet Morris and Secundus before the bonfire ceremony began. As it was a Saturday the academy was closed in any case but the senior wizards would be there, dressed in their finest cloaks and tall pointed hats, assembled in advance in order to lead the procession from the academy and along the High Street and through the Old Town to the fishing boat beach where the bonfire would be ceremonially lit.

A carnival procession was to follow the wizards as they solemnly made their way to the bonfire followed by an assortment of troubadours and the like. Immediately behind the group of wizards the town's mayor and town crier both in their official regalia always marched in front of the torch bearers who would be dressed in ancient traditional pagan costumes and with their faces painted green, blue or yellow. They had the important task to carry the burning torches with which they would light the bonfire on behalf of the wizards.

The torch bearers were usually traditionally followed by the drumming troupe who bore hand held drums and beat a slow rhythm to accompany the slow dignified march. Behind them would be the Morris dancers who always held aloft inflated white balloons on sticks and with strings of little bells tied to various parts of their traditional white costumes. They hopped first on one leg and then the other as they made their way, bells tinkling, to the bonfire. In previous years the witches brought up the rear with their giant *papier mache* effigies of wizards and other men they disliked in an effort to sour the proceedings but this year they would be strangely absent.

Chapter Five

Hardly anyone in Bilge on Sea could quite remember what it was that started the witches feud with the wizards, or when exactly that was. All that people knew was that it had been going on for a long, long time and even the witches had trouble to remember what it was all about but they carried on with the enmity as it seemed to be the right thing to do. They were increasingly frustrated and annoyed at the wizards' successes with the annual bonfires, despite their best efforts to disrupt them and redoubled their efforts to this end every year.

This year though as the wizards prepared themselves for the bonfire parade in the academy that evening the witches were also putting on their ceremonial vestments but they did not intend to tag along behind the wizards and the others as they had done in past events. In previous years they had followed the procession to the bonfire where they would throw the *papier mache* effigies of wizards and prominent townsmen on to the blazing fire as a gesture of their disapproval. This time, however, they had hatched a new secret plan in a bid to outdo and usurp the wizards' celebration.

At around the time the wizards were in the academy getting ready the witches were in their headquarters in the towns Women's Centre putting on their flimsy ceremonial white shifts and wearing willow garlands on their heads before sneaking barefooted by a circuitous route to the cliff top, not wanting to be seen, in order to better the wizards' bonfire and firework display with something much more spectacular that they had set up previously in secret.

Unknown to either the wizards or the witches a more sinister event was under way at the menacing mansion of Tiberius Mordecai who was preparing a ceremony of his own with the assistance of his acolyte Slippery Jack. Both black magicians conducted an ancient evil rite in the cellars of the mansion where they were about to conjure up a malevolent fiery demon to be sent to do their bidding.

The cellars were large, dimly lit by flaming torches, with high vaulted stone ceilings which were supported by stone pillars. At the centre on the marble floor was an inlaid silver pentagram inside a large circle, also inlaid in to the marble with silver, where Mordecai and Slippery conducted their dark rites and ceremonies. On this occasion the pair proceeded to summon a fiery monster from the depths of some unspeakable hell to be sent on a mission to bring mischief and mayhem to the celebrations due to take place in the town that night.

Groth the fire demon slowly materialised before the two sorcerers. At first as a dark smoky vapour then taking form as it grew and reached its full height just below the vaulted ceiling. Within the bright flames that the vapour had become a grotesque demonic shape emerged. A devil with twisted horns and flaming eyes as big as dinner plates which flickered above a gaping fire breathing mouth. The creature stood on cloven hooves and goat's legs below its long, broad body from which two great fiery bat like wings slowly flapped and stretched. Groth growled and emitted foul smoke and flames from his mouth as he stepped towards the two sorcerers and stopped only as he reached the edge of the pentagram, unable to cross its outer perimeter, protected as it was by Mordecai's powerful black magic.

Mordecai recited some ancient incantation several times and then commanded the demon to undertake a special task for him before allowing the creature to return to its deep subterranean lair. Groth snarled at Mordecai but nonetheless obeyed his command as he was compelled to do by the powerful spell. The demon faded back into a smoky vapour which then twisted into a tornado shape and spun away from the two men and seeped through the stonework of the cellar and on into the evening twilight to fulfil his mischievous errand.

Up on the cliff top just before twilight turned to night the group of witches had assembled, forming two circles around their own pentagram painted into the grass. A short time earlier the witches had discovered that someone had stolen their fireworks, intended as a display to better that of the wizards, and they were furious.

'I bet that lad we caught yesterday, the novice wizard, has had a hand in this!' One of the women snarled.

'We should have tied him up inside the wicker man, but it's too late now!'

Meryl, the high priestess who had earlier threatened Stumblebum as he sought out the allotments, spoke.

'Leave him to me! I shall deal with him later. Right now though we must make the best of a bad job. The main thing is that we still have the wicker man.'

She stepped into the centre of the pentagram as she lit the end of a taper with a match and touched it to the kindling inside the bundle of sticks. As the fire took hold and the kindling burst into flames the witches held hands and danced around the pentagram. Both circles of women skipped in opposite directions and sang pagan songs in an ancient language. In the centre of this Meryl performed her ceremony to pay homage to the wicker man as she was about to step up and set fire to it with her taper.

The high priestess, however, had little need to perform this task as at that moment the fire, which was now well ablaze, ignited Slippery Jack's gunpowder trail and rapidly fizzled its way up to the wicker man's feet. This set off the fireworks concealed inside and fierce flames licked up its legs. The fireworks exploded simultaneously. Coloured sparks and flames flew in all directions accompanied by whizzes and loud bangs as the astonished witches stopped dancing and looked on in disbelief.

Several witches had their flimsy robes catch fire as the sparks from the fireworks continued to splutter and fly at them. Now in a panic they ripped at their robes in an attempt to avoid serious burns and this left some of them clothed only their willow headgear as they screamed hysterically.

Then as the larger rockets took off in unison inside the wicker man's legs they momentarily became wedged in the narrower knees before they lifted the whole flaming wicker effigy high into the air, about five or six metres or so, when the entire blazing structure turned head over heels and dive bombed over the edge of the cliff.

The fiercely ablaze wicker man landed head first on top of the wizards' bonfire below causing it and the pyrotechnic display that had been set up previously to catch fire along with one or two rowing boats which had been left on the beach nearby. More mayhem ensued as the firework display, meant to last a half hour or so, exploded all at once in a noisy haphazard display as the bonfire blazed away furiously with the added fuel of the volatile wicker man.

Now the witches had lost their wicker man prematurely and thus denied their triumphant spectacle of putting on a vivid pagan display of dance, fire and sacrifice. As they grouped around the women who had been scorched to console them someone pointed to the remnants of the smoke left behind by the fireworks, near to the old beacon. The acrid smoke seemed to revolve strangely in tight spirals, spinning faster and faster until it finally burst into a glowing inferno.

Transfixed, the witches stared at the spectacle and some of them wondered if their pagan chant had caused some magic fire to appear. Perhaps this could turn into a display? Then one of the witches pointed at the flames and screamed at the top of her lungs as Groth emerged and stepped forward. He snarled and belched fire and dark plumes of smoke as he moved in the direction of the witches. The women immediately turned on their heels and fled the scene and raced back down the sloping cliff top towards the style in order to escape. Some realised that all of them would cause a bottleneck there which would slow their urgent retreat so they spread out and made for the wooden fence.

The younger and more agile of the witches vaulted clean over the fence but their long flimsy robes caught on the barbed wire nailed to the top bar as their older and plumper sisters sat on top of the fence, not realising there was barbed wire there, until the metal barbs dug in to their generous rumps as they swung their legs over the fence. The sound of loud shrieks and ripping fabric rent the tranquillity of the cliff top as the witches hastily leapt from the fence on to the steep slope below. This left most of their garments hung in tatters along the top of the fence as they flapped there in the breeze like badly made bunting.

With great haste they ran toward the winding pathway and the witches who had clambered the fence paid little heed to the thorny gorse bushes that ripped at their bare feet and legs and shredded any remnants of their garments to have survived the barbed wire. Joining the ones who had gone through the style they continued to run, still at a breakneck pace, as they descended with robes in tatters and screamed loudly in unison, anxious to return to the relative safety of their sanctuary at the Women's Centre.

Groth stood alone on the cliff top and watched the witches retreat and, task completed, gave one final snarl and evaporated back into swirling black smoke then spiralled downwards into the ground and back to his flaming lair somewhere deep in the bowels of the earth.

Down below the cliff a group of fishermen had gathered outside *The Captain Barnaby*. As they drank their cider they waited for the wizards' procession to arrive. The raised terrace outside of the pub offered them a grandstand view of the event and they sat around tables and chatted to each other as the display was due to soon commence.

The explosions of the wizards' fireworks caused the fishermen to rise to their feet and look on in surprise. Then they all laughed raucously as the bonfire prematurely blazed away until one of the men abruptly stopped his hearty laughter and shouted at his companions whilst he ran off the terrace and up to the bonfire with some haste.

'That's my boat on fire! That's my boat on fire!' he screamed as he raced in the direction of his rowing boat, now merrily ablaze at the side of the bonfire.

As the other fishermen stood there with drinks in their hands and they watched this drama unfold a new strange noise caught their attention, faintly at first but with increased levels of volume by the second. The gaggle of witches, in tatters and scorched and bleeding, raced down the steep alley at the side of the pub. The sound of three dozen pairs of bare feet as they slapped the stone flags of the steps accompanied by wails and screams blended into an unidentifiable cacophony as the volume made by the panicking witches reached a crescendo.

The two brothers Salty Sammy and Barnacle Billy turned and approached the entrance to the alleyway curious to see what might be the source this strange noise. At just that moment the now tightly packed group of witches burst out of the alleyway with loud screams and wails and sped off up the road towards the Old Town. The old fishermen stood rooted to the spot side by side as they watched the retreating rears of the largest group of near naked women that either of them had ever seen in their long lives race away from them.

Both of the men's jaws and their glasses of cider dropped at the same time as they were joined by the other fishermen, who gazed in disbelief at the spectacle. Barnacle Billy shook his head vigorously and looked down at his empty hand where his drink had been before it had dropped. He stared at his hand for a moment then marched into the pub to buy himself a much stiffer beverage than the cider in order to steady his nerves. He was followed in to the pub by Salty Sammy who needed to have a lie down on one of the upholstered benches that lined the walls of the bar. He lay on his back and trembled and muttered incoherently as his brother downed his large whiskey at the bar and immediately ordered another.

* * * * * * *

Oblivious to the events unfolding on the fishing beach Stumblebum innocently and cheerfully wended his way along the High Street as he headed towards the bonfire where he was due to meet Secundus and Morris who would also be there to see the wizards' parade arrive and the ceremonial lighting of the bonfire and fireworks.

At the end of the High Street the road curved sharply due to an old Tudor building which jutted out from the others. The cobbled road did a kind of dog-leg before it gave on to the fishing beaches and fishermen's cottages. Stumblebum stepped jauntily out and around this corner only to be stopped dead in his tracks at the horror which confronted him. The juggernaut of stampeding naked witches headed straight towards the boy and he froze rigid on the spot as the blancmange nightmare of numerous exposed bouncing breasts bore down on him at a tremendous speed.

The blood drained from the young wizard's face as the stampede galloped in his direction. He closed his eyes in terror as he expected to be trampled to death by this unexpected onslaught. The screams of the witches amplified in his ears as they thundered past and jostled and shoved him this way and that until he was left there alone and bewildered, eyes tightly shut as he shook uncontrollably.

Opening first one eye and then another he carefully looked around and then burst into a flood of tears, relieved to have survived the witches' attack relatively intact. Then his legs gave way and he collapsed onto the kerb where he sat and gibbered and babbled incoherently as the trauma turned to shock and as he stared into space he sobbed spasmodically, unable to get his legs which seem to have turned into rubber, to articulate.

A little while before Stumblebum's distressing encounter with the stampeding witches Morris and Secundus had been on their way to join him on the fisherman's beach but became distracted as they walked down one of the side streets that led on to the High Street. Morris glanced in the window of a little cafe which they were passing and stopped dead in his tracks, grabbing Secundus by the arm as he did.

'Oh, look! There's Brigitte and her sister. Let's go in and chat to them.' Morris pushed the café door open as he spoke, not waiting for a reply. Secundus followed him in to the café and went to the counter and ordered drinks as Morris sat next to Brigitte, before being joined by his friend.

'You girls don't mind if we sit here do you?' said Morris to the sisters with a cheeky glint in his eyes.

Brigitte and her pretty younger sister, Mandy, both giggled as Morris continued with his banter whilst Secundus listened to the master of the chat-up line in silent admiration. The boys soon became immersed in conversation with the girls as they drank their milkshakes, chatting and exchanging jokes with them, which made them giggle even more. Then Secundus suddenly remembered that Stumblebum would be waiting for them at the bonfire and reminded Morris of their prior arrangement.

'Why don't you girls come down to the beach and watch the bonfire and fireworks with us? We have arranged to meet our friend Stumblebum and we shouldn't really keep him waiting. It'll be a wonderful firework display, you will enjoy it. Afterwards we could walk on the beach and look at the stars if you like.' Morris oozed charm at the girls who found it hard to resist going along with this handsome youth's suggestion.

'Who is this Stumblebum we are going to meet then? Is he another student from the academy?' Brigitte asked as she finished her drink.

'Yes, I think you have met him, the lad with the really long cape and cat called Skipper. He lives with his auntie at the shop that sells crystals and stuff.' Secundus answered.

'Oh, I remember him. I saw him with his lovely little cat once in the High Street as he was going to the academy. Is he any good at magic then? What's he like to know?' Brigitte quizzed Secundus about his friend.

'He is a fairly new novice but he is alright. He can be a bit moody at times and he struggles to get his spells right, but he is a trier, I'll give him that.' Secundus went on.

'He's a nice lad right enough.' Morris agreed.

'Mind you, he does seem to be a walking disaster area continually looking for somewhere to happen.' The older lad chuckled.

'Yes, he definitely has a knack for seeking out mishaps.' Secundus said and smiled to himself as he thought of Morris's own disastrous bungled performance at his presentation in the lecture theatre at the academy some time before.

'Come on then, we'd better get down there.' he continued, making for the door, oblivious to the events that were taking place in the High Street as the others finished their respective drinks.

At exactly that moment the procession of the wizards assembled outside of the academy and set off down the High Street *en-route* to the beach to lead the procession with some dignity and pomp. All of the dignity, however, and a good deal of the pomp, fell by the wayside as the still howling witches suddenly appeared and streaked straight through the middle of the columns of wizards and knocked them hitherto and thus with some force as they sped hysterically towards safety.

Then they ploughed through the lines of torch bearers, town dignitaries, drummers and Morris dancers and knocked them into the gutter as they rushed to the sanctuary of their headquarters in the Women's Centre. They surged in through the front door and firmly bolted it behind them. As their hysteria subsided somewhat, cups of tea were made, sticking plasters applied to wounds and clothes put on as the witches calmed down a little, oblivious to the mayhem in the town that they had recently been the cause of.

Out on the street the wizards picked themselves up and retrieved their pointed hats as they wondered what in blazes had just happened. The mayor found that his official tricorn hat had been trampled out of shape and stormed off in a huff, with the town crier hot on his heels, leaving the wizards to try to reassemble the procession. This was not easy as about half of the wizards had endured minor injuries, including the Scribe Grand Magister, who lay on the cobbled road unconscious. It took half a dozen of the stronger wizards to lift him up and carry him, shoulder height, back to the Academy to recover.

In the gutter of the cobbled High Street lay an assortment of pointed hats, broken hand drums, extinguished torches and balloons on sticks along with the Scribe Grand Magister's goat's horn ear trumpet. It was some time before the bruised and battered wizards and other participants of the procession sorted out who's artefacts were who's, although the Morris dancers to a man chose to abandon their balloons on sticks and left them where they lay in the gutter as they all limped off to the nearest pub. The little bells tied around their knees tinkled mockingly as they went.

It was therefore a diminished and bedraggled procession that now made its way somewhat half-heartedly onwards to light the bonfire, unknown to them that by now it had already been fiercely ablaze for some time. They were such a thoroughly crestfallen body of men as they shuffled down the High Street with what remaining drums were undamaged beating out more of a mournful dirge than a rousing marching rhythm that they hardly noticed poor Stumblebum who was still sat on the kerb gibbering and shuffled on past him, a sorry collection of battered wizards, painted pagans and disheartened drummers.

A little after the procession had trooped past Stumblebum his friends sauntered along the street as they chatted intently to the two girls when they came across the lad, who still babbled away incoherently as he sat alone unable to either make any sense or walk unaided.

'Hello, what's happened here then?' Morris said as he looked closely at the wretched novice's dishevelled condition. The others gathered around him and discussed what was to be done.

'Well, we can't leave him here like this.' Secundus said.

'I think we ought to get him back home to his auntie's. She will sort him out.'

The girls took an arm each and hoisted Stumblebum to his feet as they held on and supported him. They followed after the two lads as they led the way back along the High Street to his auntie's shop. When they got there Auntie Maggie came to the door and let them all in, shocked at her nephews condition. They told her how they had found him sitting on the kerb but had no idea as to why he was in such a state.

'The best thing to do is to get him to bed' Auntie Maggie said after some thought.

'Will you boys help him up to his room, its right at the top of the stairs, and see if you can get him into his bed while I make us all a nice cup of tea.'

The two girls followed Auntie Maggie into her kitchen as Morris and Secundus bustled Stumblebum up the steep, narrow stairs and after a struggle got him into his bedroom where he flopped onto his bed and lay there and stared vacantly at the ceiling. Secundus threw the boy's cape over him as Morris pulled his trainers off.

'Good grief, what on earth is that foul smell in here?' Morris gagged as he spoke.

'Dunno, but it seems to be coming from over there by the fireplace.' Secundus replied, holding his nose tightly.

Both lads went over to investigate and Secundus lifted the bucket from over the mortar and its hair remedy contents. This made them recoil from the fireplace as the smell increased. The vile potion bubbled and made strange plopping noises as it fermented ferociously and emitted foul vapours as it did.

'Oh my good grief, it must be some kind of experiment he is doing.' Morris spoke with a thick, strangled voice.

'Quick, put the bucket back over it and open a window.' he went on, trying not to be sick.

Secundus replaced the bucket and went over and threw the window wide open.

'Come on, let's leave him to rest.' Secundus headed for the door, still holding his nose followed by Morris who was anxious to get out of there and back to the girls.

When they got downstairs they found Auntie Maggie in her kitchen pouring tea from a large brown earthenware teapot as Brigitte and Mandy stroked Skipper. They both cooed and cheeped at the cat as he lapped up the attention and purred loudly as he strutted to and fro.

'How is he, did you get him into his bed alright?' Auntie Maggie asked, handing the boys their cups of tea as she did. They all sat around the kitchen table and tried to fathom what exactly must have happened to Stumblebum to put him in such a state of shock.

'He must have had some kind of fright perhaps.' One of the girls suggested.

'Or maybe he has been attacked!' Secundus put in.

'He could have encountered a ghost of some sort.' Morris suggested as they explored various possibilities.

'No, he is quite used to seeing my spirit guides who often materialise in the house.' Auntie Maggie told them.

'He has even had them visit him in his bedroom so I doubt if seeing someone who has passed over in the street would bother him, I wouldn't think.'

They explored a good number of possibilities as they drank their tea but could not arrive at any firm logical conclusion.

'I expect he will tell me all about it when he is feeling a bit better after he has had a nice rest. I will take a nice cup of hot drinking chocolate up to him later and I am sure I shall find out then. Poor dear, I hope he is going to be alright.' Auntie Maggie sighed.

The others all reassured her that he would be fine and promised to call in the next day to see if he was better before they took their leave. The boys offered to walk the girls home since they believed that they had missed the start of the firework display in any case. Little did they know that it had been all but over when they had found Stumblebum as he sat on the kerb.

Stumblebum eventually fell into a fitful sleep and dreamt of strange nightmare scenarios, all jumbled up. Images of being pursued by hordes of savage, bare breasted women who bayed for his blood and hurled abuse at him disturbed his slumbers along with other strange images. Shuffling lines of zombies plodded wearily onwards in an endless march as he hid from their blank, soulless eyes and pretty girls danced around him as they jeered at him and laughed at his wispy, mousy hair.

He finally awoke to the sound of his auntie's footsteps on the stairs as she brought him a steaming cup of hot chocolate to perk him up, which he sipped at gratefully.

'Feeling better now dear?' Auntie Maggie asked as she sniffed the air with a puzzled, disgusted look on her face.

'What on earth is that bad smell in here? Has Skipper hidden a dead rat somewhere?' she said as she poked around the corners of the room.

'Oh, it's just a project I've got to do for the academy.' Stumblebum lied.

'Well I'm not having bad smells like that in the house. What will my clients think when they come to the séances? Get rid of it!' she commanded as she moved towards the door.

'It's all right auntie, it will be done by tomorrow. I will get rid of it as soon as I can after it is finished.'

'Well, be sure that you do. It's disgusting. Why don't you come downstairs when you are ready and I'll get a nice meal on for supper? Then we can watch some television together and you can tell me all about what happened to you earlier.'

'Yes auntie, I won't be too long.' he reassured her as he drank his hot chocolate and started to revive his spirits a little.

After Auntie Maggie went downstairs Stumblebum sat up and swung his legs over the edge of the bed and slipped his trainers on. Feeling better now after his troubled sleep and after he had drank his auntie's soothing hot chocolate he followed her downstairs and sat in the kitchen watching her get supper ready and he was glad to be in the warmth and safety of her cosy little kitchen.

After supper they both went into the living room accompanied by Skipper and watched television for several hours during which Auntie Maggie gently coaxed the boy to relate the events of earlier that evening. Stumblebum felt very relieved to talk about his ordeal with his aunt occasionally offering words of comfort and so it was a much happier Stumblebum who eventually turned in for bed later that night after such an eventful and horrific day.

Chapter Six

Stumblebum spent all of the following day in the house as it was a Sunday and the academy would be closed. After the events of the previous day he still felt a little fragile and had little desire to be anywhere than in the comfort of his home, so just relaxed and pottered about.

He went up to his room several times to check on his hair potion which by now seemed to have taken on a life of its own as it gave off great globs of evil smelling vapours and effervesced and bubbled away maniacally. The smell by now was so overpowering that he considered throwing it away as Auntie Maggie had wanted him to and thought about doing just that as he sat in the kitchen drinking milk and munched some biscuits until his auntie mentioned something that caused him to change his mind.

'Your friends were very nice, so polite and helpful, and it was very good of them to get you home.' Auntie Maggie said as she busied herself around the kitchen.

'Those girls were lovely. Such pretty, polite girls, both of them.' she went on.

'And the boys were bonnie lads as well, especially that Morris. He is so handsome and doesn't he have a gorgeous head of hair? If only I was twenty years younger…' she trailed off and chuckled heartily.

Stumblebum bristled at the mention of Morris's hair, especially as Brigitte had come along yesterday, and steeled his resolve to continue with the hair remedy on Monday.

'I said hasn't Morris got such lovely hair dear? I bet all of the girls fancy him, what do you think dear?' She persisted.

Stumblebum answered with a grunt and moodily drank the remains of his milk as he brooded about his own wispy hair.

As if to reinforce his decision regarding Dung Ho's hair remedy Morris, along with Secundus and the two sisters, arrived some time later as promised concerned to see if Stumblebum had recovered. Stumblebum should have been pleased to see them but following Auntie Maggie's earlier remarks about Morris he greeted them with less enthusiasm than he ought to have.

His friends put his surliness down to his not being quite fully recovered from the day before. Auntie Maggie made up for Stumblebum's sulky mood by fussing over the group and insisting they stay for some tea whilst she explained to them what had befallen her nephew the previous day. Skipper jumped up onto the kitchen table and pranced up and down again in front of the girls whilst they fussed over him as the group listened in astonishment at the account of Stumblebum's traumatic experience.

'Well, the witches have always had bad feelings towards us wizards but they have never before gone as far as to physically attack any of us to my knowledge. And why were they without any clothes?' Morris said, mystified at the behaviour of the witches.

'Perhaps it was some kind of demonstration and he just got caught up in it so they went for him.' Secundus put in as the girls listened to it all in awe.

'Well, I think I shall be having a word with those witches before long! I'm not having them attacking my lad like that. The state he was in!' Auntie Maggie said with some menace.

As they all enjoyed the sumptuous tea put on for them by Auntie Maggie the witches in question were in their headquarters holding a special 'Moot', or pagan meeting, where they discussed thoroughly the disaster of the day before. They sought to lay blame on someone for what they considered to have been the deliberate sabotage of their wicker man display and the cause of the other mishaps which had then befell them all. After they considered a number of possible theories over whom they thought to be the most likely culprits they kept returning to their arch-rivals, the academy wizards.

'I wouldn't mind betting that that lad we caught on the cliff top spying on us reported back to the old wizards and they organised the sabotage following what he told them. We should make an example of him and then go for the old wizards.' One of the witches said as the others nodded in assent.

'How shall we deal with him then so as to send a message to the wizards that we won't put up with their nonsense any further?' another of the witches asked.

'I think we should lay a trap for the little squirt and catch him, tie him up and tar and feather him, then tie him to the knocker of the front door of the academy. That would make the old wizards sit up and take notice. Show them we witches are not to be trifled with.' Someone else put in.

'That's all very well and we can get on with reprisals later but for now we must protect ourselves from future attacks by demons and other phenomena that they must have summoned to harm us, as well as protection from any hexes and curses placed on us. We must be diligent!' The high priestess addressed the meeting.

'I suggest that we all wear any protection amulets that we have already got and make more for those who don't have any. We should have a ceremony to reinforce the current protective spell we have on the Women's Centre as we must not let our guard drop. Who knows what the wizards are plotting to have in store for us next!'

After she had spoken the others readily agreed to her suggestion and after the 'Moot' concluded prepared to conduct a ritual ceremony for the immediate protection of themselves and the building.

As all of this was taking place in the Women's Centre most of the senior wizards were gathered in the academy holding an extraordinary emergency meeting of senior wizards in order to discuss the disaster of their bonfire parade in an effort to get to the bottom of what had caused such mayhem. The Scribe Grand Magister was not present, however, as he was still a little poorly and recovering in his bed.

After a heated debate the senior wizards arrived at the conclusion that the witches had set out to deliberately sabotage the wizards' celebrations and maliciously and prematurely set fire to the bonfire and fireworks before they staged the mass streak through the town in order to disrupt the procession. The subsequent battery of the participants of the procession must have been deliberate as they appeared to have taken the opportunity to inflict maximum damage.

'Who knows what else they might try. We must be on our guard from any of their spells and curses that they are known to be so fond of. We shall scour the ancient scrolls in our library and make the most powerful protection talismans for ourselves and get the others, the novices in particular, to do the same.' the academy Ipsissimus Grand Magister addressed the assembly.

'After we conclude this meeting I also suggest that we hold an impromptu ceremony to increase the protection spells on the academy building that have been in place to date and to increase their potency.'

So the witches and the wizards went about protecting themselves from each other as the real culprits, Tiberius Mordecai and Slippery Jack, sat by the roaring fire in the study of Mordecai's mansion. They drank wine and gloated as Slippery reported back to his master the intelligence he had gathered concerning the outcome of the previous day's mischief.

'Well that turned out even better than I had hoped for. Well done Slippery for finding out what you have. It seems that the old fogies in the academy and their estranged sisters of the Women's Centre are becoming more preoccupied with each other by the day! Good, good, that will keep their attention away from us.' Mordecai and Slippery snickered slyly as they took deep draughts from their goblets of wine.

'Did you find out any more about that novice whom you saw on the cliff top Slippery, during your enquiries?'

'A little.' Slippery replied.

'All that I could find out is that he is fairly new to the town and lives with Mystical Maggie from the 'new age' shop on the High Street, her nephew I think. He is also one of the newest recruits at the academy and his name is Stumblebum! Apparently the old Scribe Grand Magister misheard his wizard name and got it badly wrong!' Mordecai burst out laughing at this as Slippery gave an evil looking grin.

'Keep an eye on him anyway, Slippery. I have a feeling he could be of use to us sometime, a chink in the academy wizards' armour perhaps.'

'Perhaps!' Slippery repeated in agreement.

'What happened back in the old days, before I came to you to be trained, between you and the others in town I mean?' the apprentice quizzed his mentor.

'Many of the events from those days are probably best forgotten. Suffice it to say that things were very different in the town then, particularly amongst the occult community. There were five main powerful covens operating in the locality made up of thirteen witches each. Six male and six female witches and one priestess per coven. All of these covens were affiliated and came together from time to time to perform powerful collective rituals under the supervision of their high priest who had absolute authority over them. That high priest was Tiberius Mordecai.' The sorcerer paused for effect before he continued.

'Then the feminist movement gained momentum and influenced some of the female witches and before long they infected the other women with their ideology and their disdain for all men turned to hatred so they voted to throw out all of their brother witches. I tried to stop the madness by using my authority but the spiteful harridans all turned on me and I was out on my ear as well!' Mordecai related with some bitterness in his voice.

'So there you have it Slippery! In a nutshell! Things have remained fairly hostile since those days and the female witches still resent men doing magic in the town. They dislike the academy wizards because after they were thrown out of the covens some of the male witches were admitted into the Guild of Wizards, although most were rejected by those snotty moralising traditionalists. I offered to grace their establishment with my presence but they shied away. They said that they disapproved of some of my methods. Bloody cheek but it was their loss!'

Slippery took all of this in. He nodded as he listened to his mentor, feeling a little wiser about the situation in Bilge on Sea than he had been before, and as they say, knowledge is power!

* * * * * * *

The following day at the academy the novices were called into the Great Assembly Hall before the commencement of the day's lessons, lectures and seminars. The Ipsissimus Grand Magister relayed to them the conclusions of the previous days meeting regarding the bonfire parades shambolic disaster.

'The faculty of the Guild of Wizards have concluded after much analysis that after the attack upon our persons by the town's sisterhood of witches that they are engaged in hostile actions against the wizards of our society.' The assembly listened with full attention as the Ipsissimus Grand Magister continued with his cautionary address.

'We therefore are urging all our members, especially the novices, to be on their guard from both physical and psychic attacks from that quarter. Avoid contact with the witches where possible and make protective talismans for yourselves. All of todays' lessons are going to be concerned with the best ways to achieve protection and on advice on talismans, protective spells etc.'

The novices spent their time during the day sifting through the library's books of spells and attending seminars offering instructions on how to make for themselves talismans and other skills that would help render the perceived assaults by the witches' ineffective.

On returning home that evening after a busy day at the academy, Stumblebum devised a plan of his own to help in case he ever got pursued by witches again. He was troubled by his traumatic experiences with the witches both on the cliff top and the next day in the High Street. The recent attack on his person by the massed ranks of screeching witches had hardened his resolve to be on his guard.

Before he had left the academy that day Stumblebum had put in some levitation practice, remembering the demonstration given by Morris at that first lecture he had attended, and did indeed make some progress in acquiring this skill. On returning home he rummaged through his aunties broom cupboard where he emerged with the besom type broom with which Auntie Maggie swept the doorstep in front of the shop. If he could master the art of flying the broomstick he could use it as a quick means of escape should he need to get away in a hurry.

Taking care not to be seen by his auntie he sneaked out of the house with the broom and went around to the little beach behind the houses where he did his magic practice from time to time. He looked about him in the half light of the approaching dusk to ensure that there was no one else there and then placed the broom on the pebbles at the water's edge and began his incantations.

'What are you doing?' a child's voice startled him.

'Who's there?' he demanded, looking around as he spoke.

'Violet Veronica.' The voice answered.

'What's your name?'

'Where are you, let me see you first.' Stumblebum said as he continued to look around.

'I'm here in the *Violet Veronica.*' The voice answered again.

Stumblebum was confused.

'What do you mean, you are *in* the *Violet Veronica*? I thought you meant that was your name!'

'It is my name and I am also *in* the *Violet Veronica.* It's my Uncle Sammy's boat. He named it after me. I'm over here, look.'

Stumblebum looked in the direction of the two little fishing boats and saw a girl of about nine or ten years old stepping out of one of them where she had sat quietly and unseen. The girl came over to near where Stumblebum stood by the waters' edge and looked quizzically at the broom laying on the pebbles.

'What are you going to do with that?' she demanded to know.

'You're the wizard who lives with the crystal lady aren't you. The boy with the cat? Do you know my Uncle Sammy? He used to not mind cats but now he swears and throws things at them whenever he sees them. He seems to have gone a bit funny in the head recently so I would tell your cat to be a bit careful if he comes on to the beach if I were you. Where is your cat?'

Stumblebum opened his mouth to try to answer her but she continued with her stream of questions.

'So what's your name then? Are you going to do some magic now?' Have you got a magic wand then?'

The girl's questions came fast and furious making Stumblebum's head swim.

'I might do some magic if you keep very quiet and don't tell anyone what you have seen.'

Although he usually preferred to do his spells and stuff in secret he decided to show off his magic skills to this clearly impressionable girl as this seemed to be a good chance to amaze somebody with his newfound occult powers.

'So what do they call you then? Are you a very clever wizard?' the girl persisted.

'It's *Shtoom-bell-baum*. They call me *Shtoom-bell-baum*!' he said emphatically.

'Stumblebum! That's a funny name.' the girl replied.

'No, no, it's pronounced *Shtoom-bell-baum*, *SHTOOM-BELL-BAUM*!' he went on, a little irritated.

'That's what I just said, Stumblebum! I am not deaf you know!' Now the girl sounded annoyed.

Somewhat intimidated Stumblebum gave up on the pronunciation and focussed on his levitation spell.

‘Now you must keep totally quiet and don’t fidget or move about. I have to concentrate.’

As he continued with the incantation Stumblebum extended his hands above the broom and concentrated very hard and intoned the magic words. He soon felt a tingling sensation at the tips of his fingers which he also noticed were giving off a barely discernible faint green glow as the magic energy surged towards the broom. At first nothing happened. After a few minutes the broomstick twitched a few times and shifted on the pebbles before slowly rising about a foot or so above the beach.

‘Wow!’ the girl exclaimed excitedly.

‘That’s so awesome! How wonderful!’

Spurred on by this praise the young wizard made the broomstick raise itself to about five or six feet in the air so as to impress the girl and show off his skills at magic some more. As Violet Veronica looked on with expectation Stumblebum decided to make it revolve a few times in order to further impress her. The broomstick slowly spun around into a full revolution and then continued to spin and gathered speed as it gained height and spiralled its way upwards. Stumblebum made some frantic passes with his hands and muttered a spell in an attempt to return the broomstick back to the ground.

It was not to be, however, as the more that Stumblebum tried the higher the broomstick rose. It revolved faster and faster as it spiralled upwards into the night sky. The young wizard and his new friend both craned their necks and watched the broomstick go higher and higher until it became a mere speck high in the darkening sky before it disappeared from view completely. They both stood side by side on the pebbles with necks craned and mouths agape as they gazed towards the stars.

‘Wow, awesome!’ the girl said again.

‘Was it supposed to do that?’

Stumblebum tried to regain some composure, embarrassed at the girl’s question.

'Yes of course. I've sent it into orbit for a while to charge it with magic energy from the stars.' he lied, not wanting to lose credibility in front of the girl.

'So when will it come back?' Violet Veronica persisted.

'Oh, in a while ... sometime tomorrow perhaps.' he blustered.

'When exactly would that be then? I'd like to come along and watch.'

'Shouldn't you be running along home? It's getting rather late and it must be getting near to your bedtime.' Stumblebum had now had enough of this precocious child and her relentless questions and wished she would go away.

'No, Uncle Sammy lets me stay out as long as I like as he knows I like sitting in the *Violet Veronica.* He says it is good to know it is being guarded as much as possible.'

'Well it's time I turned in, I've got a busy day tomorrow. Important wizard business!'

Stumblebum hastily made for his home as he spoke before the wretched child could harangue him with any more impertinent questions.

When he got back indoors, minus Auntie Maggie's broom, he slunk upstairs to his room impatient to get on with the next order of business for that evening. It was time to apply Dung Ho's ancient hair thickening remedy and he had much to prepare.

First he went into the bathroom and took a mirror from the wall and hung it on the hook at the back of his bedroom door in order to admire the lush, dark hair he had been promised by his spirit guide before he cleared the books from his table and went to fetch a bowl and jug of water from the bathroom, along with a towel and some shampoo, which he placed on the table. This done he went over to his fireplace and removed the bucket from over the potion.

The smell by now was so excruciating that Stumblebum almost passed out! It was a credit to his resolve that he continued, after placing his clothes peg once again on his nose and carried the mortar and its festering contents over to the table.

Spreading the entire contents of the mortar evenly along the towel, which he had lain flat upon the table, he then gingerly wrapped it tightly around his head like a turban as prescribed and went and sat on his chair by the open window and opened his book of spells to read. It was going to be a long few hours in order for the potion to work and he needed to occupy himself until then.

Chapter Seven

Stumblebum had nodded off to sleep in his chair by the window and suddenly awoke with a jolt. For a few moments he wondered where he was before remembering the events of earlier that evening and reached up to touch the turban still tightly wrapped around his head. He glanced at the alarm clock he kept by his bed and saw that it was approaching midnight and it was now time to reveal his thick, dark locks of hair, which he hoped might now cascade down to his shoulders, just like Morris's.

He got to his feet and slowly unwrapped the towel from his head. He then rolled it and its foul contents into a ball and threw it as hard as he could out of the window and over the masts of the two little boats towards the sea. Had his eyes not smarted and watered from the fumes he might have noticed the towel unfold as it soared over the boats and he might also have noticed the corner of the towel catch on a clip near the top of the mast on the *Violet Veronica*, yanking the towel back on itself and, driven by its own momentum, winding itself into a tight ball as it came to rest precariously on top of the mast.

Stumblebum dabbed at his eyes and immersed his head in to the bowl of water and squirted shampoo onto his scalp in order to wash the remaining potion out. Still leaning over the basin he brought both hands up in order to massage the shampoo into his hair. Something did not feel quite right however!

He stood up abruptly and looked at himself in the mirror on the door and was aghast upon seeing his reflection. His head was now completely bald like a billiard ball and stained a dingy dark green colour. He rubbed his eyes and looked again then ran a hand across his now totally hairless pate and suppressed an anguished cry, not wanting Auntie Maggie to come investigating.

At this point Stumblebum went into a sort of panic, realising that his hair tonic had had the opposite effect of thickening and darkening his wispy, straggly hair, which now did not seem to be such a bad thing to have. Not only had all of his hair disappeared but his scalp was now stained a dingy shade of dark green!

The boy spent the next few hours in the bathroom washing and scrubbing his head in an effort to remove the staining. By the time he had finished all that he had achieved was to lighten the shade of green, which had become almost a fluorescent, dayglow hue. Not only this but he noticed that as he became agitated his head hummed faintly and pulsated with an eerie throbbing glow.

He marched back into his bedroom and summoned his spirit guide, Dung Ho, in order to confront him with the result of his 'hair thickening remedy' and to see if it could be put right. It was an extremely livid Stumblebum who watched the portly Dung Ho materialise, with his usual broad smile as he made his bows.

'Look what you have done to me you fool.' the boy yelled at Dung Ho, unable to contain his anger.

Dung Ho peered closely at the boy before he spoke.

'Oh my word, what's happened to you?' the spectre inquired, sounding concerned.

'What's happened to me? I listened to your advice, that's what's happened to me! Look at me, this is the result of your hair potion! Can you see any hair?'

'Ah, this is interesting. The same thing happened to the mandarin when he tried it as well. When his bride arrived on their wedding day she screamed and refused to marry him. Her father took back his dowry of a chest full of gold and took his daughter far away.'

'What, you mean this has happened before? Why didn't you tell me?'

'You never asked! All you said to me was did I know of any hair remedies and I did. I thought that the mandarin's little calamity was a one off but it looks as if I was wrong!'

'Never mind though, you might get used to it in time, and it sort of suits you.' Dung Ho beamed at the boy. Stumblebum was so agitated that his head hummed even louder.

'What about all this green stain then? As if a bald head isn't bad enough!' Stumblebum demanded to know, somewhat spitefully, from his follicle challenged spiritual advisor.

'Have you tried to rub it? That might help to get it out?' Dung Ho suggested helpfully.

'Tried to rub it! Have I tried to rub it? I have spent the last few hours rubbing it and the more I rub then the more it glows! My head looks like a giant glow worm's bum now because I tried to rub it!'

Stumblebum's head hummed and throbbed wildly and his shiny dome pulsated with an ethereal green light as he continued to rant at Dung Ho.

'I shall consult with other experts in herbal remedies back in the spirit realm and see if we can find a solution. Meantime, might I suggest you wear a hat?' Dung Ho bowed deeply and faded from view leaving Stumblebum alone. He now wished he had never set eyes on Dung Ho, let alone taken his advice.

Stumblebum climbed into his bed tired and dispirited much later than his normal bedtime and wearing his fez pulled tightly on to his head. He slept a troubled sleep that night and almost overslept the next morning, which caused him to get up too late to witness that morning's mishap outside, below his window, when Salty Sammy dragged his fishing boat into the little harbour in the half light of the late autumn dawn.

* * * * * * *

After the old fisherman's recent unpleasant encounters with noxious substances Salty Sammy no longer left things to chance. Every morning after the last violation he carried a hurricane lamp with him and inspected the interiors of both of his and Barnacle Billy's fishing boats in the morning twilight, paying particular attention to the seats of the two fishing boats.

This morning after his inspection he gave an encouraging nod to Barnacle Billy who proceeded to drag his vessel out into the harbour. As usual Salty Sammy followed and clambered into his boat as it entered the water and yanked on the line to pull the sail up as he sat down on the seat. As the sail reached its zenith it dislodged the towel at the top of the mast, which had remained unnoticed during the inspection by Salty Sammy as he had concentrated on his scrutiny of the seats and decks of the boats, but not the masts.

The old seadog turned his face upwards to watch the progress of the sail at the same time that the rolled up towel unfurled and floated downwards like some strange dream sequence in a continental art film and plopped full on to poor Sammy's face, wrapped around the back of his head and stuck to his face like glue.

Frantically clawing at the towel and making muffled hacking and spluttering sounds as he did he eventually pulled it clear and flung it and its foul contents into the sea before he leaned over the side of the boat and plunged his head under the water a number times. He finally lifted his now pallid face out of the water and looked around him in bewilderment. He then jumped out of the boat altogether and waded back up the ramp to the shore and left the *Violet Veronica* to drift aimlessly out of the harbour and out to sea, like the *Mary Celeste* of seafaring legend.[1]

Meanwhile, Stumblebum, having pulled his fez tightly down to his ears, briefly popped his head around the kitchen door and told his auntie he would skip breakfast as he was late for the academy, not wanting her to notice his green head for the time being. He slunk out

---

[1] The *Mary Celeste*: in the latter part of the 19th century the American sailing ship *Mary Celeste* was found adrift at sea apparently having been hastily abandoned. Neither crew nor passengers were ever found and it remains to this day an enduring maritime mystery. Sometimes referred to as the *Marie Celeste* after a misspelling in an account of the tragedy by Sir Arthur Conan Doyle.

of the house followed as usual by Skipper who never seemed to tire of chasing the hem of his cape.

The annoying cat also had got into the habit of clawing his way to the top of Stumblebum's cape for a rest occasionally to sit on the boy's shoulder as he walked. Sometimes, more recently, he would climb up on top of the fez and curl up for a short nap, and often Stumblebum would forget he was there. He had gone in to the academy a few days earlier and had forgotten about the cat perched on his head and again had to endure the humiliation of being evicted from the library by the Academy Scribe, this time for flaunting the rules on bringing pets into the hallowed halls.

On this particular morning's walk to the academy, however, Skipper would not climb on to the fez as Stumblebum's head faintly buzzed and hummed. The cat stared intently at the source of the noise in fascination as he sat on the young novice's shoulder. Disconcerted by the unwavering gaze at his head Stumblebum tried to knock him from his perch on his shoulder but Skipper just dug his claws in to the cape and persisted with his observation.

By the time that they had arrived at the academy Stumblebum's head buzzed and pulsated under his Fez with a few small shafts of green light escaping here and there as he struggled to release Skipper's grip on his shoulder and put him on the ground. Eventually, after he had suffered a few scratches and bites, Stumblebum got the better of Skipper and wrestled the cat off then chased him back along the street before he entered the academy by the side door, somewhat ruffled by his struggle with his belligerent pet.

Stumblebum looked for Secundus and after he had enquired in some of the usual places of study tracked him down in the spells lab. An unusually high number of novices were in attendance and their earnest attempts at some advanced magic were being executed with uncharacteristic vigour and effort. Secundus appeared to be busy waving his wand at a block of lead and getting it to change into a variety of different shapes and colours. As Stumblebum approached the lead block morphed into a brightly hued blue cauldron which then changed again into a dark grey crucible with red raspberry jam bubbled over its edges in places.

'What's this for then?' Stumblebum asked, intrigued by the experiment.

'There's a rumour going around that the Ipsissimus Grand Magister has succeeded in making gold from a base metal. It's supposed to be a big secret but you know how hard it is for news of these things not to spread like wildfire around here. Everyone else is having a go at it, encouraged by news of his success, and also driven by natural greed, so I thought I would see if I could make any headway. Looks as if I've got as far as making hot jam so far, but hey, if I keep trying I might hit the jackpot.'

'That's good, but listen, I've got a major problem and I need your advice. Is there anywhere private we can go and talk?' Stumblebum looked around the lab, which was unusually crowded with novices frantically engaged in alchemy.

'It should be quiet enough outside in the corridor. What's up?' Secundus tapped the pot of jam with his wand and turned it into a large ice cream Knickerbocker Glory as he headed for the door, followed closely by Stumblebum.

Once in the corridor Stumblebum related to his friend the mishap with his hair remedy and removed his fez to demonstrate the side effects of the treatment before hastily replacing it, looking furtively about to check that no one else had seen his problem.

'That looks rather nasty. Why didn't you go to the herbalist like I advised? That would seem to have been a better course of action.' Secundus said.

'I did, but the potions were too expensive so I took advice from my spirit guide.'

'You've got a spirit guide? Well, it looks as if it misguided you this time. You should have saved up for one of Mr Lee's remedies, it would have been better than this.'

'I know that now, but what can I do about it? Are there any spells that would help?' The tone of Stumblebums voice sounded desperate.

‘There probably are but it would be quite a complicated spell. And we would have to scour the archives to find a suitable one for this, which could take us ages.’ Secundus rubbed his chin thoughtfully.

‘Why don’t you go to the academy apothecary and speak to the Keeper of Potions? He ought to know what to do.’

‘I can’t ask him to help. I would have to admit I used the herbs and spices I got from him for my own uses instead of using them for a homework project. We need to find another way to deal with it where it can be kept from the academy authorities knowing of it.’

‘The only other thing I can suggest is that you talk to David Lee, the herbalist’s son, he’s a novice here too and I am sure you have seen him a few times at lectures before. Meet me back here after lessons and we shall look for him and ask his advice.’ Secundus returned to his alchemy practice in the spells lab leaving Stumblebum to go up to the library to look for any suitable spells, now feeling a little reassured

* * * * * * *

Across the town in the Bilge on Sea Town Hall a meeting of the finance committee of the Corporation was about to commence. A clue to this fact lay in the presence of the huge buffet of smoked salmon, lobsters, oysters and abundance of other good foods, along with dozens of bottles of chilled pink Champagne stacked up on the long wooden table which groaned under the weight of this burden, positioned along one wall of the council chamber.

The mayor, Percival Suggs, a man of ambition and guile, cast an approving eye over this imminent feast as he opened the meeting and welcomed fellow members of the finance committee to this special closed meeting which had been convened in haste. He welcomed and addressed the assembled councillors in attendance with a solemn tone.

‘We’re called to this special meeting to discuss financial matters following the recent disastrous bonfire on the beach and to ensure that any claims on the public finances receive the committee’s closest scrutiny in light of several questions which have subsequently arisen.' The mayor cleared his throat before he continued.

'The first matter on the agenda, and might I say a most important matter indeed, is the unfortunate destruction of the mayoral official tricorn hat, an irreplaceable antique and vital piece of our corporation regalia.' The mayor paused as the other committee members took in this point.

'So what do you propose be done about it since the item in question was last in your care?' Albert Trough, the treasurer and arch-rival of the mayor demanded to know, always pleased to see the mayor in a bit of a corner.

'Well it shall have to be replaced of course. It's a necessary part of the official mayoral regalia.' The mayor replied with a somewhat pompous air.

'I thought you just said it was irreplaceable!' Trough said with a sneer.

'A figure of speech! Of course we will have to replace it. What I meant was that it will not be without some sizeable expense. There is only one milliner's shop that specialises in historic ceremonial headgear in this part of the country that I know of and they would be able to make a replica, but they are expensive, although renowned for their skills in creating excellent quality items of headgear.'

'Would that be your sister's hat emporium in the High Street by any chance?' the treasurer asked, still sneering.

'What exactly are you implying? As it happens the shop does belong to my sister but that is beside the point! The fact remains that it is the only shop in these parts that can do the job, and this important item needs replacing!' The mayor bristled at the treasurer's comment.

'Well get them to send us an estimate as to costs and we shall discuss it at the next finance meeting. The corporation's coffers are not bottomless you know.' Albert Trough in his capacity as guardian of the town's finances and always reluctant to spend money unnecessarily cautioned the committee.

'Yes, yes, we'll get an estimate but it will need replacing soon before the next formal ceremony takes place.' The mayor, a little irritated at the penny-pinching treasurer's obstructive comments, moved on to the next item on the agenda.

'We have received a claim for damages from two fishermen for the loss of their rowing boats by fire caused by the bonfire debacle. I have consulted with our legal department and they advise that we, the corporation, are technically liable as we not only allow the bonfire to take place on corporation land, the beach, but are responsible also for health and safety measures, which in my opinion have been sadly lacking in recent years. As this year's bonfire has shown! However we might get away with it if we redirect the claims by the fishermen to the Guild of Wizards, who after all are the sponsors of the event.' The wily mayor concluded with a smug expression on his face.

The treasurer nodded in agreement, his tight grip on the town's finances getting the better of his dislike for the mayor. For once they found they could agree.

Unfortunately, on this matter, the secretary did not concur with them.

'Do we really want to antagonise the Guild of Wizards, who include some of the towns leading citizens and businessmen amongst their distinguished number? We would not want to lose their patronage due to any bad feeling a claim like this might cause. Perhaps it would be prudent to pick up the tab on this one for the sake of future harmony.' The mayor and treasurer exchanged furtive glances before the discussion opened up for a lengthy and heated free for all amongst the other councillors.

After much consideration and passionate debate and following a show of hands after the matter was put to the vote it was decided to reimburse the fishermen from the community funds. This brought Albert Trough close to tears as the overall wishes of the committee opted for the less confrontational solution, despite the drain on the town's coffers.

The mayor now stood up to address the assembly as he introduced the last and most important order of business on the agenda. Whether to withdraw permission of any further annual bonfires and if not how to avoid such problems in the future! He thrust a thumb under each of his jacket lapels and drew himself up to his full height in order to emphasise the importance of both himself and the proposal he was about to put to the dedicated councillors and again with a solemn tone addressed the meeting.

'It is clear that these recent problems which have never arisen before have thrown up a complex set of issues which need to be fully investigated and resolved. In order to avoid any such problems in the future it has been suggested to me that the most efficient way to tackle it would be to form a working party, with out of pocket expenses of course, so that we might look at all possibilities open to us. Do I have a proposer and seconder from the floor?' The mayor looked around the council chamber at the eager faces and had the motion duly proposed and seconded.

'Can I now have a show of hands in favour of the motion?'

A forest of hands shot into the air to be duly counted by the mayor.

'Passed unanimously. Can I now have a show of hands from volunteers to make up the working party?'

Again a forest of hands shot into the air. As a gesture of impartiality the mayor enrolled the entire committee on to the working party.

'Now that is settled we will need to discuss what action shall the working party take initially. Any suggestions?'

'Mr Mayor, I would like to propose that the working party make a visit to one of the other bonfires or parades held in neighbouring towns in order to see how they organise their events and to investigate how they deal with problems such as crowd control.' One of the councillors offered this as a solution. His suggestion was met by a stony silence.

Another councillor put forward a second suggestion.

'Why not go further afield, and I'm thinking of the Notting Hill Carnival, which might be more informative for us?'

This received a few nods of assent in the chamber before another councillor addressed the assembly.

'Last year my wife and I went to Brazil for a little holiday and we visited Rio de Janeiro during their carnival. It was very impressive and I can recommend a really good hotel where they would do block bookings for us. It could prove to be just the learning curve that we are looking for.'

The other councillors all gave vigorous approving nods at this suggestion and even the treasurer did not make any of his usual objections as the assembly collectively looked in the direction of the mayor.

'That sounds like a brilliant suggestion to me. It would enhance our knowledge of these matters greatly and also incorporate issues of ethnicity, diversity and inclusion and bring overall benefit to the town for future events. Can I have a show of hands on this last proposal, which I will propose if somebody else seconds.'

The mayor veered away slightly from rigid adherence to protocol and hastily put the proposal to the chamber. Everyone present again swiftly raised their hands.

'Motion carried, unanimously! All we need to do now is to work out the details and the secretary will make the necessary arrangements. Before we go into the matter further and work out some details however, owing to the approaching lunchtime, I will close the meeting for a short meal break and we can continue the discussion when the meeting reopens after we have partaken of some light refreshments.'

The mayor rubbed his hands together in satisfaction as he made his way over to the feast.

'Can somebody start opening the Champagne?' he instructed as everyone got stuck in to the banquet on the table.

The meeting did not make any more progress that day, on matters arising or otherwise.

Chapter Eight

After lessons ended for the day Secundus and Stumblebum met outside the spells lab as arranged and searched the usual haunts in the academy for David Lee. They eventually found him talking to Morris outside of the library as the Academy Scribe locked up.

The novices greeted one another and made small talk as they watched the Academy Scribe hang the large bundle of huge iron keys on to a hook attached to the belt around his waist after locking the library doors. He gave a disapproving sniff to the boys when they bade him goodnight before he made his way down the stairway and out of sight.

Once the Academy Scribe had left Secundus explained Stumblebum's predicament to the other two novices. David inspected Stumblebum's head with some interest, shaking his own head in disbelief.

'I've never come across this kind of problem before, it must have been a very volatile concoction you applied to have this effect. The best advice I can offer is to go and speak to my dad and see if he can find a treatment.' The herbalist's son suggested.

'There might be an ointment he has that will reduce or even eliminate the discolouring to your head but I doubt if there is a remedy for re-growing your hair. Even if there is such a remedy then I expect it would take some time for it to show a result. Have you thought of wearing a wig?' David suggested as the boys made their way out of the building and headed down the High Street in the direction of Mr Lee's shop.

The group of novices were deep in discussion about Stumblebum's head as they made their way along the High Street when they spotted two sinister looking figures walking towards them. Both men were dressed entirely in black, each wearing a long black frock coat which gave them the appearance of undertakers. The taller and stockier of the pair carried a black Malacca silver topped walking stick and wore a tall black stovepipe hat. The somewhat shabbier, skinnier young man at his side wore a battered top hat perched on his head at a jaunty angle.

The big man and his younger companion simultaneously broke into wide grins as they spotted the group of novices and walked on up to them as if they were about to enjoy some sport with the boys. The pair sniggered to each other before the older man spoke.

'Well, well, well, and what do we have here? The academy's finest! The three musketeers, Morris, Secundus and David! He said sarcastically.

'And who is this you have with you, a new member of your little gang I take it, young D'Artangion I presume?' The tall well-built man had an intimidating presence as he addressed the group with his deep booming voice whilst his creepier, younger companion sniggered in encouragement.

Morris spoke to the pair rather nervously.

'Evening Mr Mordecai. Slippery. This is Stumblebum, he's fairly new to the academy.' Morris nodded in Stumblebum's direction.

'It's pronounced *Shtoom-bell-baum* actually.' Stumblebum said timidly.

Mordecai roared with laughter at this as Slippery sneered at the group of novices.

'The boy has some spirit, I like that Slippery. Perhaps we ought to take him on as a junior apprentice, what do you think? He could prove to have hidden talents.' Mordecai sized up Stumblebum as he closely scrutinised the boy.

'Nah, he looks a bit simple to me.' Slippery replied.

‘Anyone who hangs out with this group of losers can’t be much good. Best to leave him with his academy friends where he belongs.’

‘At least we are still at the academy, Slippery, we haven’t been expelled like someone not a million miles away. So don’t talk to us about losers.’ Morris retorted, as clearly there was little love lost between him and Mordecai’s acolyte.

Mordecai laughed loudly as he walked on down the street and called to Slippery to join him.

‘Come along Slippery we have got bigger fish to fry than this little shoal of sprats.’

Before he followed his master Slippery stepped up close to Morris and prodded the young wizard in the chest as he spoke, clearly rattled by the taunt.

‘You had better watch your step Morris. I’ve had reports that Brigitte has been seen with novices from the academy a few times and I bet that you have been pestering her to go out with you. Well I saw her first so steer clear of her or I will make big trouble for you. Back off!’ Slippery snarled at Morris before he caught up with Mordecai.

‘Ooh, I’m really scared!’ Morris retorted with some bravado, as the two sorcerers walked away.

‘You don’t want to antagonise those two, they can be dangerous.’ Secundus cautioned Morris as the group moved on down the High Street.

‘Who are they, those people?’ Stumblebum asked, intrigued by the apprenticeship offer.

‘You have just met Tiberius Mordecai, a powerful sorcerer who dabbles in the black arts, and his apprentice Slippery Jack.’ Secundus informed Stumblebum.

‘A few years ago Mordecai got Slippery to enrol at the academy so that he could steal ancient scrolls and books of rare spells from the library for him. The Academy Scribe caught him sneaking books out that he shouldn’t have had access to and he was instantly expelled. Until then they had not known he was associated with Mordecai, a man with a big grudge against the academy, and very dangerous. You want to stay well away from those two, they are serious trouble.'

'I suppose the deaf old Scribe Grand Magister got it wrong at his naming ceremony then, stuck with a name like Slippery?' Stumblebum still had issues with his wizard name and was reassured to know of others in the same predicament.

'Oh no, he has always been called Slippery as long as anyone who knows him can remember. It's a nickname of course, but it's now what everybody calls him. It's because of his devious, slippery personality, a real bad apple. He's been called that for so long now that he is proud of the name. He even gave it as his wizard's name at his naming ceremony when he enrolled at the academy.'

Stumblebum stopped dead in his tracks following this revelation.

'What! You mean you can use your own name when you enrol then?'

'Yes, that's always been the case. David here for instance gave his real name but some of us like to have more appropriate names. It is a bit hit and miss nowadays though with the Scribe Grand Magister making so many mistakes. It was a fashion which began many years ago when someone insisted on being called Merlin instead of John Smith and now most enrolees like to choose their own wizard names.' Secundus explained.

I got called Secundus because my older brother Primus attended the academy before me and it seemed appropriate since I was the second of my family to attend the academy.

Stumblebum went silent as he took in this information, feeling a little hard done by.

'Ah, here we are.' David stopped the group in front of his father's shop, *The Golden Dragon*, and led the way inside as the other three novices trooped in behind him.

Mr Lee listened quietly as his son explained Stumblebum's predicament before giving the boy's head a thorough examination whilst he tut-tutted continually and shook his own head as he did. He gave Stumblebum some unction to apply to his head and as he was a fellow student with his son allowed him to put it on account and pay later, when he could afford to.

After thanking Mr Lee and saying goodbye to him and David the three remaining boys left the shop and walked on down the High Street together before going their separate ways. Secundus seemed to be in deep thought and before they parted company spoke to Stumblebum with some concern.

'You know Stumblebum, I don't think you should dabble with potions and the like until you have had more experience with them under supervision at the academy. You also need to practice your magic more when you are at home or you will never get the right skills needed for being a wizard. Try to get in some good practice before the exams.' He advised.

'I do try to practice on the little beach behind Auntie's house when there is no one about. Trouble is that recently this annoying little girl, Violet Veronica, has taken to pestering me whenever I try to do anything and I can't get rid of her.' Stumblebum told the others.

Now Secundus stopped walking, a look of shock on his face.

'Violet Veronica! Did you say Violet Veronica? Not that little horror! You want to be very careful when she is around. She can throw a tantrum at the drop of a hat and she has a terrible temper, all of her family have. You must take care not to annoy her. Everyone calls her *violent* Veronica because of her short temper. She kicks and scratches when she loses it, ask Morris here, she once kicked his shins black and blue when he was entertaining at a children's party and she didn't like the magic tricks he was doing, didn't she Morris?'

Morris nodded in agreement, a pained look passing across his face at the mention of the bad memory.

'Yes, keep well away from her Stumblebum, she is dangerous. The little wretch kept pestering me to pull a white rabbit out of a hat when I performed once at a children's party she was at. I didn't have a white rabbit with me but she insisted. When I made a balloon animal for her instead she freaked out and kicked me repeatedly on my shins. Nearly broke my legs she did!' Morris frowned at the thought of his encounter with Violet Veronica.

‘I’ll try and avoid her in future but it won’t be easy. She lurks about in her uncle’s boat all the time. Close to where I do my practice.’

‘Perhaps you could find somewhere else to practice where she won’t find you then. I’d give it some thought if I were you. See you tomorrow then.’ Secundus and Morris made their farewells as they turned off the High Street and headed away along a side street.

Before Stumblebum arrived home he passed by a hat shop and noticed that as well as hats there were a few wigs on display in the window which reminded him of what David had said about wearing one. Perhaps he could get one for now, until he found a spell or some other cure for his baldness, so that no one need know of his predicament, particularly Brigitte. On closer scrutiny he saw that the wigs were all very expensive and well beyond his means. He would have to find some way of earning extra money and would give the matter his utmost thought over the next few days, resourceful wizard as he was.

* * * * * * *

Stumblebum spent much of his time following his decision to get a wig trying to think of any schemes which would help him to earn extra money so that he could buy himself one. He considered a number of options, all of which were either impractical or beyond his capabilities. All of his schemes fell short of any positive solution to his financial problem. An unexpected opportunity presented itself however, from an unexpected source.

One evening as Stumblebum was busy in his bedroom doing some spell studies Auntie Maggie called up the stairs to him.

‘There’s a girl at the front door to see you. She says it is important.’

Hoping that it could be Brigitte calling on him he pulled his fez down tightly on to his head and scuttled down the stairs. When he got to the door he was at once disappointed and rather horrified as his gaze rested on the person of Violet Veronica who had waited impatiently for him on the doorstep.

‘You took your time!’ she admonished Stumblebum sulkily.

‘You haven’t been on the beach recently, I’ve been looking for you. What have you been doing? Where have you been?’ She demanded.

‘I’ve had a lot of studies to get on with in my room, for the academy, important stuff.’ He stammered, a little nervously.’

‘Well I’ve got a job for you. It’s for my Uncle Sammy really and he will pay you for it.’

Stumblebum’s ears pricked up at this.

‘I’ve got a lot on at the moment.’ he lied,

‘What exactly did you want me to do anyway?’ he enquired cautiously.

‘Well, you know how I said Uncle Sammy had gone a bit funny in the head recently? Well he seems to think that his boat is cursed and he hasn’t set foot in it for a while now. He refuses to go near it ever since he let it drift out to sea and Uncle Billy had to tow it back to the beach after he found it adrift and unmanned. In fact he doesn’t leave the house much now, just sits in his chair and mumbles to himself all day.’ Violet Veronica gave the young wizard a quizzical look.

‘I mentioned it to my Uncle Sammy that I knew someone who might help with the boat and he said he would pay well to get the curse removed. Can you take curses off things? I expect that you can. I’ve seen you do some awesome magic before so I should think that to remove a curse would be easy for you. Well, will you do it?’

Now here was an opportunity that presented itself out of the blue which Stumblebum had not expected. He could feel his head pulsating under his fez as he took in all that Violet Veronica had just told him and looked for a way to maximise his advantage with this situation.

‘Actually I specialise in curses, both to remove and bestow them, but it takes a lot of skill and there would be a sizeable fee involved.’ he lied, with some satisfaction.

‘I think Uncle Sammy would pay well to get his boat un-cursed. He hasn’t been out in it fishing for ages. Will you do it then? How soon can you do it? How much will it cost then?’ The precocious child persisted in questioning him.

'Oh, let me get back to you on that, and when I can fit it in with my schedule too. I will let you know when I have worked it all out.'

'Oh, goody, that's settled then. I can't wait. I shall come along and watch when you do it. It will be awesome!' Violet Veronica ran back to her uncles' cottage as Stumblebum went back up to his room and rubbed his hands together with satisfaction. He tried to remember the price of the wigs in the shop and then sat down to work out how to make it look as if he was doing curse removal magic to impress these superstitious fishing folk.

Chapter Nine

Winifred Closet was a serial gossip! She was also many other things, few of them very nice! She could not help herself. It was in her nature to be obnoxious. She was also long past the first flood of youth to say the least! A long, long way past. She had never possessed classic good looks but made up for this by having a misguided belief in her own perceived beauty, importance and great talent, which, alas, were all also sadly lacking.

She put herself about a bit. If there was an organisation or society that had the potential for her to display her 'gifts' and to enable her to show off and feed on attention at the expense of others then she would join it. She enrolled on to painting classes, pottery 'workshops', creative writing 'workshops' and the like in the delusion that she was competent in all of these endeavours, which sadly she was not, but nonetheless expected great praise and much massaging of her enormous ego from the other members and participants.

Along with many other talentless, bored and aging matrons of Bilge on Sea, she had discovered that the most important skill necessary for the pursuit of these pastimes was the ability to apply for funds, of which success was largely dependent on paying lip service to whatever political ideology was currently prevalent no matter how asinine or banal. Hence the bank balances of the arts societies and 'creative' groups of Bilge on Sea were swollen from the taxes paid by the hard working to ensure that the idle and talentless of the town had ample outlet for promoting their misguided and grotesque offerings.

Another of these 'outlets' that Winifred frequented was the Bilge on Sea Old Town Amateur Repertory Theatre Society, which liked to be known by the acronym of the 'Old Town A.R.T.S.', but which was more generally referred to around the town as the 'Old T.A.R.T.S'. This was a society consisting almost entirely of self-promoting prima donnas of whom Winifred was the leading and most dominant amongst others, mainly women of a certain age and several fey men, with thespian ambitions, and it was a major recipient of the towns arts funding.

Several other 'workshops' of which Winifred attended were put on in the Women's Centre in the High Street and it was here that she learned of a snippet of information useful for spreading as gossip, particularly as it involved someone she knew well who ran another of the events to which Winifred was a frequent visitor.

It was therefore with some haste after leaving her latest 'workshop' at the Women's Centre that Winifred scurried down the High Street towards the little 'New Age' gift shop run by Stumblebum's Auntie Maggie and where séances were put on of which Winifred often attended.

Winifred sat at the kitchen table as Maggie poured them both a cup of tea. Winifred's eyes were glistening with the effort of keeping her gossip in until she had Maggie's full attention, waiting for the appropriate moment to drop the bombshell to its maximum effect. The effect, however, was not entirely as she had hoped for when she finally finished relaying the rumour that the witches were planning to set a trap for Maggie's nephew and catch him and paint him with tar and feathers as revenge for what they believed was his part in the recent sabotage of their wicker man ritual.

Winifred concluded her account with a look of delight and smug satisfaction on her face at being the first to deliver bad news and hoping for a grateful response for her diligence in the matter. The supercilious expression soon fell from her countenance when Maggie, who had listened to her gossip in total silence, slowly got up from her seat and fixed Winifred with a piercing gaze and with a look of thunder on her face, before she then addressed her in a sombre, measured tone.

'You are a spiteful and vindictive woman without a decent bone in your worthless body!' Maggie snarled at the now worried Winifred.

'Do you expect me to be pleased with you for telling me this silly nonsense? The witches in this town, as well as anyone else for that matter, know better than to get the wrong side of me and that is just what you have achieved by your account of this fanciful boasting from them. You would have done well to have kept it to yourself but that is not in your nature is it Winifred? I have never really liked you, less so now, and would be grateful if you would go away and never trouble me with your presence again. Now leave!'

Winifred opened her mouth to say something but was checked by the fierce look on Maggie's face and so closed her mouth again without speaking until she had got up and was about to step out of the door.

'What about the séances? Surely you can't…' Winifred hastily stepped into the street before finishing her sentence and scurried away as Maggie stepped menacingly towards her.

After her visitor had left Maggie sat at her table thinking about what had been said for a long time before she put on her coat and tied her headscarf on in a sort of 'no nonsense, cross me at your peril' kind of manner before heading for the door out of which Winifred had so recently hastily departed and then marched on up the High Street in the direction of the Women's centre.

* * * * * * *

After that morning's last 'workshop' for women had ended and trestle tables folded and stacked against the wall of the large hall along with about half of the chairs, the remainder of the chairs were reorganised into a semicircle so that some of the witches from the five covens who had been present at the 'workshop' could have an impromptu Moot.

Meryl, the high priestess, seated herself roughly centre with the others either side of her as the Moot got under way.

The little gathering had hardly begun with its business as the chatter and small talk subsided and Meryl was about to conduct a small blessing on the assembled sisters when the door of the hall burst open and Mystical Maggie came in and strode purposefully straight over towards where Meryl sat, which caused the group of women to fall silent in their surprise at the interruption.

'Why, Magnolia, what a lovely surprise, it's been some time… arrrrgh!!!' Meryl yelled loudly as Maggie seized hold of her ear with a vice-like grip and heaved her to her feet before she turned on her heel and headed back to the door and dragged the poor woman along in her wake.

'A word in your ear Meryl. Outside. In private!' Maggie said, missing the irony, as she dragged Meryl back through the doorway and into the street. The other witches sat in silent shock too frightened to help their leader for fear of the formidable Maggie turning her wrath on them. They sat stunned with mouths agape as they wondered what on earth had just happened.

After about ten minutes or so Meryl came back in to the Women's Centre alone and looked somewhat shaken, face pale and body trembling, with a look of contrition on her face. She returned to her seat and after she had composed herself for a few moments addressed her companions.

'Apparently we have been misled into believing that Magnolia's nephew was responsible for sabotaging our wicker man ceremony. Magnolia, whom I have known for many years and is not one to mince words, has put me right on a few things and I must ask all of you to refrain from harming the lad in question in any way.' Meryl seemed a little sheepish as she spoke.

'It has been pointed out to me that any such an action would have consequences for us. So let's draw a line under this sorry affair and move on, and I repeat, do not under any circumstances attempt to harm the academy novice Stumblebum in any way as we are now being held responsible for his wellbeing.'

* * * * * * *

Later that day after Stumblebum returned home following a productive afternoon at the academy where he had done some levitation magic practice along with some new spells he found his auntie drinking tea at the kitchen table and chatting to a stranger.

The man was a rum looking cove to say the least, a short fat man with a shock of vivid red hair which protruded from under a tweed deerstalker hat and a pair of gilt *pince nez* perched on the end of his button nose. Cascading down from his several chins a long red beard plaited neatly into a pigtail hung down almost to his rotund waist. To say that he was short and fat was something of an understatement. His little legs barely touched the floor below his chair, but it was his enormous girth which emphasised his shortness. His body was almost spherical in shape and it had often been said of him that, were he to fall over, he would remain at exactly the same height!

'Ah, good, you are home dear. I want you to meet an old friend of mine. This is Mr Roland Ramsbottom, from the north originally but has lived down here in Bilge on Sea for a long time now. He has kindly offered to take you under his wing as a sort of mentor and help you with your studies. He is a freelance wizard, a pagan and an authority on druids, Celtic culture and witchcraft. I thought it might broaden your outlook and add a new dimension to your studies if he were to guide you a little and he has agreed.'

'Ay up youth, reight glad to meet thee. I'll show thee summat tha waint learn at yon college tha nuz, just stick with me kid an' tha'll be aw' reight, sithee.'[2] His mouth was moving and some noise was coming out so he must be talking, but Stumblebum hadn't a clue as to what he actually said.

---

[2] This loosely translates into normal English as: Good afternoon young man, I am delighted to make your acquaintance. I can give you some insight into skills over and above those taught at your current place of learning. I shall look out for your general wellbeing in these matters.
[Ay up = hello. waint = will not. summat = something. thee = you. tha nuz = you know. tha'll be aw reight = you will be just fine. There is no equivalent translation for 'sithee', an ambiguous utterance often used after a statement by people who live in the north.]

Stumblebum looked blankly at the strange man then turned to his auntie with a puzzled look on his face.

'Bless you dear, are you finding his northern dialect a bit hard to understand? You will get used to it, they all talk a bit like that in the north. Mr Ramsbottom has invited you to lunch at his house on this coming Sunday and afterwards you can learn some of his pagan spells and magic. That will be nice won't it dear?'

'I suppose so.' Stumblebum wasn't too sure, but it wouldn't hurt to go and check it out, he might pick up some useful tips and Auntie seemed to think highly of him. Perhaps he could do his spells practice near to his house, away from Violet Veronica and her persistent pestering.

Stumblebum and Auntie Maggie spent a pleasant couple of hours as they chatted with Stumblebum's new mentor. Auntie Maggie explained to her nephew the gist of what was being said from time to time a bit like an interpreter. By the time that he retired to his room he had almost got the hang of this strange dialect and hoped that he would be able to understand the conversation on his own the following Sunday when he was to visit Mr Ramsbottom and his wife for lunch.

When he got in to bed that night he lay for some time staring at the ceiling and going over in his mind the day's events. It had been on the whole a productive day. He had made good progress with his magic practice at the academy, particularly the levitation, of which he was becoming quite confident in doing to a good level of success and with very few mishaps.

He had also called on Salty Sammy on his way home and secured a hefty advance on his curse removing fee which would cover the cost of a wig from the hat emporium. Finally, he now had a personal wizard tutor and mentor and he felt that this would be a great help in his preparation for the coming exams for his subsequent grade review at the academy.

Stumblebum drifted into a comfortable sleep as he mulled over these positive developments, sure in the knowledge that things were finally better, after all of the recent setbacks he had endured. Yes, things were definitely looking good for the future. Surely nothing could spoil things now? After all, what could possibly go wrong?

* * * * * * *

Something hovered above him as he slept which caused him to awake with a start and in the dark of the room detected that something illuminated the space above his bed. As his eyes adjusted to the dim light and focussed on the apparition he was startled to see what appeared to be three Dung Ho's as they leant over and peered intently at him.

'Arrrrgh!!!' he yelled in shock and sat up in bed abruptly as the three beaming spectres' bowed in perfect synchronicity as they hovered just above his head.

'What are you doing here lurking over me like that? You nearly gave me a heart attack. And why are there three of you?' Stumblebum was livid at having his sleep interrupted in this manner, particularly as it was Dung Ho whom he still had not forgiven for his hair loss.

'I think I see why you are confused.' The Dung Ho on the left of the group beamed at Stumblebum as he spoke.

'Allow me to present my two younger brothers, Ho-Ho and Yo-Ho. They are twins and we all have a strong family resemblance so everyone gets confused.' The other two apparitions smiled and bowed again at the introduction.

'You mean to tell me that your father, whose family name is Ho, has called his sons Ho and Yo?' A bewildered Stumblebum looked at Dung Ho's brothers, identical to him apart from their wispy beards and drooping mustachios whereas Dung Ho had no facial hair. In fact, just like Stumblebum now, Dung Ho had no hair at all!

'Oh no, that would be silly. Their full names are Ho-Ho Ho and Yo-Ho Ho, Ho being the family name. Ho-Ho, Yo-Ho and Ho had completely different meanings in ancient China.' Dung Ho explained somewhat confusingly.

‘Like with me, if you should wish to summon them just say their names three times each and they will appear before you.’ He went on, as if to clarify matters.

‘Why would I want to summon them? One of you is bad enough, and I am not saying Ho-Ho Ho and Yo-Ho Ho three times under any circumstances. If Auntie were to hear me she would think I had lost the plot!’

‘Anyway, why are you all here at this time of night? You nearly frightened the willies out of me just then, don’t ever do that again!’

‘Sorry if we startled you. I didn’t think you would wake up and I wanted my brothers to have a look at your scalp. I said I would consult with other experts from the spirit world didn’t I? Lucky for you Ho-Ho and Yo-Ho are experts in herbal remedies just like me. Now we have had a look we shall go back and mull it over until we find a solution. Until later then.’ Dung Ho and his brothers all gave a deep bow before fading from sight leaving Stumblebum sitting up in bed feeling bewildered, annoyed and wide awake, wishing yet again he had never set eyes on his annoying spirit guide.

Chapter Ten

The following morning before he left for the academy Stumblebum stuffed the money he had got from Salty Sammy into one of his trouser patch pockets and carefully buttoned the flap down on it so as to keep it secure. As usual Skipper pursued him down the street and attacked the hem of his cape like a feline from hell until they both arrived at their destination and Stumblebum chased his pet back down the road.

After his disturbed sleep he felt tired and found he couldn't concentrate properly on his studies, annoyed because he wanted to work out a magic performance for the beach that night and make it look as if he had removed the imagined curse from Salty Sammy's boat.

He decided to put on a little display in order to impress these gullible fishing folk and get them to believe it to be serious magic. By the end of the day he had devised a suitable routine with several special effects that ought to suffice and left the academy for home rather tired but pleased with his ideas.

Stumblebum's mind was preoccupied with a more pressing matter however. As he made his way along the high street after he left the academy that afternoon he called in at the hat emporium on the way home. The shop had a double-fronted aspect with a large display window either side of a glass door, which was recessed a little and through which he entered the shop. Inside was a long counter the length of the shop with shelves neatly stacked with boxes behind and hat stands and wig stands arrayed along the glass display counter at intervals.

A plump matronly lady wearing a navy serge skirt and frilly white blouse approached Stumblebum as he browsed amongst the various wigs on display and asked if she could be of assistance. Stumblebum was rather embarrassed and looked down at his feet as he spoke to her and avoided any eye contact.

'Er, yes, I'd like to buy a wig please, only I noticed you sold wigs and I'd like one.'

'Do you know your hat size or shall I measure your head for you to be sure?' she asked, to Stumblebum's horror, as he did not want to remove his fez and reveal his green head, which was now beginning to throb and hum slightly under his headgear due to this current anxiety.

'No, no, that's alright, I know what size I am.' Stumblebum blurted out a hat size which he hoped was about right and the shop lady led him over to where a selection of wigs were on display.

After browsing for a couple of minutes he settled on a dark brown wig with a fringe and soft tumbling curls which he guessed were about shoulder length. The shop lady spent some time rummaging amongst boxes on the shelves behind the counter until she found one in the appropriate size, wrapped the box in brown paper and tied string around it, leaving a loop for carrying, like a handle. Stumblebum paid her for the wig and hastily carried the package out of the shop and set off for home impatient to try it on in the privacy of his bedroom.

After Stumblebum arrived home he again took the mirror from the bathroom and hung it on the hook on the back of his bedroom door and then unwrapped his parcel and tried the wig on. It was perhaps a size or so too big and slipped down a little towards his eyebrows but overall it was a big improvement on his appearance and Stumblebum was pleased at the result and posed for a long time in front of his mirror admiring his new look. Eventually satisfied with his purchase, he removed the wig and placed it on the wooden wig stand which had accompanied it in its box and stood it on the end of his table.

He decided he would first wear it on the visit to the Ramsbottom's that coming Sunday when he was to go over for lunch. He would have to introduce his new look to his auntie after he had a little talk to her about his hair mishap predicament, though he thought she would no doubt disapprove and see wearing a wig as an unnecessary extravagance.

Before going down for some tea Stumblebum busied himself making preparations for that evening's curse removing demonstration as he laid out a number of items he would need on to his bed. He placed his wand and a pouch of flash powder beside each other and then took from his casket a quill, ink bottle and a piece of parchment.

He sat down and scribbled some impressive looking magic symbols on to the parchment and left it on the bed with the other items as he went over to his bookshelves to get a couple of drawing pins and chuckled to himself under his breath at the thought of how easy it was to separate these simple fishing folk from their money.

Just then the bedroom door creaked open a few inches and Skipper entered, curious to see what Stumblebum was doing, as, like all cats, it was in his nature to be inquisitive. Skipper took a couple of steps into the bedroom before he stopped dead in his tracks and stood stock still for several seconds before his tail shot into the air and his fur puffed out as he hissed vehemently and his eyes glazed over and glared maniacally.

Hearing Skipper's hissing caused Stumblebum to turn and look for what had troubled the cat. Too late he followed to where Skipper's gaze rested as the cat launched himself into a fearsome and impressive pounce.

'No, no Skipper, leave it, no, it's all right!' Stumblebum called out as Skipper pounced on the wig and dragged it to the floor and furiously bit, kicked and clawed at it as if it were some intruding animal of some sort.

'Oh no!' Stumblebum wailed, though he knew better than to try to retrieve the item, as recent experiences had taught him that he could suffer grievous injury in the attempt.

The wig and Skipper were embroiled in a *battle royale* as claws and fur whirled in a frenzied flurry. Patches of wig hair flew off in tufts as the cat kicked, shook and savaged the mysterious creature that had dared to intrude on his domain. After what seemed to be an age, but in reality just a few minutes, the cat stopped his onslaught and dropped the creature at his feet, satisfied that it was now quite dead, and proceeded to wash his face with a look of triumph.

Stumblebum picked up the vandalised and vanquished wig and sat on his bed with it on his lap as he gently stroked it and sobbed quietly, feeling thoroughly defeated. Yet again the world had turned against him and delivered a cruel blow just as he was feeling full of hope and optimism.

* * * * * * *

At exactly that moment in the old repertory theatre in the Old Town one Quentin Claymore, amateur thespian, playwright and self-appointed stage manager was preparing to receive several visitors. His mind too had become pre-occupied with wigs of late and now he was taking a bold stance. He had opened the little theatre up a few hours before that evening's meeting and rehearsals of the Old T.A.R.T.S. was due to begin as he attempted to achieve something of a *fait accompli* for the good of the society.

Quentin was one of the two long standing male members of the society and passionate about preserving and promoting the success of the little theatre in which it put on its productions. Quentin also stood alone amongst the other members, all of whom were well past their sell-by dates, in his desire to inject new 'blood' into the ageing ranks of this self-preservation society of geriatric poseurs.

Recent years had seen a stubborn resistance to change and renewal from the hard-core of old and pretentious women who promoted their own self-aggrandisement as they hogged the best roles for themselves. This strategy was now getting a bit strained as recent productions had shown when Winifred Closet insisted on taking the most prominent of female parts in every play. As she had access to the large selection of wigs donated by her to the society she felt that they were all that were needed to transform herself into a beautiful young heroine and therefore could not see what the objections were.

Winifred's portrayal of Blanche in *A Streetcar Named Desire* solicited from the audience outright mockery and hoots of derision as did her part as Desdemona in the disastrous production of *Othello* in last year's offerings of the Shakespeare season, which was important to put on as it increased the scope of funding revenue upon which the society was dependant.

What was needed was an influx of younger players but every attempt by Quentin in the past to encourage this was met by hostility and resistance. Things had now arrived at an impossible impasse following the choice of the next production, *Romeo and Juliet*. Winifred as usual demanded the eponymous role of the young and beautiful teenage Juliet. No amount of stage make up, flamboyant wigs and clever use of stage lighting would be able to conceal this latest affront to the beloved Bard!

Quentin's covert strategy was rewarded when several bright young things entered the auditorium and approached the stage where he sat on a chair as he read a copy of the script. He excitedly called them to join him up on the stage and introductions were made. A young novice wizard he was acquainted with, Mooning Mike, whom Quentin had approached some time earlier to ask if he might get some of his young friends interested in amateur dramatics and bring them along, introduced two pretty, fresh faced girls, sisters Mandy and Brigitte and their friend Morris, a young man with dashing good looks.

Quentin was absolutely delighted at these new additions to the society and in his mind's eye visualised Morris and Mandy, the younger of the girls, with her natural waist length blonde hair, in the title roles of the upcoming Shakespeare production. Now all he needed to do was to enrol the newcomers and introduce them to the older members and suggest them for the leading roles.

*   *   *   *   *   *   *

Later that evening as dusk turned to night and the stars shone bright in the sky Stumblebum knocked on the door of Salty Sammy's cottage. The door of the cottage opened and Violet Veronica peered out at Stumblebum.

'I'm ready to remove the curse from the boat now so if you would like to tell your Uncle Sammy to join me on the beach I shall begin.' He told the girl.

'Oh, awesome! Wait here and I'll get him.' Violet Veronica went back indoors and Stumblebum could hear several voices as he waited.

Violet Veronica, Salty Sammy and Barnacle Billy all trooped out of the house and followed Stumblebum to just opposite where the boat, the *Violet Veronica*, rested on the pebbles and they all stood together as he made his preparations. The fishing folk watched silently in awe and anticipation.

Stumblebum dramatically drew his wand out from beneath his cloak and pointed it at the boat with a flourish and then twiddled it around for effect before he appeared to concentrate hard and muttered a levitation spell whist making mysterious passes with his free hand. The boat shifted slightly on the pebbles as Stumblebum continued with his spell and this display of magic made the fishermen gasp in astonishment.

Encouraged by their response he caused the boat to rise slowly to a few feet in the air before getting it to float steadily over the harbour wall and hover just above the ramp, which was now almost fully submerged under water. He then got the boat to ease back down and settle into the water before he delivered his spectacular finale.

As he walked along until he was opposite where the boat was now floating the two old fishermen and their niece followed him and all three stood in a line and watched Stumblebum with fascination and amazement. The young wizard then took the parchment from one of his pockets and went over to the boat and fastened it to the bow with the drawing pins and with his back to the group used his concealment to fling the flash powder at the boat for effect.

A large puff of smoke followed his action. This brought more gasps of amazement from the little group. Stumblebum then strode back towards them from out of the swirling smoke and turned to face the display in order to conclude the show with an even more extravagant trick.

He loudly invoked, so that the others would hear, that the curse be removed and that the boat be cleansed as he made plumes of water rise up and cascade down over the vessel as he chanted his incantation. He got the boat to rise into the air once again as he prepared to return it to the place on the beach beside Barnacle Billy's own boat. The fishing folk all gasped again in unison. They watched Salty Sammy's little boat float above the ramp unaided. Pleased with their reaction to the show so far he decided to show off and end the spectacle with a flourish.

As he made the *Violet Veronica* rise into the air and just before he returned it to its usual resting place on the pebbles Stumblebum cockily got it to spin around a few times, which prompted more admiring noises from the onlookers. He then pointed his wand at the boat and attempted to steer it back through the air and over the harbour wall again but this time it just continued to revolve faster and faster as it rose upwards in the air with each revolution until it spiralled swiftly on and upwards becoming smaller and smaller to see, until, just like Auntie Maggie's broom had done before, it disappeared completely into the night sky.

Stumblebum, Violet Veronica, Salty Sammy and Barnacle Billy all stood silently in a row, scrutinising the heavens with necks craned and mouths agape. They all remained like that for a long time until Stumblebum was aware of the three pairs of eyes that stared quizzically at him, as if they awaited some explanation.

* * * * * * *

It was a chastened and crestfallen Stumblebum who climbed into bed that night. The complaints of the fishermen regarding the disappearance of their vessel still rang in his ears. The reaction he got when he had asked Salty Sammy for the rest of his fee made his head spin at the memory. Suffice it to say that Violet Veronica was indeed not the only one in her family to have a fierce uncontrollable temper and Stumblebum felt lucky to have beat a hasty retreat from the scene of his latest mishap relatively unscathed, physically at least!

The language the old mariner had used as he hurled his own curses and oaths at the hapless young wizard is far too strong to repeat. Not only did Stumblebum not receive the rest of his fee but a full refund of the deposit was demanded with menace.

Stumblebum stared at the ceiling above his bed for a long, long time trying to work out where he could find the money to pay back to Salty Sammy, which he had spent on the wig he bought from the hat emporium earlier. Since Skipper had all but destroyed the wig he decided it might not be a good idea to return it to the shop for a refund as he might be disappointed at the result of such a request.

Things now had moved from bad to worse as his every attempt to improve his position ended in failure and humiliation, and now he found himself plunged into debt. 'Why does everything keep going wrong?' he reasoned, 'Why do I always come unstuck? Why me? Why me? Why?' The boy eventually fell into a troubled and fitful sleep.

Chapter Eleven

The following Sunday before he left for his appointed lunch with the Ramsbottoms Stumblebum finally revealed to Auntie Maggie his scalp problem from under his fez, which he had taken pains to keep on at all times, even in the house. She was very understanding and told him she had guessed that something was amiss but did not want to pressure him at all. He said that he felt much better now that he had got it off his chest as a problem shared was a problem halved.

'I thought you were having some problems dear' she said gently, 'that's why I asked my old friend Mr Ramsbottom to look out for you. He is a very accomplished freelance wizard and is held in very high regard around town. I expect he will help you find a good solution, so don't worry dear, I'm sure he will take care of you and help as much as he can. I have every confidence in his abilities dear so don't you fret anymore.'

Before he set off for the Ramsbottoms Auntie Maggie drew Stumblebum a little map showing how to get to his house, which was along the outer road and on a hill behind the corporation allotments, just some small distance away from the main road. It was a good walk and following his map he left the main road as directed and walked up a steep hill with modern semi-detached houses on either side of the street. Upon arriving at the crest of the hill, as the street curved around, an unexpected sight came to view.

The area in front of him resembled a Second World War bomb site with rubble and red bricks covering a large area just below the rolling hills of the downs, an unexpected desolation of some magnitude.

Exactly in the centre of this desolation stood three little streets of redbrick terraced houses, all of them collectively standing out amongst the surrounding rubble *like a dunny in the desert* as our Australian cousins would say, apparently still occupied despite the scene of utter chaos surrounding them.

A little perplexed by this vista Stumblebum nonetheless continued his progress towards the terraced houses and found the street name he was looking for on the side of the central terrace. This consisted of seven or eight late Victorian houses with front doors opening straight out onto the pavement and as he approached he could see that they all had backyards enclosed with high redbrick walls with door sized gates set into them as back entrances to the properties.

Puzzled by the door number he had got written on his instructions as it was number 33 he realised that a good portion of these last streets had been demolished which left the remainder still with their original house numbers, so he made his way along until he came to the right numbered door and knocked on it in the hope that he was not mistaken.

The woman who came to the door seemed to expect him and welcomed him inside into a narrow hallway which led to a door to the side. Stumblebum entered a small cluttered drawing room where Roland Ramsbottom sat in a leather armchair at the side of a small fireplace as he read a book and smoked a long churchwarden pipe. He wore a velvet smoking cap with a tassel on his head and was dressed in a large baggy kaftan which almost reached the sandals he was wearing on his feet.

Mr Ramsbottom looked up from his book and his face lit up at the sight of Stumblebum. He bade his guest to sit down on the armchair opposite his by the little fire whilst his wife went into the small adjoining kitchen and put the kettle on to make some tea. As they waited for the tea to arrive the two made polite small talk between themselves and it was at this point that Stumblebum realised that something was quite different from his previous meeting with Mr Ramsbottom. He could now understand every word that he said!

‘Your manner of speech has changed a bit since I first met you. I can understand you easily now, I couldn’t before?’ Stumblebum quizzed his new mentor.

‘Ah, yes, you noticed, that’s good. I only talk with a broad northern accent and quaint mannerisms because it is expected of me down here. That’s how everyone thinks we talk in the north but the truth is that people haven’t spoken quite like that for over a hundred years or so. We only do it to keep the tourists happy. There are a few people still stuck in their ways who still speak northern, like the poet of Pontefract, but they are few in number these days. Your auntie expects me to talk northern so I keep it up so as not to disappoint her, as I do with most folks I know down here. When I’m in the house I have to speak as I am now or my wife, who is local, would not understand me.’ Mr Ramsbottom explained.

‘Oh, Mrs Ramsbottom isn’t from the north then?’ Stumblebum seemed surprised.

‘No, I met her down here. In fact she was one of my clients originally. She had booked a course of hypnotherapy with me to cure her smoking habit.’ Ramsbottom puffed on his pipe as he spoke, apparently oblivious to the blatant hypocrisy. He pointed proudly to a row of certificates on his wall each of which proclaimed an impressive qualification verified by dubious accreditors, including one naming him as being proficient in hypnotherapy.

‘And did you, cure her I mean?’ Stumblebum enquired.

‘He’s very clever my Roly, he got me to stop after a short course of hypnosis and I haven’t had a cigarette since. He is wonderful at that sort of thing.’ Mrs Ramsbottom answered Stumblebum as she came in carrying a tray with some steaming mugs of tea on it.

Ramsbottom flushed to a bright red and beamed at this praise as he took a mug of tea from his wife.

‘It’s funny how it all happened, really. I didn’t like the look of him when I first met him at my initial appointment and had decided not to come again. The funny thing was that after the hypnosis session was over I found my craving for a smoke had lessened and I had become a little attracted to my Roly.' She smiled lovingly at her husband as she handed him his tea.

'I suppose I had relaxed a bit by then. Anyway, by the end of the hypnosis course I was head over heels in love with him and never wanted to smoke another cigarette again. We married shortly after that, a sort of whirlwind romance! Strange how it all worked out really, but it did and I'm so lucky to have my gorgeous Roly Poly for a husband.' Mrs Ramsbottom twittered on as she handed Stumblebum his mug of tea, barely pausing for breath.

'Anyway love, enough about us, lunch will be ready soon so we can relax and have a good talk afterwards. It's lovely to have a visitor, we don't get too many these days. You must call me Freda. We don't stand on ceremony in this house, do we Roly?'

'No, we're very informal at home. You can call me Roly if you like or Roland if you prefer that. I am not an academy wizard so I am not obliged to use an academy name in all circumstances as they insist from their students and guild members. A bit too formal for our liking, but hey, each to their own!' Ramsbottom went on as his wife went back into the kitchen to prepare lunch for them all.

'I understand from your auntie that you have had some trouble with the town coven witches in the past and she is worried that they might try to put a curse on you so she has asked me to protect you with one of my spells.' he continued.

'Your spells are strong enough to combat the witches then? Only I have heard that they can be very powerful when they put their minds to it.' Stumblebum was now a bit concerned.

Ramsbottom gave a knowing smile as he sucked on his pipe, blowing several smoke rings before giving a little chuckle.

'They may have *some* power!' he said sombrely, with a look of superiority on his face.

'Don't you worry young man, my protection spells are legendary for their effectiveness. I use them all of the time. In fact I have a powerful one covering this house at all times so that nothing can ever penetrate it.' He sat back with a smug expression on his face as he knocked the charred contents of his pipe into the hearth and replaced it on to a rack, which contained several other pipes, on the mantelpiece.

As Ramsbottom was imparting this information a movement outside in the backyard caused Stumblebum to look out of the window behind where Ramsbottom sat.

'Does that protection extend as far as your backyard also?' he asked and nodded in the direction of the window where he could see a couple of scruffy young boys who had just climbed over the top of the wall help themselves to the last of the season's rhubarb growing against the back wall.

His new mentor looked over his shoulder at this, before jumping to his feet with a start and running to the back door in the kitchen, shouting to the boys as he opened the door.

'I'll swing for you, you thieving little buggers, just see if I don't.' Ramsbottom shouted, enraged at this affront as the boys scrambled back over the wall clutching their spoils.

He returned to the house and sat back down and puffed and panted, face bright red, a look of indignation clouded his features before eventually he regained his composure.

Freda called them into the kitchen just then as she had finished laying out the kitchen table for lunch, which was quite a lavish affair, and Ramsbottom cheered up a little as the meal got under way. Afterwards Freda cleared up whilst the other two returned to the drawing room where Ramsbottom filled more tobacco back into the bowl of the pipe he had been smoking earlier and the two wizards settled back again in their armchairs.

'I noticed that there has been some demolition going on here.' Stumblebum commented, trying to get the conversation moving again.

'That's putting it mildly!' his mentor replied with a tremor in his voice.

'What happened to all of the other buildings, were they condemned?'

‘Oh no, not at all, they were all perfectly good houses, like this one, streets and streets of them. Until a supermarket chain wanted to build a mega-supermarket here and the scoundrels on the corporation saw a chance to feather their own nests and started compulsory purchases in order to implement the scheme. They put out the usual propaganda that it would be good for the town and would create a handful of jobs, so therefore the beautiful houses would have to be cleared.’ This was clearly a topic that Ramsbottom felt passionate about.

‘About two thirds of the homeowners took the money they were offered and moved out. The corporation sent in the bulldozers to clear them and expected all the rest to follow suit, but they did not reckon on Roland Ramsbottom!’ Ramsbottom drew himself up in his seat as he continued and his eyes glistened with indignation.

‘I organised a petition and forced a halt of the demolition work whilst their legal team tried every trick in the book. Bribery, bullying, appealing to public opinion for the supposed good the development would bring to the town, but we resisted and dug our heels in!’ he continued his saga.

‘There were seven complete streets that had not been knocked down by the time we had stopped the destruction. Good solid Victorian terraces with some character, but the rot had set in. Over time the corporation offered larger and larger amounts of money to get people to move out, and most did, but I stepped in again and persuaded the rest not to give in. I also organised a residents committee and we held out against the scheme.’

‘So what happened then to the seven streets?’ Stumblebum enquired.

‘Well, the corporation knocked down the houses as soon as the bribe takers moved out and then it reached the point that the demolition had gone too far with only three streets partially standing and so our committee decided that we would have to go the same way and take the money. However, I persuaded the remaining householders to stand firm and resist as I was sure that the corporation would offer lucrative amounts to get the last of us out if we all stood together. If we were going to be forced to leave we might as well maximise on our compensation.’

'And did they offer lucrative amounts?'

'Er, no. The supermarket chain got fed up with all the delays and pulled out and built a giant supermarket complex in a nearby town instead. The corporation just gave up with the demolition and left it as you find us now. We did approach them and asked for the compulsory purchase to go ahead but they refused, said they had wasted enough of the town's funds on the project already and would spend not a penny more.'

'Did you try to appeal the decision?'

'I called a meeting of the remaining householders to explain the situation and they became very ugly and hostile towards me. They said it was my fault for interfering and most of the ingrates haven't spoken to me since. I even strengthened the protection spell on the house as I was rather concerned after I received death threats and the like.'

'Well, I think you have a lovely house here, very cosy!' Stumblebum tried to placate Ramsbottom, who had become somewhat agitated with the telling of the sorry tale.

'Yes, it's a good solid house, we like it, though I don't get too many clients coming here now, they find it all a bit spooky, but on the plus side it's reasonably peaceful for doing my outdoor magic spells, not too many distractions.' Ramsbottom said as he scowled out of the window towards the back yard.

'I was wondering if you could advise me on a particular mishap I have experienced.' Stumblebum tentatively approached the delicate subject of his hair loss.

'Do you know how to reverse spells and potions that have gone wrong? Only I have fallen victim to some bad advice and have been caused some personal injury. Well, to be frank, I have lost all of my hair.' Stumblebum's bottom lip trembled for a few moments at the thought of the effect of Dung Ho's hair remedy.

'Oh my dear boy how upsetting. Do let me have a look and tell me more details. I'm sure I will be able to help, I've been at this magic game a long time now.' Ramsbottom smiled at the boy as he refilled his pipe again, wearing a sage like look on his face.

After a lengthy explanation during which several more mugs of tea were drunk and several more pipes smoked, Stumblebum finished telling what had happened, watching Ramsbottom's reaction closely as he took it all in whilst giving his head a thorough examination. Ramsbottom nodded at intervals and smiled sagely as the account unfolded.

'Hmm, I think I can see where you went wrong, or rather your spirit guide. He was on the right track but some of the ingredients were too potent, the fermented pigs manure in particular.' He explained with the air of one with great authority on these matters.

'Some years ago two labourers who worked on a poultry farm and processed chicken droppings for use of as fertilizer noticed that they were growing thick dark hairs on their arms and foreheads and put it down to the dried chicken droppings that their job put them in contact with, and of course chicken muck is not as strong as pigs muck, and it has to be dried to a powder, not fresh.' Ramsbottom paused and took a long draw on his pipe.

'To be really effective of course the application has to be put on during the correct phase of the moon and with a healing spell to reinforce it. It is a very specific procedure. You are in luck, however, what with my expertise in these matters. Look out of the window again towards the back of the yard.' He leaned back in his chair wearing a superior look on his face as he puffed away on his pipe.

Stumblebum got up and went over to the window and wondered what he was supposed to be looking for until he spotted about six or seven hens clucking about the yard.

'If you give me a couple of weeks I shall keep their droppings and dry them out and mix them with other necessary ingredients for you to apply. You will find, unlike your misguided guide from the other side…' he paused and chuckled at his own humorous quip '… I will do the job properly with the benefit of my own special expertise.'

Stumblebum felt as if a huge weight had been lifted at the thought of his problem being put right, encouraged by the older man's self-confidence.

'Are there many 'independents' doing magic in town then.' Stumblebum enquired. He was intrigued by Ramsbottom's unconventional approach as opposed to the rigid adherence to strict protocol at the academy and wondered if there were many others of his ilk in the town.

'Oh there are quite a few of us, a mixed bag of pagans, wizards, witches, clairvoyants and healers and others who defy any category. A friendly bunch, we get together regularly at a moot we hold in the pub on the main road, *The Smugglers Rest*. Some of the witches who join us are in an old fashioned traditional coven, thirteen men and women, a really friendly lot, unlike those harpy's from the town's women only covens.'

'You must come along to the next moot we have, you will enjoy it, and get to meet some nice, independent occultists from the town. I'll let you know when the next one is being held.'

Stumblebum liked the idea of all this and was in a cheerful mood as he bade the Ramsbottom's goodbye and thanked Freda for the sumptuous lunch. He felt it would do him some good to mix with Roland's friends and get another angle on magic and perhaps learn some useful spells from these people.

By the time he had walked home he was feeling better than he had for some time, what with having a new mentor to advise him, and the promise to restore his hair to its former condition lifted his spirits immensely. Auntie Maggie commented on how happy he seemed when he got back home and they talked for a long time about his visit to her friends before they settled down to finish off the evening relaxing in front of the television in the drawing room for a couple of hours before he retired to his bed.

Now all he needed to do was to work out how to make some money to pay Salty Sammy back what he owed to him. Perhaps his new mentor might give him some advice on that matter. He was sure that he would know what to do. Things were finally looking up at last.

Chapter Twelve

The next day, Monday, there was a renewed energy at the academy. Most of the students now feverishly engaged in intense studies as they continued to search for the secret of transmuting base metal to gold. Stumblebum was also swept along with this race to find the secret of making gold. A successful outcome would get him out of his debt and help to return Salty Sammy his money as well as fulfilling the young wizard's innate dreams of great riches. After his failure to properly master the art of levitation, considering his most recent blunder on the beach, Stumblebum decided to focus his studies on other spells, magic and alchemical processes.

The library was filled with students who earnestly scrutinised ancient scrolls and dusty tomes in their desire to be the first to uncover the secret process with which the Ipsissimus Grand Magister was apparently arriving at some success, although he refused to discuss the topic. On top of all of the gold fever some older novices anxiously prepared for the impending upgrading assessments to the next level of competence and promotion to full wizard status.

The upgrades were to take place over the next few weeks and when the results were assessed an elaborate ceremony was to be put on in the Great Hall of Wizards with the newly promoted wizards each giving short displays of their magical prowess. This would be followed by a feast in honour of the new graduates and speeches would be given by some of the Magisters and Grand Magisters to round off the celebrations.

The novices to be presented for this event had to pass their assessments to a good level and so were busily engaged in some serious research, intense study and time spent on practice in the spells lab. Stumblebum followed everyone else's example and focussed intently on his studies, particularly as he was keen to make bucket-loads of gold for himself, but also as he was aware that his first assessments would take place in due course and he needed to keep on the ball.

During that afternoon, Stumblebum encountered Morris hurrying down a corridor and tried to stop and talk with him.

'Can't stop, busy, lots to do, I'll catch up with you later!' Morris told Stumblebum breathlessly as he scurried away to some spell practice or another. Stumblebum had never seen the usually laid back Morris so stressed out. He resolved to make sure that he would allow enough time to prepare for his own assessment a bit better when it was due.

During the day he also encountered several other senior novices, including David Lee, who rushed about too busy to stop and say more than a few words in their haste to attend to their studies in earnest. Thankfully Secundus was not due to be assessed at this time and so when Stumblebum encountered him leaving a lecture theatre later that afternoon was relieved that he had the time to stop and talk for a while.

'Hello Secundus, it's all getting a bit manic around here right now, does it always get this hectic before the assessments?' Stumblebum enquired.

'It usually gets a bit tense leading up to the assessments but not to this degree. The business over the gold has got everyone running themselves ragged, I expect that it will settle down before too long as soon as they realise how difficult it is to transmute base metals into gold.' Secundus said, with a slight smirk on his face.

'You don't think it can be done then, making gold from lead?'

'Oh, it can be done, it's just not that easy, otherwise everyone would be doing it and either they would all become incredibly wealthy or gold would have little value!'

'But it can be done?' Stumblebum persisted.

'Yes, but the key to doing it is in finding the philosopher's stone, a vital component that very few have knowledge of. Most of the novices and students busy in the spells lab right now are wasting their time unless they can unlock the secret of the philosopher's stone themselves.'

'So you think the Ipsissimus Grand Magister has the secret of the stone then?'

'Possibly, but he is keeping his cards close to his chest over the matter, so no one else really knows. It is after all only a rumour.' Secundus smiled at Stumblebum.

'Don't get too obsessed with it, remember we have our own assessments coming up soon so I would concentrate your studies on the easier magic that we can learn about without too much difficulty if I were you. You don't want to fail when the time comes because you have placed all of your energy on this wild goose chase.'

'Mmm, I suppose you are right. It won't hurt to have a stab at it every now and again though, surely?'

Secundus laughed before he changed the subject.

'I hear that Brigitte and her sister have joined the Old Town amateur dramatics society along with Morris and Mooning Mike. No wonder Morris is so stressed out, he is spreading himself a bit thin right now. Bad timing!

Having Brigitte and Morris spoken about in the same breath caused Stumblebum to again feel pangs of jealousy as he was still carrying a light for the town's foremost beauty. In fact he was so completely smitten by her so was not happy to hear of her and Morris doing things together.

'I think that Mooning Mike is meeting her after lessons in that coffee bar that novices like to hang out in, the big one in town. Why don't you meet me there for a drink after and you can talk to them about joining in with the drama society, if that's your sort of thing, you never know.' Secundus gave a wink as he spoke, giving Stumblebum food for thought.

* * * * * * *

Bilge on Sea's *Beverage Bliss*, a popular coffee bar on a busy street adjacent to the High Street, buzzed with customers, many of them novices going over their notes they had brought from the academy. Stumblebum looked around to see if either Brigitte or Mooning Mike had arrived yet and as this was not the case bought a cappuccino for himself and sat at a small table by one of the two large windows looking out onto the street since Secundus was also not here yet.

Before long Brigitte and Mooning Mike did indeed enter the café and took a table nearer to the service counter after they bought two milkshakes. Brigitte looked especially lovely. She brightened up the place with her pleasant demeanour and turned a good few heads with her stunning good looks. Stumblebum was about to get up and go over to join them when a youth he vaguely knew from the academy, one Silas Suggs, a senior novice originally from the north, stood up and went over to the table at which Brigitte and Mooning Mike were seated and engaged in conversation.

Silas Suggs was a strange looking chap and to say that he had fallen out of the ugly tree was not an exaggeration! In fact it appeared that not only had he fallen from the tree but had repeatedly climbed up again only to be rudely ejected back to *terra firma* a good few times.

He was tall and ungainly, a loose limbed youth with a large head topped with muddy red hair. His pale eyes bulged and reminded one of a fish and his long bulbous nose defied analysis, suffice it to say that it hovered above the most horrendous feature on Silas's face. His mouth was unusually wide with fleshy red lips and when he opened it to speak had the appearance of a large letter box.

'Ay up Brigitte' Silas said indignantly as he prodded a sausage-like finger in the direction of Mooning Mike's face, 'you waint go out wi' me but you'll go out wi' this fat wazzock!'[3] Startled at this intrusion Mooning Mike rose to his feet to placate the intruder.

'Oh aye, fat wazzock's standing up is he!?' Silas thumped his right fist into his opened left palm.

'Fat wazzock wants to feight does he? Fat wazzock thinks he's ret 'ard does he?'[4] Silas thumped his palm after each statement and squared up to a perplexed Mooning Mike as Brigitte looked on in astonishment at this affront.

Stumblebum wanted to get up and intervene so as to impress Brigitte but was a bit scared of Silas. In a reckless moment he decided to cause a distraction to the fracas by making something levitate and float around the café, which was about the extent of his magic skills thus far. The first thing that his eyes fell on was a ceramic plant-pot containing a yucca plant and almost without thinking he attempted to levitate it.

It was probably his nervousness due to the hostile situation! The plant pot together with its resident yucca did not gently glide around the room as intended but instead it shot across the cafeteria at some speed and struck Silas squarely on the back of his head with a sickening thud as the pot split in two and fell to the floor. Silas's bulging eyes crossed and glazed over and his blubbery mouth twisted into a sickly grimace as he stood completely still, silenced. He then swayed to and fro for a few moments, keeled over backwards and landed on the floor unconscious with a loud whump.

As Brigitte was clearly upset at this confrontation and its unexpected outcome Mooning Mike hastily ushered her out of the café before Stumblebum, who was in something of a state of shock by now, could go over and join up with them. By the time that the proprietor had appeared to see what all of the commotion was about Stumblebum thought it might be prudent to also exit at this time and also made a hasty departure, half of his cappuccino left on the table undrunk.

---

[3] Translation from northern: [Ay up = now then. waint = will not. wi' = with. wazzock = obscure archaic word usually used in a derogatory sense in the north, often as an insult, as in 'fat wazzock'.]

[4] [feight = fight. ret 'ard = extremely rugged (right hard!).]

In a dark corner of the *Beverage Bliss* a sinister figure who had quietly observed these events from behind a newspaper quite unseen by the others in the café put his paper down and took out a little note-pad into which he scribbled something before he also got up to depart. He glanced down at where Silas Suggs lay, still unconscious, and then gave a snigger as he stepped over him whilst the angry proprietor muttered something about hooligans and swept up the mess left by the broken plant-pot. Slippery Jack stepped into the street deep in thought and then he made his way back in the direction of Tiberius Mordecai's mansion.

* * * * * * *

Later that afternoon Slippery was seated on one of the leather armchairs in Mordecai's study making his report. Mordecai listened intently as Slippery related the events from earlier in the café and interrupted occasionally to ask for more details. When Slippery had finished talking Mordecai leaned back in his chair with a thoughtful look on his face as he went over in his mind what his acolyte had reported to him.

'This novice who was knocked out sounds like a rum character, not the usual sort of novice they get in the academy, do you know who he is?'

'Yes, he's called Silas Suggs, the mayor's nephew. Thinks he's the bee's knees, a cocky fellow but not very bright.' Slippery replied. He smirked at the memory of Suggs being struck down by a yucca plant.

'And you say it was young Stumblebum who laid him out with magic and he reacted with lightning speed to the situation?' Mordecai seemed quite interested in the young wizard's skills.

'He certainly sorted it out pretty fast. I reckon that he had been expecting Silas to kick off by the way he reacted right on cue. It looked very much like a set up or a trap if you ask me.'

'Good, good, I like that Slippery, he sounds as if he is very devious, excellent! He seems to have more talent than he realises, we shall have to keep a close eye on him from now on. He could prove to be very useful to us! We ought to try and entice him over to our little circle. What do you think Slippery?'

'Well, we ought not to be too hasty. I shall have to observe him some more and see how he pans out but you could be right, he could turn out to be one of us. He certainly isn't typical of the usual academy wizards that's for sure! But let's give it some time and I'll keep a close watch on him.' Slippery reassured his boss.

'And what about this other fellow, the mayor's nephew you say? Hardly surprising, stupidity runs in that family along with lots of low animal cunning to make up for the intellectual shortfall. Keep an eye on him as well will you Slippery, we might be able to make use of him to get to his uncle, a man who could do with being cut down to size if ever there was one.' Mordecai got up from his chair and poured them both a goblet of wine each, satisfied with his acolyte's report. Things were looking up in Bilge on Sea from Mordecai's point of view. Things were definitely looking up.

* * * * * * *

Stumblebum kept a very low profile the next day at the academy just in case Silas Suggs had made it in, which of course depended on how bad his injury from the previous day was. He spent much of the day immersed in study in the library so as to keep away from other areas of the academy where he might run into Silas, not sure how much he would remember about Stumblebum's attack on his head. He decided to err on the side of caution and keep out of sight in any case so scoured books in the library in order to do this.

Whilst he browsed through the pile of books of spells he had stacked on the table in front of him he came across a spell on how to repair fabric with magic and this gave him an idea. Perhaps he could apply this to his damaged wig since it is at least part fabric. It might be worth a try and would be a good magic skill to acquire since his main magic repertoire to date had largely been focussed on levitation, which he still had not quite got the hang of, as recent events demonstrated.

A bit of news from Auntie Maggie earlier that morning also gave Stumblebum some cause for concern. She told him over breakfast that his parents had been in touch and were due to come down for a visit soon, which caused him something of a panic as they were not aware that their son was now completely bald. His only hope would be either to succeed to re-grow his hair under Ramsbottom's supervision or to somehow have his wig repaired, so discovering the fabric repair spell was a positive outcome.

Stumblebum took a sheet of parchment and a quill from one of his pockets and then went over and asked the Academy Scribe to lend him a pot of ink, which he did only after he gave several deep sighs of disapproval and with a sorrowful shake of his head in a dramatic display of reluctance, as if Stumblebum had just asked him to give him a sack full of gold coins as an indefinite loan. Unfazed by these histrionics Stumblebum took the ink back over to his table and copied the spell from the book.

It was advised that the magic be performed under a night sky as the moon was on the wane, where the item to be mended was to be laid down near earth and water so the beach at the shoreline would do. The magician was then to draw power from the water with a wand which must be lifted high to absorb energy from the moon and the air before pointing its tip at the item in question as the magician intoned a spoken spell. Stumblebum copied the spell with great accuracy! The energy of the moon, air, water and earth, under the light of the waning moon was thus to be discharged directly on to the item from the tip of the wand when said item would undergo an instant renewal and repair.

Elated at this find he read up on a few other new spells also in order to add to his growing repertoire and resolved to practice them to perfection as his upgrade assessment would require a fairly broad display of knowledge in order for him to reach the standard set by the academy and hopefully pass with flying colours.

He usually had some lunch around midday in one of the common rooms but this time he gave it a miss in order to stay out of sight so spent his time more productively than normal in the library reading up on a number of different disciplines within the scope of wizardry.

It was during this prolonged study session, about mid-afternoon, whilst he browsed in an ancient dusty bookcase that he noticed a small, very old battered book that had been stuffed underneath a broken, loose fitting shelf in order to wedge it in place. Intrigued, he removed the book and replaced one of a similar thickness in its stead to support the shelf and carried the leather bound book over to his study table.

The pages inside the book were yellowed and cracked parchment and the ink was faded to a barely visible brown colour. As he thumbed through this ancient manual he began to realise that page after page described the method of transmuting base metals to gold, as prescribed by some wizard from antiquity. Although faded, he could just make out the script and the diagrams of the spell tables, pentagrams and other symbols.

Realising that he had stumbled on a vitally important book, apparently forgotten or not known about by the others, he sat back in his chair and pondered how best to take advantage of this precious find. He looked around him furtively to see if anyone had noticed him. Apparently not as the other students were deeply engrossed in their own studies and the Academy Scribe was preoccupied as he stacked some books back onto their shelves.

The proper thing to do would be to bring the book to the attention of the Academy Scribe, who would no doubt claim credit for its discovery, or at best Stumblebum would receive some praise for pointing it out but would never be allowed to set eyes on it again. No, that would not do. Perhaps he could steal the book and take it home but he remembered that the reason for Slippery Jack's expulsion was for a similar crime and he dare not risk that outcome. After a long and anguished struggle with his conscience he came up with a little plan, a sort of compromise.

Stumblebum began to copy each page of the book and faithfully reproduced every symbol, spell and table described but as time went on he realised it would take him ages to reproduce the entire book. He copied the pages he had time for that day and then, as he took great care not to be seen, he replaced the little book back to where he had found it underneath the loose shelf as a support in the hope that no one else might discover it. He would return over the next few days and weeks, however long it would take, until he had copied the entire book.

* * * * * * *

Later, back in his bedroom, Stumblebum prepared to sneak out of the house at around midnight in order to repair his wig with his newly found magic spell. He placed in his various pockets his wand, wig and a piece of parchment with the incantation written out on it. Filled with anticipation and hope he carefully made his way down the wooden stairs as quietly as he could so as not to disturb Auntie Maggie and to make sure that Skipper did not follow him, then crept out of the house and on to the little beach.

It was a crisp, frosty night and the stars and moon where shining bright overhead as Stumblebum placed his damaged wig on to the pebbles close to the water's edge. This done he took the parchment from his pocket and read it several times over so as to memorise the spell before he drew his wand from another pocket to point at the gently lapping waves as close as he could without actually touching the water. As he concentrated very hard he felt the surge of energy from the water charge his wand and after a few minutes of this lifted the wand high above his head. He then chanted the spell by memory and immediately felt the energy being discharged from his wand prematurely.

As the magic flowed from his wand Stumblebum remembered it had to point at the wig so he leaned over and brought his wand down to just above the wig. The wand crackled with an eerie green magic light which surged out of the wand and lit up the wig in a swirl of vapours as Stumblebum continued with his incantation and the wig clearly appeared to transform into its original new condition.

Stumblebum put his wand away when suddenly, just as he stooped down to pick up the wig, he sensed a whooshing sound as something passed by his ear at speed. Startled, he jumped backwards, and as his fez fell forward over his eyes tripped and landed on his behind on the pebbles.

The bewildered young wizard got to his feet, adjusted his fez and blinked a couple of times as his eyes sought out what had caused the upset. Embedded deep into the pebbles just in front of him was Auntie Maggie's besom broom, shaft first, embedded into the pebbles and had pierced through the newly repaired wig dead centre, having chosen that particular moment to return to earth from its orbit of the heavens. It took Stumblebum quite some time and not without a struggle before he managed to free the broom from where it had buried itself in the pebbles. Exhausted from the effort he laid the broom down and picked up the wig, which was now in an even worse state than before he had started with the spell.

Stumblebum felt a little deflated by this setback and so began the whole procedure again determined to get the wretched wig repaired and wearable but for some reason he seemed unable to get the spell to work properly again despite several attempts. Finally he abandoned his effort and picked up both the wig and the broom, which he carefully sneaked back into his auntie's large broom cupboard, and crept back upstairs to his bedroom.

He sat at the table by his bedroom window for a long time and gazed at the damaged wig before a deep weariness overcame him and he climbed into bed feeling a sense of defeat yet again. He knew he had to do better with his spells if he was going to pass his upgrade exams. He must increase his efforts to a much higher level in order to be an effective wizard and, of course, to succeed with his desire to make gold. Lots and lots of gold!

Chapter Thirteen

Over the next few days Stumblebum spent most of his time at the Academy in the library copying pages from the book on how to transmute gold from other stuff. He took great pains to ensure that nobody watched him as he removed and replaced the book from where he had discovered it, underneath the dodgy shelf in one of the bookcases.

By the end of the week he had copied a large part of the book with only several final pages left to do. As soon as he had got the full transcript copied he would have an attempt to make gold since he was under such financial pressure from Salty Sammy. As he left the academy that night his mind turned to another matter. What was he to do about his hair problem, particularly in light of the imminent visit by his parents?

He had tried to wear the wig in its damaged state but the hole through the centre of it proved to be too large for this to be practical or effective. The only successful way he had found to wear it was with his fez clamped down on top of it, though the wig did have a tendency to slip around which made both the wig and the fez liable to fall at any time.

His attempt to wear it without his fez made him look like a medieval Trappist monk with a tonsure and if he became agitated for any reason a solid beam of green light would escape from the large hole in it, like a laser, which would draw unwanted attention to his cranium.

Stumblebum decided to discuss the matter further with his mentor, Ramsbottom, during his visit for lunch that coming Sunday in the hope that perhaps he had collected enough ingredients for his remedy by then. With a bit of luck the treatment might produce a positive result in time for his parent's arrival and they would not be any wiser about the matter

When he had almost arrived back home from the academy his heart sank as he spotted Violet Veronica sat on the doorstep in wait of his return. He was about to turn around and head off back down the street but she spotted him and jumped to her feet and called out to him.

'Yoo-hoo, yoo-hoo Stumblebum, yoo-hoo! I've waited ages for you to turn up, what took you so long?' she shouted to him. 'Didn't you see me just now? Uncle Sammy sent me round to ask when he can have his money back 'cos he has seen another boat he wants to buy and he will need the money soon to go towards it. Have you got it for him?'

More pressure! He had deliberately kept out of the way of the fishermen since he had not the means just yet to pay back the deposit he had secured from Salty Sammy and the alchemy skills for making gold would take him some time to master and organise.

'I've got the payment of some fees for other spells to come in and as soon as I have it I will bring it round to your house. No need for you to call again as I have not forgotten.' He lied, wanting to get rid of the wretched child.

'I haven't seen you do any magic on the beach lately, why is that? Don't you like it on the beach anymore since you lost Uncle Sammy's boat? I thought it was awesome the way you made the boat fly away but Uncle Sammy doesn't look at it like that, he just swears now whenever you are mentioned at home. But I still think you are an awesome wizard!'

'No, no, I still go on the beach. I was there the other night but it was way past bedtime, around midnight. Some spells are very specific about when they are to be done you see. And that one had to be done at midnight.' Stumblebum did not want them to think he had tried to avoid them, which, of course, he had!

'Well I'll tell Uncle Sammy that you will have his money soon. That should stop him from grumbling about you all the time. How soon do you think it will be then, when you get your money?' She persisted.

'Oh, it won't be too long. Don't worry he will have his boat, no problem.' He glanced at his wristwatch. 'Oh my word is that he time, I have to go in now. I am running late.' He lied again as he pushed open the front door anxious to get away from Violet Veronica and her never ending questions.

Relieved to be indoors and away from the girl's continual interrogation Stumblebum went and sat in the kitchen. Auntie Maggie kneaded some dough in a large bowl on the big kitchen table ready for the oven.

'Did you have a good day at the academy dear?' Auntie Maggie asked, out of habit.

'Yes Auntie, not bad. I've nearly finished an important project I have worked on in the library all week, it should be done in a few more days. How was your day?'

'Well, it was quite busy in the shop this afternoon, a good day's trade and some of my clients came in for a chat, as they do, a lovely day really. A funny thing happened though, remember some time ago I asked you if you had seen my broom that I swept the doorstep with? It had just disappeared and I looked everywhere for it but it had gone.' She gave her nephew a curious look as she placed a tea towel over the dough and placed the bowl on the floor by the oven. 'I even briefly thought that you might have messed about with it and lost it or something but it has reappeared now in the broom cupboard, very strange!'

'You must've overlooked it before then. Perhaps it was amongst all of the other brushes and stuff.'

'No, I turned that cupboard inside out before and there was no sign of it. It's all a bit strange if you ask me.'

‘There must be a poltergeist haunting us then. Hardly a surprise what with all of those spirits who hang about all the time, it’s a wonder there hasn’t been more odd stuff like that happen.’

‘You could be right. Anyway, I have got the broom back now so that’s all right.’

As Auntie Maggie sipped her tea Skipper jumped up onto the stool he usually sat on at mealtimes so she went and found some treats for him and placed them in front of him in a small bowl.

‘You don’t half spoil that creature you know!’ Stumblebum glared at Skipper, still annoyed about the wig.

‘He’s no trouble, bless him, and he is good company for me when I am in the shop. He’s as good as gold he is, aren’t you Skipper?’ She tickled the cat under his chin and behind his ears as Stumblebum tutted in disapproval and spread his notes from earlier in front of him on the table and then tried to work out the instructions for making gold as he felt he was under some pressure to refund Salty Sammy’s curse removing deposit.

‘I found this old book in the library with some instructions for alchemy in it. I think I’ll have a go at it.’ He told Auntie Maggie, in an effort to sound mysterious.

‘Alchemy, that’s all a bit too scientific for me dear. You clever wizards are the best ones to dabble in all that stuff, the only ones who can make head or tail of it all,’ she chuckled. ‘I’ll just stick to what I know, spirits and clairvoyance!’

‘Do you think that Mr Ramsbottom would know anything about alchemy Auntie? He seems to have a wide range of expertise, perhaps he could point me in the right direction?’

‘Well, it wouldn’t hurt you to ask him. I’m sure he will give you whatever advice he can, he does seem to know a great deal about all sorts of things. Are you there for lunch again on Sunday?’

‘Yes, there are a number of things I need to ask his advice on. I’ll go there a bit earlier when I do, so as to talk things over. He seems to like to offer advice. I’m so glad you introduced him to me.’

'I have known him for a long time. I rather hoped you would both get on together as he could be a great help to you.' Auntie Maggie topped up their teacups from the teapot before she carried her cup of tea into the drawing room to watch some television, followed by Skipper, leaving Stumblebum to try and make sense from his copious notes in his quest to make lots of gold.

* * * * * * *

Stumblebum spent much of Saturday doing some spell practice for small spells he could do in his room, away from distractions, with various outcomes. He was pleased when he successfully did an invisibility spell on his quill, which happened to be in front of him on the table, and made it fade from view altogether. He went around the bedroom and tried the same spell on several other small objects with similar success. He had not, unfortunately, got the hang of how to reverse the spell and became frustrated some time later when he could not find where he had left his quill, until the spell wore off in due course and it again became visible.

He had found a spell for inducing sleep upon others which he thought could be handy if Silas Suggs ever confronted him. He had been worried that Silas might find out who had caused the yucca plant to hit him on the head and thought it would be a good defensive spell to use if he ever tried to attack him. He could simply make him fall asleep so that he could then get away unhurt. He practiced the spell on Skipper but realised that as his cat spent much of his time asleep in any case that he was not the best subject to measure success against.

After this he spent most of the rest of the day immersed in study of the alchemy from the pages he had copied from the book in the library. There was a lot to learn and he realised that it might not be without some difficulty for him to make this work. He considered asking Ramsbottom for help with it but by now Stumblebum had fallen victim to the inevitable 'gold fever' affliction, inexplicably reluctant to share any of the gold with others. '*It's my formula to make gold and no one else shall get their hands on any of it! It's all mine! Mine!'*

He decided it would be best to keep his discovery a secret for now at least. His obsession to hoard gold increased as did his suspicion that others might take his share from him if he involved them. No, he must keep it all to himself at all costs, after all, people could be very fickle and untrustworthy couldn't they? He even took care to hide his notes in his room for fear that Auntie Maggie might look for them and steal them from him!

* * * * * * *

That Sunday it was a very furtive Stumblebum who knocked on the door of the Ramsbottoms' house as he arrived for lunch and he found it hard to relax straight away but after another magnificent meal he found his reservations were possibly a bit over the top and he settled into a comfortable and pleasant afternoon as he chatted with his genial hosts. With his confidence in his mentor restored the young wizard brought up the matter of his hair treatment with him and asked if his treatment was ready to apply just yet.

'I might just about have enough stuff from the chickens dried out for you for now. I have mixed a powder with other things in it to speed up the process. If you like we can apply it tonight after it gets dark as the moon is now on the turn and in the right phase for the spell.'

Stumblebum's spirits improved a lot at this news and he couldn't wait to begin the treatment and spell.

'That's great Roland, such a weight off my mind. How long does it take for its effects to show?'

'Once it has been applied and the magic spell invoked you should see some growth show in a few days, within a week at the very least. Of course it will take longer to get back to normal but at least you will find you have some results.' Ramsbottom leaned back in his chair with the look of a man of great knowledge and authority on his countenance and gave a long pull on his favourite churchwarden pipe as he smiled benevolently at his young charge.

Stumblebum was so pleased at the reassurance from his mentor that he almost asked him if he knew anything about how to turn lead to gold, intending to seek guidance on this matter, but he checked himself as he did not want his secret to fall into others' hands. No, he must work out himself how to do the alchemy, he must guard it at all costs.

'A penny for your thoughts?' Ramsbottom interrupted his reverie.

'*Mine, it's all mine!*' Stumblebum blurted out. Then as he realised where he was and noticed the startled reaction from Ramsbottom at this outburst he giggled nervously and went on to cover his tracks.

'Oh, sorry. I was thinking about something someone said at the academy earlier. I was miles away. What were we discussing?' he stammered, a little embarrassed.

'The hair transformation spell, remember, I said it should show results within a week.'

'Oh, yes, that's right. I am so grateful to you for this, I can't thank you enough.'

'Oh that's all right, I'm here to help all I can. What's the use of all of my years of expertise in these matters if I can't do some good occasionally?' Ramsbottom said, smugly.

'I have another surprise for you also. Since it will be several hours before we can do the spell I thought we might use the time until then at the moot. It's on tonight at *The Smugglers Rest* and it will be good for you to meet some of the other pagans and such before we can come back and sort your head out. Your auntie knows you are with us so she won't worry if you return home a little late.'

'But I'm not old enough to go in a pub yet, they won't let me in will they?'

'Not a problem, you can go in, you just can't drink alcohol. They are pretty laid back at *The Smugglers* in any case. It won't be open for a few hours and the moot usually starts early, I'm sure you will enjoy it.' Ramsbottom reassured Stumblebum as Freda brought some mugs of tea and a plate of biscuits for them all and they relaxed by the fire and chatted amiably together and talked about various magic skills of which Ramsbottom claimed to excel in.

Several hours later Ramsbottom donned his deerstalker cap and a tweed Inverness cape and Freda and Stumblebum accompanied him down the hill to the pub. *The Smugglers Rest* had several bars and the pagans held their moot in the cosy lounge bar with its upholstered fake leather seats and pine topped cast iron tables with stools and chairs around them. Logs blazed fiercely in the fireplace and added to the cheerful atmosphere of the room.

As they went in to the lounge of the pub a few people greeted Ramsbottom as he ushered his party over to where they sat around tables cluttered with drinks and empty glasses. Before Ramsbottom went to get a round of drinks in for his own little group he introduced Stumblebum to several of the others, an eclectic mixture of individuals, aged from early twenties to some who seemed to be late middle aged. They were very friendly and Stumblebum soon relaxed and listened with interest to their conversations and occasionally answered a question about himself.

When Ramsbottom came back from the bar with a tray of drinks, he handed a glass of cola to Stumblebum and as he and Freda sipped a pint of beer each explained to his friends that he was acting as Stumblebum's guide and mentor in all things occult.

'Stumblebum is Mystical Maggie's nephew. He is staying with her in her shop. He enrolled at t' academy o' t' guild wizards earlier this year and I am helping him wi t' advice about magic.' Stumblebum noticed that Ramsbottom had slipped into speaking northern again, presumably for the benefit of the company.

'Mystical Maggie? She hasn't been to a moot for ages, do say hello to her from us all and tell her we all miss her good company. I shall have to call in her shop when I can to catch up with things with her.' One of the older women spoke to Stumblebum as the others chatted to each other and discussed what they had been up to since the last moot and passed bits of information between them.

Stumblebum was taken by how jolly and informal a group of people they were and noted the enthusiasm with which they knocked their drinks back. He thought how friendly the atmosphere was. He did wonder though how different their approach to magic was from the more formal, serious training of the academy. These people appeared to have no visible structure or system of organising themselves apart from meeting in the pub from time to time and then apparently most of them went their own sweet way to dabble with whatever their chosen field of the occult was.

'You see yon tall blonde feller over at that table, the one wearing a kaftan and beads, well he's king o't' witches and yon lass sat next to him is his wife. She's his high priestess. They got married at a pagan ceremony at Stonehenge a couple o' years back before they came to live here in Bilge on Sea.' Ramsbottom nodded towards the man in question.

Stumblebum looked over at the handsome couple who appeared to be holding court around their table, along with a small group who hung on to the man's every word as they all drank copious amounts of beer. He wondered how the man had come to be king of the witches and what this role involved. He turned to Ramsbottom and quizzed him about this.

'Who is he and how did he get to be the king of the witches then? What does he do?'

'He's called Calvin Pendragon and his wife is called Meredith. They organise their own ceremonies and anyone from t' occult fraternity can join in. They sometimes join t' wiccans and other pagans so as to officiate in their rites as well.'

'How long has he been king then? What did he do before?' Stumblebum was intrigued.

'He's been king a good while now after he anointed himself at a ritual him and his wife did in t' woods not far from here then he announced his kingship at our next moot which we attended here. Everyone celebrated that night doing lots of singing and drinking. It warra ret good do!'[5]

'But how does he earn his living? Does it all come from magic and stuff? How long has he been doing it?' Stumblebum persisted.'

'Well, he charges for doing spells for folk and charges fees for performing some ceremonies for private events and he writes books of advice on magic which he sells. Before that he was a window cleaner but he got fired so had to find another income and that's when he became king o' t' witches.'

'Oh, I see!' Stumblebum wasn't sure if this was a valid way to become a king, but then again, what did he know of these matters. None of his business really, he supposed.

After about an hour or so Ramsbottom indicated that it was time they should head back and stood up to make his farewells to his friends, who were all now fairly well inebriated.

'We'll be off then.' He took his leave with an air of mysterious northern wisdom. '*There's many a mickle's mackled wi' out a muckle tha nuz, so until t' next time, sithee.*'[6]

By the time they had returned to the Ramsbottom's house Roland had reverted to speaking in normal English again much to Stumblebums relief and they got straight on with the treatment for Stumblebum's problem.

Ramsbottom and his wife both left Stumblebum alone whilst they went upstairs to change into their ceremonial vestments. As he waited for them to return he browsed amongst the knick-knacks and books on the shelves and sideboard, an interesting collection of items and books relating to the occult, including a crystal ball, various dried herbs in labelled boxes and several incense burners of elaborate designs. And candles, lots of candles!

When the Ramsbottoms came back downstairs they both wore long flowing gowns with magic symbols printed over them and Roland had on his head an extremely long pointed wizards' hat, so tall that he had

[5] It warra ret good do! = it turned out to be a splendid event.

[6] Mostly pure unintelligible gibberish, even in the north!

to duck his head down to get through the door despite his own lack of stature. He had a polished hardwood wand in one hand and carried a small box in the other which he placed on the coffee table and opened to reveal a greyish powdery mixture inside.

'I've mixed some ashes of elder root, a very potent natural ingredient, along with some other effective herbs and, of course, the dried chicken droppings.'

'We'll do this out in the backyard under the sky. It's nice and private so we won't be disturbed.' Ramsbottom picked up the box and Freda got them a candle each which she lit before they all went out into the yard by way of the back door in the kitchen.

It was a bit cool outside and the sky was slightly overcast. A few stars twinkled above as the clouds drifted along to reveal them. Occasionally the thin sliver of the moon made a brief appearance before it disappeared again behind the next cloud. The light from their candles dimly illuminated the yard and flickered in the slight breeze as Ramsbottom led them to the space at the bottom below the kitchen, where a small ramshackle chicken coop leaned against a wooden shed which he entered and emerged again with a small wooden stool.

'Sit on the stool and hold your candle up in front of your face and concentrate on the flame.' Ramsbottom instructed Stumblebum as he opened the little box and gave it to Freda to hold for him as he began his magic spell.

He held his candle above Stumblebum's slightly glowing head and moved it in a rough circle three times as he intoned the words of the spell. He then carefully placed his candle on the ground before taking a scoop of the powder from the box held by Freda and rubbed it all over the boy's scalp as he continued to mutter a magic incantation. He then waved his wand over Stumblebum's head several times and brought the little ceremony to a close.

Before they went back into the house Stumblebum helped his mentor to put the wooden stool back in the shed and as they did this he noticed in the dim light row upon row of demijohns, bottles and jars containing coloured liquids on several shelves at the back of the shed.

‘Are they magic potions in those jars, you seem to have quite a lot of them?’ he asked, curiously.

‘Er, no, well not exactly. They contain home brew beer and home-made rhubarb wine. Those flagons on the top shelf are a special mead done to an ancient secret druidic recipe known as *Druids Delight*. Very potent stuff! Lethal!’

‘If you like you can try some of the rhubarb wine when we get indoors. Here take my candle and wand will you while I go and get a bottle. Ask Freda to get us three sherry glasses would you please.’ Ramsbottom handed him his wand and candle as he went back into the shed and returned with a dusty bottle of wine.

Back in the house they warmed themselves by the fire and sipped the rhubarb wine, which Stumblebum found to be surprisingly pleasant, and chatted together, in fairly high spirits due to the successful ritual they had just completed outside. After having a second glass ‘for the road’ Stumblebum got up and put on his cape and fez before he bade goodnight to his hosts and thanked them for the wine after which he set off back towards home feeling a warm glow of contentment and wellbeing.

It had been a very good outcome to the evening all in all. At last some positive progress had been made by Stumblebum and so he was in a very buoyant mood when he got back to his auntie’s place. Success at last!

Chapter Fourteen

The following Monday at the academy saw a flurry of heightened activity on a number of levels. First of all preparations were under way for the wizards' novice upgrade ceremony being held at the end of the week on Friday, which would be followed by a celebratory feast in the Great Hall of Wizards.

The novices themselves who were to be upgraded were still frantically engaged in some last minute study before their imminent assessments. It would appear that the novices not being assessed this time were even more frantically engaged in a furious search for the secret of the transmutation of base metals to gold, such was the level of gold fever which seem to have gripped the minds of the remaining novices.

It was this maelstrom of furious activity into which Stumblebum stepped on that Monday morning and, not himself immune to the obsessive search for untold riches, made his way with some haste to the library with the intention of copying the final pages of his hidden book. The library was busier than he would have liked it to be, certainly much busier than usual, as Stumblebum secured a table for himself in an obscure corner of the room near to some of the bookcases.

Stumblebum went back to retrieve the concealed book from under the bookshelf. He took great care not to be observed as he brought the book back to the table and then opened it and found the page where he had left off on Friday. This part of the book referred to the philosopher's stone and his heart raced with anticipation. To his horror he discovered that someone had removed most of the last chapter, the rough remnants of these pages barely visible, showing where they had been torn out.

He had to stifle a howl of disappointment which would have drawn unwanted attention to his task. Stumblebum just sat there in silence for a long time as he gazed at the stubs of the absent pages. On close inspection it seemed that they had been torn out some time ago as the ripped edges were faded like the rest of the pages and not more recently done. At least it did not look as if he had been seen replacing the book so it must have been done some time earlier. But why?

Stumblebum slipped furtively back to the bookshelf and put the book back under the shelf since it seemed to be the best place to conceal it from others. He then went down to the spells lab to do some wand practice for the rest of the day but his mind went back to the mystery of the missing pages again and again. At least he had taken accurate copies of the remainder of the pages and had them safely concealed between his own books at home but it was a shame he had not managed to complete the formula in full.

As Stumblebum left the academy for home that afternoon he decided to spend the next few weeks in search of any other books which there might be on alchemy in the library so as to complete his notes on the subject. He was now in urgent need to get some money for Salty Sammy's boat so it would be good if he learnt the secret of how to make gold sooner rather than later. It could be the end of all of his troubles if he could pull it off!

* * * * * * *

Tiberius Mordecai and Slippery Jack were busy with a plot designed to achieve several outcomes, all of them devious! Mordecai was deep in discussion with Slippery and touched on a past matter which now could be pivotal to their plans.

‘It was a good move of yours Slippery when you took the formula for the philosophers’ stone out of that book that you hid before you got expelled. It was wise of you not to try to steal the entire book until you had let me see those pages first. It‘s a shame they caught you the next day with the other books, though. Do you think it will still be there?’ Mordecai enquired.

‘It should be, I stashed it in an unlikely place and I doubt if it has been found yet. It’s a pity I couldn’t get it out that first time, but as you say, as well that I didn’t try.’

‘We could do with getting our hands on that particular book and since neither of us can gain entry to the academy we must find someone to do it for us. Off the top of your head who do you think would be mug enough to get the book for us? And I am thinking novice guild wizard here!’

‘Well now, let me see! I don’t think any of the three musketeers would co-operate with us as they are far too straight laced but their young friend Stumblebum could be a possibility. We might be able to entice him round to our way of thinking.’ Slippery looked thoughtful.

‘On the other hand I think that the mayor’s nephew, Silas, would be better. He is even more of a misfit than Stumblebum, and stupider! It would be fairly easy to get him to do things for us if he thought there was a good piece of the action in it for him. He seems to be just like his grasping uncle in that respect. In fact we could probably simply pay him to do our bidding!’

‘Keep an eye on both of them for now then, particularly that Silas, he could be the one.’ Mordecai rubbed his chin thoughtfully. ‘We might do well if we get Silas to assist us, we could use him to get to the mayor and kill two birds with one stone. It’s high time that our not so ‘honourable’ mayor got his come-uppance, and we could bring mayhem to the town if we play this right! What do you think Slippery?’

Slippery sniggered as he mulled this over in his twisted mind.

‘It’s a good idea, retrieve the book and entice the mayor into a trap at the same time! I like it! What sort of situation did you have in mind?’

‘I’m not sure yet but we ought to come up with something appropriate. I’ll check out what schemes the mayor is currently abusing his position on and which other corporation members are in his little mafia. It could prove to be good sport, Slippery, and at the least we should get his nephew to get the book for us. We could do with another spy entrenched in the academy since your cover was blown. There are a few possibilities for us.’

Slippery grinned widely in anticipation of his tasks ahead as he really enjoyed enticing people into traps, a real labour of love for him, without a doubt!

* * * * * * *

The next day Slippery lurked about close to the academy just before it closed and watched the wizards and novices come out of the building as he looked out for the ungainly person of Silas Suggs. His patience soon paid off and Silas emerged from the building on his own and headed off toward the town centre. Slippery followed at some distance behind and watched with interest as Silas went into a small café. It looked as if he had chosen to avoid the more popular *Beverage Bliss* since his recent mishap in the place. Slippery grinned devilishly at the memory of the yucca plant incident.

Slippery hung about on the street for five minutes or so then entered the little café where he found Silas seated on his own with a cup of tea. He nodded to Silas in acknowledgment and joined him at his table.

‘You don’t mind if I sit here do you Silas? We have met before but I don’t expect you will remember, no matter though. My name is Slippery, you’ve probably heard my name around town? I’m glad to bump into you as I could be of assistance to you in a certain matter.’

Silas looked up at the newcomer with suspicion.

‘What matter’s that then? And why should you help me?’

‘Well, let’s just say that we have mutual interests and goals and I could help you to achieve some of those goals if you were to help me in one or two matters. That way we shall both win and everybody will be happy. Think about it, no rush!' Slippery got up from his seat as if to leave.

'Hold on a minute, what do you mean, 'mutual interests' and what have you got in mind?'

Slippery sat back down, now that he had hooked Silas's interest.

'Well, have you heard of Tiberius Mordecai? He is my associate, an extremely successful and capable magician, and very wealthy!' This struck a nerve with Silas.

'Go on.' He prompted, as Slippery reeled him in.

'How would you like to meet him at his mansion for a drink? He might be able to put some good fortune your way if you help him in a small matter and I know that you like Brigitte so it would impress her if you were to make a good sum of money, with our help of course, you know how girls like to be pampered with expensive gifts, never fails.'

'How do you know about Brigitte?' Silas looked suspiciously at Slippery.

'Oh, I happened to be in the *Beverage Bliss* the other day when you suffered your mishap with the yucca plant. I heard everything.' Slippery grinned widely.

'Yeah, well when I find out who was responsible they'd better watch out…!' Silas punched his open palm in his favourite hostile gesture. 'So do you know who did it then? I'll make them wish they hadn't been born, so I will!' Again he punched his palm menacingly.

'Well, I can only speculate really and I can tell you what I saw, but not here. How about coming over to Mordecai Manor tomorrow evening after college? I can introduce you to Mordecai and we will discuss many things over a drink of wine.' Slippery rose his feet and made for the door as Silas seemed to have taken the bait, hook, line and sinker. He quickly stepped outside before Silas had a chance to question him further, having now got his full attention.'

'I'll meet you in here after you leave the academy. Then I shall take you over to meet Mordecai. Until tomorrow then?'

Silas was left on his own to mull over the conversation he had just had, intrigued by the offer of help from a wealthy and successful magician and with a glimmer of hope for gaining the affections of the lovely Brigitte. He still could not understand why she turned him down in the first place but now here was a chance and he must take it.

* * * * * * *

Stumblebum at about this time relaxed lazily in his room after a hard day of study at the academy and idly watched the activity out on the sea from the window, though first making sure that neither Salty Sammy nor Violet Veronica were outside where they might see him.

He opened the box of powder that Ramsbottom had given him along with instructions to rub it into his scalp twice a day and removed his fez. He gently massaged the mixture in as he absently gazed out across the little harbour. As he rubbed his head a tinge of excitement came over him as he detected that already a result was in evidence. His fingers rubbed the powder onto his bald pate before he felt the beginnings of growth all over his head, a sort of soft down clearly in evidence.

He immediately ran into the bathroom to look in the mirror and to his absolute joy confirmed that a barely visible downy growth had appeared, indication of his return to a full head of hair and normality. Elated, he went back into his bedroom and rubbed some more of the powder in for good measure in the hope that this might speed up the process. Too excited to study Stumblebum replaced his fez and went downstairs to join Auntie Maggie and Skipper in the kitchen for tea in the hope that she would also notice the return of his hair.

Auntie Maggie looked up from feeding tit bits to Skipper who was as usual seated on his stool as Stumblebum came into the kitchen and gave him a warm smile.

'What are you looking so pleased with yourself about dear?' she asked.

‘Oh, nothing really Auntie.’ Stumblebum smirked as he looked for the best moment of impact with which to surprise her with his good news.’ He removed his fez and placed it on the table in front of him and stroked his head several times, still grinning exuberantly.

‘So what’s for tea tonight, I’m rather famished?’ He pointedly stroked his head some more so as to draw attention to the new growth of his hair.

‘I was just going to do some scrambled eggs with salad but if you like I can make something else dear, what do you fancy?’

‘No, no Auntie, scrambled eggs sounds fine, just do me plenty please.’ Stumblebum couldn’t stop grinning as he continued to stroke his head in the hope that she would notice his hair.

‘Don’t forget to wash your hands dear, and don’t touch your head before you eat, it’s not very hygienic dear is it?’

‘Not as bad as touching that wretched cat all the time, Auntie, that can’t be very healthy when you are cooking!’ Stumblebum glared at Skipper, still perched on his stool at the table.

‘I always wash my hands before I handle food dear, you know that. What’s made you so grumpy all of a sudden then? You seemed to be really cheerful a minute ago!’

‘I was going to show you something but it doesn’t matter now. It can wait ‘till tomorrow I suppose.’ He said somewhat petulantly.

‘Suit yourself dear, do you want any bread and butter with your tea?’ Auntie Maggie fussed about making the meal, which Stumblebum ate in a sulky silence, after which he declined to join her and Skipper in the drawing room as they went in to watch some television.

Stumblebum stomped loudly back up the stairs to his bedroom in a massive huff. ‘Doesn’t she ever notice anything?’ He thought, annoyed that his surprise had gone unnoticed during tea. ‘What does a fellow have to do to get some attention around here? Perhaps I should just purr and roll on my back like Skipper does. That blasted cat gets all of the fuss and attention around here and he doesn’t do anything! Just takes!’

* * * * * * *

Over at the little theatre clouds of discontent also gathered and the storm was about to erupt into a major tempest as a certain bombshell was to be dropped.

Terry Philpot had some diplomatic manoeuvres to conduct in his role as productions director for the Old Town Amateur Repertory Theatre Society due to Quentin's reckless award of the part of Juliet to one of the newer and younger members of the society.

Terry, known by the nickname 'Teapot' partly because of his habit of standing with one hand high up on his hip whilst reading from a script held theatrically high in his other hand, had been given the unenviable task by Quentin of breaking the news to Winifred and the other older female thespians that the upcoming leading role had been awarded to the lovely young Mandy. As expected, Winifred Closet was not happy.

'But this is absolutely outrageous, she has only just joined. This ought to be a matter of seniority and as the longest standing female member of our society the part should be mine.' Winifred protested. Some of the other older women also muttered their dismay, though secretly pleased to have Winifred knocked from her perch for once.

'Well lovey, we must give the new arrivals a chance to get into the swing of things and they will not be able to unless they get straight into some challenging roles. Plus we really do need to attract new, younger players into our little family or we will lack range and scope.'

'And besides,' Teapot went on, 'Young Mandy will make a splendid Juliet, what with her beautiful long blonde hair and all.'

'Well I've got my wigs,' Winifred retorted, 'and my invaluable experience in delighting our audiences with my performances over many years! What experience has this slip of a girl got, ask yourself that Terrence, what experience does she have?'

'The only way she is going to get any experience is if we let her have a go at a good part and I say that this part is just right for her. We shall just have to give her a chance that's all. If you like you can play Widow Twanky in Aladdin when we put on the pantomime this year, how does that sound love?'

'Widow Twanky? Widow bloody Twanky?' Winifred nearly choked on the name.

'That's hardly the same as playing Juliet is it? And besides it is usually played by a man in drag! You and Quentin take turns with it don't you?' Winifred was now completely livid.

'I'm sure Quentin won't mind if you have a stab at it this year. We have all got to make some sacrifices for the overall good of the troupe lovey and I'm prepared stand aside this once, it is a central character in Aladdin you know, an important part, ...but if you don't think you are up to it dear...' he trailed off.

'Of course I can do it but I wanted to do Juliet. I have a perfect wig for the part and my years of acting experience make me perfect for this role, you can't deny that can you Terrence?'

'Yes, well, wigs are all very well but they can't compete with natural healthy bouncy hair for impact on the stage. No, the decision has been made Winifred and that's the end of it. Start thinking about how you are going to play Widow Twanky dear and let me worry about the Shakespeare production this time.' Teapot was adamant.

Chapter Fifteen

Healthy bouncy hair was very much on Stumblebums mind as he got up from his bed the next morning. Hoping to detect some improvement on yesterday's happy discovery he again ran his hand across his head and was delighted to feel that not only had the stubble grown but it seemed to have more body and substance than before, if not a little stiff to the touch. This was good since he had always hated his limp wispy hair before and now it seemed as if it would grow back with much more substance than ever.

He chatted cheerfully to Auntie Maggie over breakfast and even made a fuss of Skipper afterwards before leaving for the academy. On his walk there Skipper climbed up his cape and on to his shoulder and stared unblinking at Stumblebums head as they made their way to the little door in the alley at the side of the academy where he chased the cat away after the usual struggle to knock it from his shoulder.

'At least Skipper has noticed my new growth of hair so I suppose that's something!' Stumblebum thought, still slightly annoyed that his auntie hadn't noticed, although it might be a laugh for him to see how much it would grow before she did. He chuckled at this thought as he made his way through the old academy's labyrinth of passages and corridors to the library where he was to resume his search for the elusive philosophers' stone.

The library was even more crowded than the previous day with novices occupying every table as they furiously scoured parchment scrolls and old books in the quest for the secret of transmutation of a base metal into gold. Stumblebum had to share a study table with several other novices and although they were immersed in their own research nonetheless he was a little uncomfortable doing his secret research in such a close proximity to others, worried that should he make a discovery it would be observed. After about an hour or so he got up and left the library as he found that he could not concentrate so well with others at his table close by.

Despite the preoccupation with the search for the formula to make gold there was also a buzz of excitement around the academy in anticipation of the upgrade ceremony due to take place on Friday, which by all accounts would be a very lavish affair. Rumour had it that His Grand Eminence the Magister Magus, a powerful and reclusive wizard and the current patriarch of the Guild of Wizards and chancellor of the Academy, was to put in a very rare appearance and oversee the proceedings.

Stumblebum visited the apothecary and secured several rare herbs from the Keeper of Potions in order to practice a number of new spells which he had not attempted before and then went on to the spells lab to practice them, which he did with not much success, although he was getting slightly better at his spells he noticed, so his recent intensive practice had improved his skills to some degree. After this he attended a lecture on wand maintenance followed by a seminar discussing the merits of science over superstition in the application of magic.

After his busy day at the academy he left for home a little tired but full of that kind of satisfaction brought on by hard work and study. When he got home he watched television with Auntie Maggie and Skipper after the evening meal and then he turned in early to bed as he had difficulty in staying awake. Although he intended to resume his search for the secret of making gold the next day at the academy he also looked forward to Friday and the feast at the novice upgrade ceremony which he expected to be an enjoyable, relaxing and interesting end to a week of mixed fortunes and intensive studies.

*   *   *   *   *   *   *

Silas Suggs also had much on his mind that evening as he left Mordecai Manor following an interesting few hours where he had been plied with wine and had engaged in friendly conversation with the great sorcerer Tiberius Mordecai, along with Slippery Jack, who had put to him a proposition that could do him much good, financially and otherwise. As he walked home from the mansion he thought about how he might maximise his advantage from this situation, although he little realised how much he already was being manipulated by his two new devious partners in crime.

On his way home he made a detour and called in on his Uncle Percy, the mayor of Bilge on Sea, and relayed to him the gist of the conversation he had just had at Mordecai Manor and the scheme that had been discussed.

The mention of gold made the mayor's ears prick up and suddenly he gave his full attention to what his nephew said to him. His years of manipulation of expenses and other public funds had given him a huge appetite for the accumulation of wealth for himself, particularly when it properly belonged to others.

'So what are you telling me then Silas? This book they want you to secure for them has instructions on how to make gold in it?' The mayors already beady, pig-like eyes narrowed as cogs in his head turned and creaked into 'operation acquisition' mode, an automatic response from his brain whenever the possibility of financial gain was brought to his attention.

'Yes but it will be an elaborate system of magical procedures. They will require a great deal of skill and experience. Not at all easy.' Silas explained.

'Well what's the problem lad? You've been at that academy long enough now to do this sort of thing and since you will have the book in your possession just follow the instructions. We could all be rich if we approach this right.'

'What about Mordecai? He will want me to take the book to him as soon as I get it out of the academy and he expects me to get it soon.'

'Bring it to me to see first. We will look at it together and if the task is too much for us then we shall have to devise a plan 'B' and that might involve you and me having a secret meeting with this Mordecai. First it would be better if just the two of us manage to pull it off. That way we won't have to share any gold with them!'

Silas had to agree as this was more or less what he had hoped for when he had decided to let his uncle in on the situation. He knew that he would use all of his years of guile and experience in such matters to squeeze the maximum benefit for them both and it was better to divide the gold between two rather than three or four. In fact Silas would have to watch that his uncle did not try to keep it all for himself but he would go along with his plan for now until they succeeded in making the gold and then be on his guard.

After Silas took his leave of his uncle and headed home he gave some thought to the conversation he had had with Slippery Jack at Mordecai Manor earlier that evening regarding the incident with the yucca plant in the *Beverage Bliss* which had caused both insult and injury to him in front of his fellow novices.

Although Slippery had taken care not to definitely identify the culprit directly he did indicate that it could very likely have been the work of a young novice called Stumblebum who was at a nearby table when the assault took place and was also was known to Slippery to be a secret admirer of Brigitte! This theory made sense if this was indeed the case as Silas knew only too well the passions inspired by the lovely Brigitte and how they could drive a fellow to commit violence if deemed necessary. He would make a point to watch out for this Stumblebum character the next day at the academy and try to observe him secretly and see if he could get the measure of him.

And then if it turned out he was the culprit, and was also after the affections of Brigitte, well, he had better watch out!

'This Stumblebum youth is about to find out what happens to those who get in the way of Silas Suggs and it won't be very pretty!' Silas mused as he walked home deep in thought.

'Stumblebum beware!' Silas growled, 'Silas Suggs is not a wizard to be trifled with. So beware!' Silas thumped his right fist into his opened left palm time and again as he made his way home.

* * * * * * *

The following morning Stumblebum felt a little uneasy as he prepared for his day at the academy before breakfast. Nothing felt quite right that morning. His hair had continued to indicate some more growth but had a strange feel to it and an air of impending disaster seemed to occupy his thoughts. He wracked his brain but could not quite put his finger on what might be behind this sense of foreboding other than perhaps his urgency to acquire some funds in order to repay Salty Sammy his money. He could not rid himself of this expectation of doom no matter how he tried to put his mind to it.

By the time that he had arrived at the academy his mood had lifted, caught up with the buzz of excitement about the following day's upgrade ceremony, an important event held several times throughout the year when selected novices were presented with their upgrade awards before the brotherhood of wizards. A demonstration of their skills to the assembled wizards and fellow novices would take place before they all enjoyed a glorious elaborate feast.

These events were a welcome punctuation to the year's hard work and always full of spectacular magic displays after which the wizards would party on through the rest of the day as they indulged in good food and drinks. Stumblebum was excited at this prospect but nonetheless decided to knuckle down to some more serious study for the rest of the day so made his way to the library hoping to find a table to himself for a change.

The library was still busy though not quite as crowded as it had been of late as novices were now taking a more relaxed approach to their studies, gold fever or not, as their minds were on the next day of magic demonstrations and the subsequent feast. Excited novices chatted in groups in the corridors around the academy and a general expectation of Friday's fun and debauchery informed their light hearted conversations.

Stumblebum found an unoccupied table to sit at and glanced around the room at others immersed in their studies before he resumed his search for books about alchemy and making gold. After he carried a number of such books from the bookshelves to his table he knuckled down to some serious research for most of the morning, too preoccupied to notice that he was being observed from across the library from behind a large pile of books that Silas had stacked high in front of him in order to conceal himself from Stumblebum.

Silas found his observation of Stumblebum boring and tiresome but persisted in this line of action as he wanted to see what made the younger novice tick and whether he might have been capable of the yucca plant-pot attack in the *Beverage Bliss*. At one point when Stumblebum had gone behind some bookshelves looking for more books Silas sidled nonchalantly over to the table which Stumblebum had recently vacated and slyly glanced at the pile of books he had been reading. They were all concerned with alchemy and transmutation of base metals into gold! Interesting!

The picture Silas was building of Stumblebum looked very much like Slippery Jack's assessment of the lad was correct. He would watch him more intently from now on and discretely ask around to find out his habits and places he hung out at. Towards the end of the afternoon, as the novices gradually trickled out of the library, Stumblebum finally closed his books and also left.

Silas had one more bit of business to conduct. He pulled a sheet of paper from his pocket with a rough plan of the library and some instructions scribbled on to it by Slippery. He then waited until the Academy Scribe busied himself at the opposite part of the library that Silas needed to investigate and quickly found the row of bookshelves described on his map.

He found the loose shelf propped up by a small leather bound book which he removed and hastily stuffed down the front of his trousers as he watched out for the Academy Scribe in case he saw what he was up to.

Mission accomplished he made his way quickly out of the library and down the stairs and corridors to the little wizards' door in the alleyway and hastily left for home, pleased to have secured his prize with such ease. He would deal with Stumblebum in a day or so but first he had to focus on his upgrade ceremony the next day, after which he would consult with his uncle on how best to proceed with the gold making enterprise.

Chapter Sixteen

Friday! The day of the upgrades and the celebratory feast. Stumblebum awoke with eager anticipation of that day's celebration at the academy. As he lay in bed he felt the weight of Skipper, who sat on his chest much to his annoyance. The cat stared with some intensity at Stumblebum and his eyes followed the young wizard as he got up from the bed, yawned and scratched his head. Something did not feel right! He ran his hand all over his head and his new growth of bristles definitely felt very wrong.

Stumblebum marched immediately to the bathroom and looked at his reflection in the mirror and confirmed what his touch seemed to indicate, contrary to what logic would suggest. To his absolute horror he saw that the new growth on his head, far from the lush dark bouncy hair he desired, was not in fact hair but feathers! Feathers! His previously bald scalp now had a cluster of reddish brown feathers which sprouted thickly all over like an American chieftain's war bonnet.

Stumblebum's first reaction was to panic! His next reaction was to panic some more! He returned to his bedroom and continued to panic. What should he do? How could this happen? He tried to appeal to reason and to look for a solution.

‘Surely this can’t be real, perhaps I am still asleep and having a bad dream!’ He wondered, as he pinched himself hard in an effort to wake up.

‘Arrgh!’ Stumblebum yelled with pain and realised that he was indeed very awake and still had feathers growing out of his head. What could he do?’

‘Ramsbottom!’ It suddenly occurred to him what might be the cause of this recent calamity.

‘Bloody Ramsbottom and his dried chicken droppings! I thought it was all too good to be true. Bloody pagan magic! I might have known something like this would happen. Why does everything keep going wrong for me? Why? Why me? Why?’

Stumblebum sank onto the edge of his bed and sat for some time until his sense of panic calmed slightly. What should he do about this? He could not ask the senior wizards at the academy for help since they disapproved of pagan magic and would likely to give him a black mark against his wizard assessment results. He would have to ask his friends for their advice again and hope that between them a solution could be found.

Stumblebum nonetheless was determined to enjoy the day as he had so much looked forward to its arrival and the subsequent attendant jollifications at the academy. He would try to put the problem out of his mind for the day, although this would not be easy since the problem would accompany him everywhere as it was on top of his head.

He dressed in his favourite top with the Superman logo across its chest and put on his best half-mast cargo trousers and coolest trainers. Then he spent some time as he attempted to ram his feathered growth into his fez until he was sure that no feathers were visible before going down for breakfast.

Auntie Maggie need not know about his latest mishap for now he decided. So as not to appear foolish yet again he wore his fez pulled down tight in order to wear at breakfast, as he often did, though this time he checked frequently to reassure himself that it was still secure and tightly seated on his head.

On the short walk to the academy Stumblebum felt self-conscious about the feathers under his fez, a feeling not helped by Skipper, who declined his usual assault on the hem of his cape but instead scrambled straight up on to his shoulder to stare intently at the rim of the fez as if waiting for some prey to emerge. Stumblebum and Skipper engaged in their usual struggle to separate the cat from his shoulder before the young wizard composed himself, took several deep breaths and entered the academy.

* * * * * * *

As soon as the little door from the alleyway slammed shut behind him Stumblebum sensed the atmosphere of expectation and excitement which permeated the old academy building and which heightened as he made his way along the corridors to the Great Hall of Wizards, where the current upgrade ceremonies and celebratory feast were about to take place.

Upon the approach to the hall Stumblebum felt the increased buzz of excitement amongst the groups of novices and the other wizards who thronged the corridors up to the tunnel which led to the great oak door. The tunnel itself was blocked by a glittering array of transparent crystal pillars, a splendid display with each pillar radiating a different rainbow colour and with magic life-size images of previous eminent alumni as they slowly revolved inside them in an eerie choreography of excellence.

The wizards and novices chatted excitedly as they awaited the commencement of proceedings and jostled for position along the corridors nearest to the tunnel. Stumblebum elbowed his way toward the front of the crowd, impatient to make a start on the day's celebrations. He had looked forward to the demonstrations of magic from the upgraded novices, usually quite an impressive spectacle.

As the figures inside their crystal shrouds revolved one by one the crystal pillars disintegrated into small shards which fell to the ground in a symphony of tinkles and chimes. The images of the alumni of past wizards evaporated into multi-coloured clouds of vapour and then swirled under the great oak door and disappeared into the Great Hall.

The last wisp of smoke vanished and the huge door creaked open to reveal the interior of the hall, now set out with rows of tables and benches brightly illuminated by the wall sconces and candles and the enchanted vaulted ceiling as it shimmered with a magical glow of kaleidoscopic coloured light.

The assembled company of wizards and novices shuffled into the hall and took their places at their tables, laid out below the raised rostrum and set with platters, cutlery and goblets for wine. Already seated on the rostrum on magnificent gilded thrones behind a large oak table were five of the most senior wizards of the guild. His Grand Eminence the Magister Magus was seated on the largest of the five thrones, in the centre, flanked by the other high ranking wizards, with the Ipsissimus Grand Magister and the old Scribe Grand Magister either side of him.

All five of these dignitaries wore their finest robes and headgear, the tallest of the hats on the head of the Magister Magus, a large, imposing man of indeterminate age who sported a long white beard and long white hair below a very tall white triple crown. These were worn only by the wizards of extremely high rank. It was emphasised by its height, so high that the tip of the hat almost touched the high vaulted ceiling of the hall. He wore a long white robe with a large silver talisman on a chord hung from around his neck and his impressive silver embossed wand was worn suspended in a special ornately decorated scabbard slung from the knotted chord tied around his waist.

At one side of him sat the Ipsissimus Grand Magister, bedecked in a rich adornment of heavy gold chains, gold medallions, chunky gold bracelets and solid looking gold rings on each of his fingers. He even had a solid gold band hooped around the base of his wizard's hat, a purple pointed affair almost as tall as that worn by the Magister Magus although more elaborately adorned with symbols and small gold studs.

The Scribe Grand Magister rose to his feet and addressed the assembly in his usual solemn tones.

'We, the Academy of the Guild of Wizards, do hereby welcome all assembled to this most auspicious occasion of the grade ceremony of our newest graduated wizards.'

'Hail to our Great Academy!' came the enthusiastic reply from the collective voices of wizards and novices.

'I invite you to extend your most heartfelt welcome to our patron and chancellor His Grand Eminence the Magister Magus upon gracing this assembly with his esteemed presence.'

'Hail to His Grand Eminence!' the wizards roared loudly.

'Before we begin the demonstrations and grade awards I would like to first offer a few words of advice to our novices and younger wizards regarding their studies.'

'It has come to the attention of the governing body of the academy that many young wizards, especially novices, have employed much of their time and studies recently in their attempts to transmute base metals into gold. This, although commendable enthusiastic approach to the study and practice of magic, is felt to be rather premature in your studies as this advanced alchemy is rarely met with success other than by those of our number with many years of experience and competence.' The scribe Grand Magister paused at this point as he cast a sideways glance to the Ipsissimus Grand Magister before he continued.

'Although we are encouraged by the enthusiasm from our young scholars in their application to this subject we do advise, however, that your efforts would be better spent on the less demanding tasks on the curriculum at this stage. Bear in mind that success in this advanced alchemy is rarely achieved and then only after many years hard work and utter selfless dedication for the sole purpose of the pursuit of knowledge.'

The Ipsissimus Grand Magister gave an embarrassed cough and shuffled uncomfortably on his throne as he folded his arms across his chest in a vain attempt to conceal some of the bling which dripped from his person as he shot a brief withering look at his colleague the Scribe Grand Magister.

'To assist the novices in returning to their more appropriate studies it has been decided that all books and scrolls containing advice on this area of alchemy be removed from the library to the archives where they will only be issued by special permission. To this end the Academy Scribe has undertaken this task already and these gems of knowledge are now safely under lock and key.' The old Scribe Grand Magister concluded and returned to his throne accompanied by a collective moan of disappointment from amongst the novices.

The Magister Magus now rose to his feet and addressed the assembly in his role as academy chancellor. He opened the celebrations and invited the upgraded novices to begin their demonstrations whilst food and drink was brought into the great hall by a legion of caterers and waiters and distributed amongst the tables. The mouth-watering aromas as the feast arrived lifted the spirits of all present and a party atmosphere of excited wizards soon ensued.

As the wizards chatted and dined the novices to be graded were outside the hall in the tunnel preparing their entrances. The commencement of the demonstrations of skill by each novice in turn was heralded by a signal from the Scribe Grand Magister who rang a ceremonial hand-bell, after which the noise in the room became somewhat more subdued as the wizards waited with anticipation.

After a few moments a movement was seen near to the door and the mystified brotherhood of wizards watched as something appeared to float through the air into the hall. As the object glided towards the front of the rostrum it became clear that it was in fact a red novice's fez, apparently floating unaided as it came to a halt below the row of dignitaries.

The fez remained suspended for several seconds before a large pair of ears suddenly appeared beneath the rim followed by a pair of bulging eyes, nose and blubbery lips as the facial features of Silas Suggs emerged from below the headgear. This caused each of the dignitaries to simultaneously jump in their seats, startled by the sudden appearance of the countenance of Silas, not a pretty sight in normal circumstances, but to appear without warning and also without visible means of support was, to say the least, rather unsettling.

The remainder of Silas continued to slowly manifest until finally his large feet took shape on the floor in front of the rostrum, Silas gave a low bow to the Grand Magisters and then removed his fez and placed it on the table in front of the row of five grade one wizards hats previously arranged there. At this the Scribe Grand Magister came to the front of the table and placed one of the hats on to Silas's head and again intoned to the assembly.

'I hereby promote Silas Suggs to the rank of wizard grade one. May his magic never fail to astonish!'

'Hail Silas Suggs! Hail Silas Suggs!' Came the loud response.

Silas swaggered to his table to join his fellow wizards to polite applause, a smug look on his face, pleased as he was by his successful demonstration of invisibility.

As the claps and cheers subsided David Lee entered the hall in a more conventional fashion and carrying with him a large bronze oriental incense burner. He placed the object on the floor in front of the rostrum and tapped it twice with his wand. At this a column of blue smoke emerged from an opening on one side of the lid followed almost immediately by a column of red smoke out of the opposite opening. The two columns of smoke swirled and twisted upwards and became denser and larger before they took the shape of two large dragons engaged in a ritual battle close to the vaulted ceiling, giving off sparks and coloured vapours as they fought.

At the close of this impressive mock battle the two dragons exploded into a myriad of bright burning fragments which cascaded down over the heads of the watching assembly. The exotic spicy scent of the smoke permeated the room as it swirled back into the incense burner, which now transformed itself into a bronze statue of the two dragons, intertwined in their fierce combat, and now a beautifully designed *object d' art*. David lifted the statue up on to the table and presented it to the Magisters and gave a low bow, before he removed his fez, as Silas had, and placed it in front of the row of wizards' hats.

The assembly applauded enthusiastically after this colourful display as David was presented with his grade one wizard's hat and took his place at the feast. A long pause followed which caused an atmosphere of expectation amongst the audience as Morris, the next candidate, deliberately took his time in order to maximise the dramatic effect of his entrance. The Scribe Grand Magister rang his little hand-bell several times and looked rather annoyed at the lack of response.

As the waiting wizards and novices wondered what the delay could be Morris suddenly flew into the hall flamboyantly dressed in a red embroidered waistcoat, yellow baggy silk trousers and with a pair of red velvet slippers which curled up to a point at the toes. His fez was surrounded by a white silk scarf he had wound around its rim to give it the appearance of a turban and he was seated on what looked like a magic Persian carpet which bore him around the hall and knocked a few wizards' hats to the floor as he passed over the wizards heads.

Morris completed several circuits of the hall and flew higher and higher until he had to duck quickly in order to avoid bumping his own head on the vaulted ceiling, and nearly lost his fez as he did so. He then glided to a halt on the floor just before the rostrum with the five dignitaries and, like his predecessors, gave a low bow before he disentangled his fez from his makeshift turban and eventually placed it on the table as he waited for it to be replaced with his wizard's hat.

The grade one wizards hats were conical in shape and a bit taller than the fez's but coloured orange with a broad silver band around the middle. On Morris it looked as if he had a traffic cone on his head, though like the others, he was pleased to wear his new symbol of achievement. He pushed in between Stumblebum and David at their banquet table and took a long draught of wine from one of the goblets.

'So what did you think of my demonstration lads? Spectacular or what?'

'Where did you get the outfit from? You certainly looked the part, straight out of *The Arabian Nights*. Very impressive!' Stumblebum replied.

Morris gave a wide grin and answered in a hushed voice.

'I "borrowed" it from the little theatre. It's from the props for the upcoming production of *Aladdin*. They have got loads of costumes. Oh, before I forget, I found loads of wigs in a cupboard. I shall see if I can liberate one for you, I'm sure they won't miss one.'

Stumblebum involuntarily put his hand on his fez and checked it was still covering his feathers. The magic energy in the hall seemed to have caused them to grow some more but they were still contained under his fez, thankfully. He would keep a check on the situation as the party continued.

Secundus moved down from another table to sit next to Stumblebum and the others.

'So what do you think about the upgrade ceremony then?' he asked Stumblebum

'It's great so far, and the feast is something else, even us younger novices are allowed to drink wine!' Stumblebum took a swig from his goblet.

'Yes, but go steady with it, we don't want to have to carry you home.' Secundus grinned.

'By the way, how is your magic practice getting on? Did you find somewhere else other than the little beach by your house? Only if you work hard and practice you might get a chance to be assessed for the next batch of upgrades, along with me.'

Stumblebum put his goblet down and wiped his mouth on his sleeve.

'No, I was going to ask Ramsbottom to let me use his backyard for practice but I am not sure I am going to be friends with him for much longer.'

'Why, what's up?'

'Oh, I'll tell you later. Anyway I go on to the little beach behind auntie's house most nights around midnight now when there is no chance of being pestered by Violet Veronica. Even that little tyke is in bed by then.'

Silas Suggs, who was seated at a table behind Stumblebum's group of friends, quietly listened in to the conversation as his big ears flapped and twitched like radar antennae. He noted what Stumblebum's group said with some interest before he returned to his food and drink as he slyly formed a sinister plot in his mind.

'Who's on next then?' Stumblebum asked.

'It's supposed to be Tweedledum and Tweedledee doing a joint presentation but before I came on they were busy arguing in the tunnel. I expect they will be along soon.' Morris grinned again as he tucked into his food.

Sure enough, Mooning Mike and Breaks Wind appeared in the doorway, giving directions to several other novices they had recruited to help with their presentation. Two small groups of novices struggled with a large wooden throne apiece which they dragged with much difficulty to the back of the hall and set them up opposite each other at some distance. The two brothers seated themselves and took up their positions facing each other with their respective wands held aloft.

'They are going to have a wizard duel like that one in the film *The Raven* between Boris Karloff and Vincent Price. Apparently they have been practicing it for weeks and trying to keep it a secret to boot.' Morris informed them knowingly.

The chatter in the hall became more hushed as the wizards turned in their seats to watch the display. Breaks Wind made the first move. He formed a complete circle in the air in front of him with his wand, then twisted it up and down as he muttered his spell. The circle of green magic energy he had made to appear turned into a long dagger which hovered in front of his face for a few seconds before it flew in the direction of Mooning Mike at a good speed, accompanied by a loud whoosh of air.

Mooning Mike quickly responded to the attack. He waved his wand in a circular motion and formed a shield of magic energy which the ethereal dagger thudded into, its progress halted and Breaks Wind's attack thwarted. The shield and dagger were next transformed into a long plume of energy which flew across the divide between the two brothers and wrapped around the neck of Breaks Wind before it changed into a large serpent slithering around his neck, squeezing tighter and tighter.

Breaks Wind nervously reached up and cautiously touched the writhing serpent and turned it into a length of rope which he hurled towards his brother, along with an angry look of hatred. The rope now became a large net which hovered above Mooning Mike but he acted swiftly and changed it again into a rain cloud and sent it hurtling over Breaks Wind's head where it discharged a large volume of water, completely drenching him to the skin.

A scream of rage emitted from Breaks Wind's lips as he threw his wand to the floor and ran over to his brother with arms flailing and punched him viciously about the head. Mooning Mike grappled his soggy enraged brother to the floor where the two of them continued to pummel each other in a fierce scuffle until they were separated by several of the older wizards who had realized that this was not a part of the demonstration. Once apart the two stood and glared at one another and puffed and grunted angrily as they attempted to regain some composure.

At the insistence of one of the older wizards they begrudgingly shook hands and were led to the rostrum where the award ceremony continued and they were given their grade one hats, after which things seemed to calm down somewhat. If the senior wizards on the gilded thrones had noticed the presentation had become a little heated they did not display awareness of it and continued with the awards as if it was all a part of the show. The brothers then took their seats, at separate tables, and the party got into full swing.

* * * * * * *

It was a satisfied and slightly tipsy Stumblebum who made his way along the cobbled High Street that afternoon following the upgrade celebrations at the academy. The young novice had thoroughly enjoyed every minute of it, especially the wine. As he got home he put his head round the door to tell Auntie Maggie he had had a great time but was a little tired and as he had eaten plenty at the academy he would not be coming down for dinner but would have an early night instead.

Before he retired to bed Stumblebum went into the bathroom to inspect his head. As he had expected the feathers had grown quite a bit more so he decided he would confront Ramsbottom the next day, instead of Sunday, and see if he could reverse the spell.

As Stumblebum lay in bed he revisited the events of the day in his mind. It had been a wonderful feast and one of great merriment. Wizards having fun! He stared at his ceiling for a long time as he recollected all that had happened and sometimes chuckled out loud at a memory, like the brawl between the two brothers, which he had found to be immensely entertaining.

'So this is the life of a wizard!' he said to himself, feeling happier than he had for a long time, despite the feathers that sprouted from his head and rustled against his pillow, before he fell into a long, deep sleep.

Chapter Seventeen

Stumblebum awoke the next morning with a headache. Skipper sat on his pillow and stared intently at the feathers which now completely covered the boy's head and occasionally tapped at the feathers gingerly with his paw as if they were some new kind of creature. Stumblebum shooed the cat away and went into the bathroom to inspect the progress of the growth in the mirror and noted it had increased a good deal. He tried to stuff it all under his fez but after a lengthy struggle gave up as the feathers were now too long and springy and refused to be contained beneath the headgear.

In the end he had to wear an old hoodie he had brought with him when he had first come to stay with Auntie Maggie, though he had not worn it much since then as he usually wore his cape and fez when going out and about. He managed to contain the feathers under the hood and he decided to waste no time in confronting Ramsbottom with the outcome of his pagan magic spell and hopefully get him to put it right.

After the long trudge up to the Ramsbottom's house Freda answered the door to him and invited him in. Ramsbottom sat in his usual armchair by the fire as he smoked one of his pipes. He looked up and greeted Stumblebum with a friendly smile.

'We weren't expecting you 'till tomorrow but it's nice to see you anyway, you are always very welcome. How did your grading party at the academy go?'

‘Oh, that was great, I’ll tell you all about it later. The main reason I am here is that I have had a problem following your hair restoration spell. Look!’ Stumblebum lifted his hood to reveal his now magnificent mane of feathers.

Ramsbottom started forward in his chair and nearly dropped his pipe.

‘Good heavens above how on earth has that happened? This is most unusual! Not the usual outcome. There must have been some interference with the spell from somewhere, let me have a close look at it.’ Ramsbottom stood up and scrutinised Stumblebums scalp at some length and occasionally uttered the odd ‘Hmm’ before he eventually shook his head and let out a lengthy sigh.

‘No, I’m not sure what we can do about that. I shall consult my books for a solution. There must be a solution, we can’t leave your head like that.’ He concluded, stating the obvious much to the annoyance of Stumblebum.

Freda also had a good look at the feathers, after she had got Stumblebum to sit down in the other armchair by the fire whilst her husband thumbed through some of his many books of pagan spells.

Several hours later Ramsbottom was no nearer to finding a remedy to the lad’s plight so closed his last book and shook his head in defeat.

‘No, there doesn’t seem to be a spell to cover this kind of thing, most unusual. I am not sure what we can do about it, not sure at all.’ He lit another pipe and sucked thoughtfully on it for some time as Stumblebum became more and more agitated about the situation.’

‘Why don’t we just pluck it?’ Freda suggested, ‘after all that works with the chickens when they are being prepared for the pot.’

Stumblebum and Ramsbottom dismissed this at the same time. They both shook their heads and said ‘No. That won’t work.’

‘Why not?’ Freda replied as she walked over to behind Stumblebum before she reached over and grasped a single feather tightly and then quickly yanked it out.’

‘Aaaarrrrgh!’ Stumblebum screamed loudly at the top of his voice, taken by surprise and left in some pain.

‘Ow, ow, ow! No, don’t do that, it really hurts.’ He pleaded, tears in his smarting eyes.

Freda looked at the feather in her hand thoughtfully.

‘Well, it seems to have worked, but I don’t want to cause you distress or pain dear. If only we could find a way to numb your head for a while I think I could pluck all of the feathers out. What do you think Roly?’ She looked at her husband quizzically.

Ramsbottom stroked his beard as he sucked on his pipe and pondered the situation. He suddenly sat bolt upright and looked out of the window to the backyard.

‘Druids Delight!’ he exclaimed. ‘Druids Delight! It can work as an anaesthetic after a few draughts. If he drinks some before you pluck his head he should be oblivious to it.’

Ramsbottom sat back in his seat with a self-satisfied look on his face, pleased with his solution.

‘I don’t know about that. Are you sure that would work?’ Stumblebum had his reservations.

‘Oh yes, it will work all right, potent stuff. The ancient Druids used it for all sorts of things, not just recreation. Amputations, operations, subduing human sacrifices, they knew what they were about. Let’s give it a try, trust me!’ Ramsbottom gave one of his knowing looks.

After going to the shed in the backyard and after he had rummaged through the clutter in there he returned with a dusty demijohn of the cloudy golden coloured fluid, Druids Delight.

Stumblebum was then dosed up with several mugs of the stuff which he drank hesitantly as he was a little disturbed by two things that Ramsbottom had said earlier, “subduing human sacrifices” and “trust me!”. He had once been cautioned by his father to ‘never trust anyone who says “trust me!” son.’ and this troubled him a little as he drank the Druids Delight.

Freda brought a dining chair in from the kitchen and sat Stumblebum on it before she placed a large bowl in his lap. She wrapped an old bath towel around his neck and got him to drink the rest of his doses of Druids Delight. The stuff did seem to have worked to an extent as

Stumblebum now had little awareness of his head, or anything else for that matter. The room spun around slightly and he could not focus his eyes properly.

Over the next couple of hours Freda plucked away at the feathers whilst Stumblebum occasionally cried out in pain and his head bled in places. Eventually his head was devoid of any feathers although it smarted and had to have a good number of sticking plasters slapped on to stem the trickles of blood. It also glowed green, pulsated, hummed and throbbed as the procedure went on, much to the surprise of the Ramsbottoms. He sat on the chair and held the bowl full of feathers with mixed feelings. Relief at the success of the endeavour and severe trauma at having had to sit through what seemed to be an eternity of having his head plucked.

He was completely bald again which seemed to be preferable to the feathers. His head now also emitted a low hum as the green glow faded before it returned to a normal pinkish colour.

He stared at the bowl full of feathers for some time, still a little vague from the effects of the Druids Delight. Ramsbottom fished out a large feather and held it up in front of the boy with a benevolent look on his face.

'Do you want to keep one to make into a quill?' He suggested.

Stumblebum had had enough of feathers by this time so shook his head vigorously.

'No, no thanks, just get rid of them please. Enough already!'

Ramsbottom offered the boy some more Druids Delight to drink.

'Here, get this down you, it will help to calm you down after your ordeal.'

Stumblebum gratefully took the drink and sipped at it as his host poured himself and Freda some of the potion to drink also, in a recreational mode.

The day wore on and the contents of the demijohn of Druids Delight were duly drained as the Ramsbottoms and their guest chatted and became light headed with the drink. They spoke of many things as they drank and Stumblebum recounted the events at the upgrade ceremony with relish. Ramsbottom quizzed him about the academy and Stumblebum proudly explained the magic lessons, facilities and curriculum.

Ramsbottom was very interested in the library and the books of spells that were kept there and Stumblebum, tongue loosened by the Druids Delight, explained the way it worked and described the Academy Scribe and other officials. Then he recounted how the recent gold fever had been thwarted by the removal and transfer to the archives of all books on alchemy.

'That's a great shame' Ramsbottom said, 'it would have been a useful skill for you to learn, what with your financial difficulties.'

'Ah, but I managed to copy some pages of spells and pentagrams from a little ancient book I had found concealed in a place in the library. I have still got the pages hidden at home. They must be the only instructions on alchemy that haven't been locked in the archives.' Stumblebum boasted proudly. He blabbered on and explained how he had hoped to make enough to pay Salty Sammy his deposit back.

Ramsbottom exchanged a quick glance with Freda and stroked his beard thoughtfully before he filled another pipe bowl and lit it.

'You know, you could sell those pages and raise the money that you need. A more experienced wizard might be able to make the process work.' He suddenly brightened as if a great idea had just come to him.

'Why don't you let me discretely ask about amongst my mates at the next moot? I am sure some of them might be interested and I could sell them on your behalf if you like.'

Although he was reluctant to let the pages leave his possession, on the other hand he was getting desperate to find the money to replace Salty Sammy's fee, and besides the pages were incomplete. Perhaps if he did not mention this and since all of the formulae were on different sheets of parchment he might get away with it.

'All right, if you are sure you can sell them for me it would help no end.' He said, gratefully.

'Can you get them to me soon and I will make enquiries for you at the next moot?' Ramsbottom pursued the matter as he tried to sound nonchalant.

'I can bring them over tomorrow lunchtime if you like, only I will have to cut my visit short as I have been invited to attend the opening night of *Romeo and Juliet* at the little theatre in the Old Town. Why don't you come along too? I think there is a party after the show. Some of my friends are in the production.'

The Ramsbottoms agreed that they would enjoy a visit to the theatre with him and made arrangements for Stumblebum to call in for lunch the next day as usual and they would leave from there when it was time for the play to start.

They both came to the doorstep to wave goodbye to Stumblebum and as he left Ramsbottom reminded him to not forget to bring the parchment pages with him. Stumblebum staggered back home still a little light headed from the Druids Delight, glad to have resolved the feather problem and pleased to have found a way to pay back the money to Salty Sammy.

When he got home, once again he headed for his room to have an early night and to sleep off the effects of the Druids Delight. He quickly fell into a deep, heavy sleep, and dreamed of being chased by angry chickens and short fat wizards stuffing pillows full of feathers, and Druids, many Druids, watching with interest.

* * * * * * *

The next day Stumblebum again walked up to the Ramsbottom's house and joined them for Sunday lunch. Before he sat down to eat Ramsbottom enquired as to whether he had remembered to bring the pages, which he had, and he took them from him with a gleeful smile before he flipped through them, looking at each page with interest.

'Good. I'm sure I will be able to find someone interested in these and get you some money before too long.' He reassured the boy.

The Sunday lunch was its usual sumptuous affair and afterwards the two wizards joined each other on the armchairs by the fire. Freda fussed about in the kitchen as she cleared up the dishes and made some tea whilst her husband lit his favourite churchwarden pipe and puffed away at it with satisfaction and chatted with Stumblebum.

'So who is in the play then? You say some of your friends are in it?' He asked.

'There are two academy wizards who are recently upgraded novices and two girls I know.' Stumblebum replied, blushing a little as he thought of Brigitte and her sister.

'Oh aye, oh aye, I see.' Ramsbottom teased, 'so that's why you are so keen to go, there are some girls you fancy in the play! I get it.' He chuckled as he called to Freda in the kitchen, to Stumblebum's further embarrassment.

'The lad has got himself a young lady Freda. She's in the play we are going to see.'

Freda carried a tray of mugs of tea in from the kitchen with a wide grin on her face.

'Well, who'd have thought it, such a quiet lad and all? He's a dark horse right enough isn't he? Is she very pretty then dear and are we going to meet her?'

Stumblebum now wished he had kept his big mouth shut about the girls and could feel himself turn bright red with embarrassment.

'No, no, I've not got a girlfriend they are just friends that's all and they are girls, very pretty girls. We are not going out, well, not yet anyway.' Stumblebum stammered on as he made a mess of his explanation and ended limply with 'they are just some girls.'

Freda and Ramsbottom exchanged a knowing look and grinned some more.

After they had teased him about the girls for some time he managed to get off the topic and asked about when the next moot at *The Smugglers Rest* would take place.

‘Oh. I think there is one this week sometime’ Ramsbottom said vaguely ‘they hold them very frequently.’

‘You do think someone will want to buy the alchemy pages don’t you? Only I really could do with the money soon.’

‘Don’t you worry your head about it, just leave it with me, it will be fine. Trust me!’

After he reassured Stumblebum that he would easily sell the pages Ramsbottom turned the conversation to other matters. He enquired about Auntie Maggie and they talked generally about how he liked his life in Bilge on Sea and whether he was comfortable at his auntie’s house.

A few more hours or so were passed with friendly chatter until Stumblebum reminded his hosts that it was getting near to the time for the start of the play. Ramsbottom put on his tweed Inverness cape and deerstalker hat as Freda put on a coat, scarf and woollen hat. She brought Stumblebum his cape, which she had hung on a peg in the hallway and the three of them made their way down the hill to the little theatre in The Old Town.

Upon arriving at the theatre they managed to get some good seats close to the front of the stage. Teapot popped his head around the curtain to introduce the play. Due to a shortage of male players the play had been abridged and shortened a little with the actors taking on more than one role where it was possible.

Mooning Mike appeared as Abram, sporting a large black eye from his recent scuffle with his brother. Even the best efforts of the make-up lady could not completely conceal it. It seemed appropriate however since he soon gets into a quarrel in the play with the servants of the Capulets, played by Quentin and Teapot, with much biting of thumbs and other insults.

Quentin then did a quick costume change and gave a somewhat camp performance of Juliet’s nurse which he played with relish in drag. Both Morris and Mandy looked stunning in their costumes as Romeo and Juliet and Brigitte looked gorgeous playing Lady Capulet. They each put their best efforts into their respective parts and their lack of acting experience was compensated for by their natural good looks.

By the end of the play they had won the audience over and the play came to a close to thunderous applause.

After most of the audience had shuffled out of the auditorium Stumblebum took his guests backstage where the players now relaxed with glasses of wine. A long trestle table had been set up laden with little snack sized nibbles, which a tall fat man at the end was busy munching his way through at an alarming pace. Ramsbottom seemed to know the man and attempted to engage him in conversation but gave up after it was clear that the man was too busy stuffing his mouth with food to have time to talk.

'Who on earth is that?' Stumblebum asked Ramsbottom as they filled a side plate each with the little snacks from the buffet table whilst some still remained.

'Oh, just someone I know from town. He's a reporter. I expect he is doing an article on the play, *when he finds time to stop eating that is*!' Ramsbottom sounded a bit miffed with the snub he had just received so Stumblebum introduced him and Freda to Morris and Mooning Mike, taking care not to approach the sisters for the time being, fearful of being embarrassed by any suggestion that he fancied them.

Eventually he could not avoid the girls but Ramsbottom and Freda didn't say anything out of turn and they all enjoyed what was left of the drink and food. Teapot was in his element and Quentin, delighted at the performance given by his new protégées, fluttered about and praised the newcomers at every opportunity as the party wore on.

After a while the Ramsbottoms said their goodbyes and took their leave having had a really good time. Stumblebum stayed for a short time longer as he enjoyed the company of the girls in particular, but as he had a busy day planned at the academy the next day also decided to head for home.

At about the same time that Stumblebum arrived back home across the town a couple of figures lurked about on the roof of the town hall under the cover of nightfall. The mayor and his nephew were busy stripping lead from the roof and lowering it down to the ground in a canvas sling attached to a rope. The town crier unloaded the burden and laid it on a wooden hand cart he had borrowed from his wife's brother, who sold fresh crabs and shellfish from it on the beach in the summer season.

The town crier also acted as a lookout as he had been recruited by the mayor with a promise of rich rewards and now kept an eye out for anyone who might come by and see what they were doing. The lead was for the mayor and Silas to transform into gold as he understood that to be the way forward with the alchemy. He reasoned that the more lead they could secure the more gold would be produced. So he and Silas stripped most of the lead that there was to be had in a display of greed typical of the mayor.

'So when are we going to turn this lot into gold then Silas?' The mayor asked his nephew.

'I can't do it tomorrow as there is a little matter of some importance I have to attend to.'

'What's that about then?' The mayor demanded to know.

'I'll tell you all about it when I have finished. We shall have to have a go at the alchemy a bit later in the week. Can you stash the lead somewhere until then?'

'Well I suppose I could keep it in my shed at home but we don't want to hang about for too long. The sooner it is done the better.'

'I think I know where the last chapter of the book is, or rather who has got it, and I aim to get it from them. I will see you on Tuesday and we shall have a go at it then.' Silas said.

The mayor's piggy eyes narrowed at the thought of untold riches and even now was working out how to cheat Silas and the town crier out of their share once the job was done.

'Good. Let's get this lot off of the roof and on to the cart before anyone comes along. We will sort it out on Tuesday then! I can't wait!' The mayor had the gold fever in a bad way.

Several hours later in the middle of the night the three shifty figures strained as they pushed the heavily laden barrow through the dark streets to the mayor's backyard and shed. Mission accomplished the lead was concealed under an old tarpaulin sheet and the three conspirators all skulked off in different directions, job done.

Chapter Eighteen

Winifred Closet had been a force to be reckoned with before the neighbourhood watch scheme came to her street. Her flat, pasty, yellowy-white face was made even pastier by having an alarming amount of makeup slapped on in her vain attempt to conceal the ravages of time and it would hover at her window, just behind the net curtains like a malevolent moon, watching, noting and disapproving.

The neighbourhood watch scheme had much to answer for. They had given her a notepad and asked her to keep an eye out for problems and jot them down. They appointed her as neighbourhood information officer. They even made her the 'information gathering sub-committee', mainly because no one else could be bothered to do it, but they had a willing guardian of the street's moral wellbeing in Winifred who liked to feel important by being on many committees and thus empowered she was always watching, noting and disapproving.

She had always twitched her chintz curtains and tut-tutted at the children when they kicked balls in the road or rode their bikes on the pavement but now that she was an official of the neighbourhood watch she believed she could wield a degree of authority over others.

It was in this role as guardian of the street's morals which caused Winifred to peer through her window from behind her curtains one evening. Her gaze rested on the form of a stranger who behaved, to Winifred's mind, in a manner that was of a highly suspicious nature.

The stranger in question hovered about outside her gate. He was a stranger indeed in these parts and he appeared to be somewhat perplexed with regard to his whereabouts as he scratched his shiny pink bald dome of a head and looked this way and that in an agitated manner. It was not so much this behaviour, peculiar though it seemed to be, that aroused Winifred's suspicions but rather his appearance. Winifred always had judged people by how they looked, woe betide someone with eyes which were too close together or with chin in recession, and now her judgemental gaze settled upon the strange form of Harry Grubdyke.

His appearance was indeed something of a paradox by anyone's standards let alone those of Winifred. He was an exceptionally tall man who appeared to be, when viewed from behind, quite slim. It was only when he turned around however that the seeming contradiction of his proportions became apparent. His shoulders and hips appeared to be ridiculously narrow for such a tall man but in fact he possessed an enormous stomach which protruded like the prow of a ship and gave his perambulations the sense of sailing forth rather than walking. This manner of motion was emphasised by the fact that he had a backward leaning posture, developed over the years to counterbalance his ever increasing corpulation. The further out that his stomach protruded the more he leaned backwards and the slower he progressed in getting from A to B.

His gait was awkward and ponderous. He moved with slow, plodding, deliberate steps and paused at regular intervals in order to regain both breath and equilibrium. It was during one such halt in his progress that found him in front of Winifred's bungalow and he took advantage of his temporary delay to re-assess his position. He was in something of a quandary as he appeared to be lost. This did not bode well for Harry who generally preferred to conduct his business in familiar surroundings and became agitated, like a fish out of water, when not in his usual neighbourhood.

Harry paused to scratch his sweaty pink head as he looked around in order to find some clue as to his whereabouts. He seemed to refer to a scrap of paper bearing the address he was seeking for guidance and looked about him again until his gaze finally rested on the numbered door of Winifred's bungalow. As he scrutinised the door number and again checked it against his piece of paper he caught sight of Winifred's flat, pasty face glaring at him from behind her windowpane. A huge almost gleeful grin passed over his countenance and he walked toward the front door much to the horror of Winifred.

Harry Grubdyke was a freeloader. He was also a gossip, a glutton and a slob, but first and foremost he was a freeloader. He had honed this skill down to a fine art and had a sort of instinct for where to find any event where copious amounts of free food and drink would be available.

His appointment as 'Roving Reporter' for the community rag although voluntary and therefore without pay nonetheless brought with it many perks. None of these perks was more valued by Harry than the invitations to the many opening events in the town such as artists' exhibitions. Little expense was usually spared on these lavish buffets thanks to various generous funding schemes and which were all enthusiastically attended by Harry, the town's leading freeloader outside of the corporation council.

So it came to pass that Harry Grubdyke, freeloader and roving reporter, had wangled an invitation to attend the opening night of *Romeo and Juliet* being put on at *The Little Theatre* in the hope that mountains of free food and rivers of wine would be on offer at the after performance party. In order to justify his lusty enjoyment of the buffet he felt obliged to interview the producer of the play, Terry 'Teapot' Philpot, with a promise to give a good review in the next publication of the local news-sheet.

After the interview Teapot had asked Harry to visit Winifred and discuss her role as Widow Twanky in the coming panto season, since Winifred had made a point of staying away from the opening night of the Shakespeare play in a massive self-righteous huff. He scribbled her address and instructions of how to get there on a scrap of paper which Harry read several times before he put it safely in his pocket.

Teapot, knowing her huge ego would not be able to resist being put in the spotlight this way, hoped she would perhaps cease to behave in such a petulant manner if she was to receive a mention in the local paper. He prided himself on his skills of diplomacy, much needed with all of the prima donna would-be thespians whom continually jostled for attention and felt that this was one of his better manoeuvres. It might serve to calm feelings down a bit and restore a semblance of harmony to the theatre troupe once again.

So after Harry had consulted his scrap of paper again and he was sure that he had found the right address he knocked on Winifred's front door and listened as the sound of footsteps approached followed by the rattle of a security chain being fitted into its slot before the door opened several inches and Winifred's shallow eyes viewed her visitor with suspicion.

'Shoo, shoo, we don't deal with hawkers here. I'm in touch with the police you know, shoo, shoo, get off my property.'

Harry beamed at her as he fished into his pocket and produced his business card, which he handed to her through the gap in the door. Winifred hesitantly took the card and looked at it, her plucked and re-drawn eyebrows arching upwards in surprise as she read the card:

Harry Grubdyke
Roving Reporter
C.R.A.P.P.
(Community Regeneration Arts Project Press.)

'Oh, I see,' Winifred turned the card over and over and read it several times. 'So you are from the paper, do come in young man, come in.'

she undid the security chain and opened the door fully as she led the way into the front room.

'Do take a seat in the parlour and can I get you some tea?' she enquired as she invited Harry to sit down in an armchair.

When she returned with a cup of tea for Harry he was busy removing a dingy knotted handkerchief from his pocket which he unfolded on to his lap to reveal a hard-boiled egg. He then took the egg and tapped it firmly on his bald head several times before he peeled it and carefully placed the fragments of eggshell on to his handkerchief and commenced to eat the egg.

Harry chewed his egg slowly and noisily with his jaws rotating in exaggerated chewing motions whilst he stared glassy eyed at Winifred who found the situation to be somewhat unnerving. After some time he seemed to have finished his egg, to Winifred's relief, but then he pulled a brown speckled banana from his other pocket and methodically peeled it and then bit chunks off and chewed them in the same manner as he had the egg. Finally he finished the banana and folded the skin into a neat little bundle which he added to the eggshell in his grubby hanky. He then tied it into a little parcel before he placed it back into his pocket.

Winifred observed all of this with some disgust, yet patiently waited for him to finish his little meal before she prepared to give her interview. She was about to speak when Harry reached over to the little coffee table and picked up his cup of tea and sipped at it with a loud slurping sound. This went on for what seemed an age before he drained the cup, placed it back on its saucer on the coffee table and gave the now cringing Winifred the sweetest of smiles.

'So you are to play the Widow Twanky in *Aladdin* at the theatre. Mr Philpot tells me that yours is the star role in the pantomime and the success of the play depends largely on your performance.' Harry produced a little note book and pencil from his pocket.

'I have been asked to give a write up in the community press solely devoted to your interpretation of the role and I am to set aside a whole page to you. If you don't object we can begin the interview now and do excuse me as I take down some notes.'

Spurred on and flattered by this encouragement Winifred talked at some length about herself and discussed some of the plays she had been in. She spoke emphatically and dramatically of her many years of experience treading the boards at the Old T.A.R.T.S. *Little Theatre*.

'I was in the last Shakespeare production of *Othello* last season and after that took a star part in *A Streetcar Named Desire* which brought the house down.' She informed Harry.

'Oh I remember that, I went along to do a review. The production was rather good. It's a pity it was spoiled by the wooden performance by the old granny who had been miscast as Blanche. She was terrible, and the awful wig she had on! It looked like an old hearthrug on her head! Yesterday's production of *Romeo and Juliet* was much better. The young girl who played Juliet had such natural healthy golden locks of hair. You just can't get the same look with a wig.' Harry rattled on oblivious to the look of indignation on Winifred's face.

'So where were we?' he glanced at his notebook. 'Oh yes, *A Streetcar Named Desire*. And what part did you take in that production? I can't seem to remember seeing you in it, remind me.'

'Blanche, I played Blanche,' Winifred was seething with fury 'and furthermore it was my skilful portrayal of Blanche that held the play together. Also, that "hearthrug" that you so emphatically derided happened to be one of my best wigs, top quality and very expensive!'

Harry listened to this tirade in silence before he then attempted to change the subject.

'I don't suppose I could have another cup of tea, this interviewing is thirsty work, and any chance of some cakes or biscuits?' He said brightly.

'No young man, there will be no more tea for you, and definitely no cakes or biscuits! I would very much like you to leave now and if you see that Terrence Philpot you can tell him I would like all of my wigs returned to me. Tell him "good luck" from me on the future productions. And he can find someone else to do Widow bloody Twanky! Perhaps that new girl with the natural golden locks of hair can do it!' She ranted on.

'Please get out of my house now. Shoo, shoo! I want you to leave.'

Harry got up and sheepishly crept to the front door and let himself out, as he did he turned and said, rather timidly,

'No chance of any biscuits before I go then?'

* * * * * * *

Stumblebum had set off to the academy with something of a spring in his step and with thoughts of Brigitte and Mandy foremost in his mind that morning. He had been bowled over by their appearance in their costumes the night before and had enjoyed his chats with them at the party after the play. As he had taken his leave to go home both girls gave him an affectionate peck on his cheek which caused his heart to miss a beat or two.

'If I could perfect my magic skills I might be able to impress them and be in with a chance!' He mused, seeing the girls in his mind's eye overawed by his future demonstrations of great wizardry.

He had plans to work hard that day on a project that had come to him as he had thought about the previous day's events at the Ramsbottom's house. After he had reluctantly given his parchments with the spells that he had copied to Ramsbottom he had been troubled with second thoughts. It occurred to him that he ought to have made more copies before he had handed them over and wished he could kick himself for not doing so.

He had then formed a plan to spend much of the day in the library to once again copy the pages out after he got the book from its place of concealment, so would therefore, after Ramsbottom had sold the other pages for him, have his cake and eat it.

Unfortunately Stumblebum's plans for his day at the academy did not pan out quite as he had wished. Upon his arrival at the library, armed with several bottles of different coloured ink and a wad of parchment pages he had procured from the academy stationary office, he then found to his dismay that the little book was no longer in its hiding place where he had left it.

'Drat! The blasted Academy Scribe must have found it and moved it to the archives when he did his purge of the alchemy books the other day.' He thought with some annoyance. Although this put him in a fairly foul mood for the day he decided nonetheless to fill his time for the rest of the day in the levitation section of the spells lab, since his skills in this area urgently needed some practice and polish.

The door to the levitation section had a plywood board nailed over what had been a glass window in it which had been smashed so many times by out of control flying objects that nobody bothered to replace the glass anymore due to the futility of the exercise.

As Stumblebum entered he quickly had to duck low in order to avoid being clouted on the side of his head by a flying leather satchel someone had lost control of. There were a few novices immersed in their practice and a variety of objects hovered about close to the ceiling somewhat precariously. The instructor had removed his pointed wizards' hat and replaced it with a hard hat of the type worn by builders, though the sturdy fezzes were deemed to be sufficient protection for the novices.

Stumblebum had brought several items with him to practice on, including a tennis ball, a heavier billiard ball and several books of different sizes and weights. He had sort of got the hang of this magic skill but as events on the beach with his auntie's broom and the *Violet Veronica* had demonstrated, not to mention the debacle in the *Beverage Bliss* with the yucca plant, there was some room for improvement!

At the moment levitation was his best skill in magic and so he determined to improve until it would be good enough to perform for his upgrade assessment, so that he would be ready when that time came. He intended to now spend most of the day in the levitation room since there were no other classes or lectures for him to attend that day and since his plans to work in the library had come to nought, so he would practice, practice and practice. He also intended to practice some more at home on the beach around midnight, as was his habit recently, in order to avoid the real Violet Veronica and be left in peace.

Stumblebum found a space at one of the long teak benches used for practice and placed his objects in a row in front of him. He took out his wand and pointed it at the tennis ball as he quickly muttered an incantation at the same time. The ball gradually rose to about a foot or so above the bench and hovered in front of Stumblebum's face as he made it spin on its axis. As had happened with the broom and the *Violet Veronica* on the beach the ball rose higher and higher as it spun until it was pressed up against the ceiling, since it could rise no further.

Stumblebum tried in vain to get it to return but it stubbornly remained rammed against the ceiling as he frantically waved his wand and muttered a variety of spells he had memorised from his little red book. Finally the tennis ball shot across the room at an angle then hit the wall behind the wizard instructor before it rebounded and knocked his hard hat off his head as it then ricocheted around the room. This caused some mayhem as surprised novices were struck about their heads as the ball continued on its destructive trajectory.

The instructor finally intervened by bringing the tennis ball to a halt in front of Stumblebum with a flourish from his wand. He came over to where Stumblebum was and went over his technique several times to show him where he had been in error and how to effectively control the object as it levitated. He also explained which incantations and spells were more effective for which types of objects, to the delight of Stumblebum, who now felt that he could see where he had got it wrong. He was about to practice with the billiard ball until the instructor spotted this dangerous levitation attempt and urged him not to at this stage.

Stumblebum instead got the books to levitate one by one until they were all lined up in a row about a metre or so above the bench. He practised changing the order of them round, shuffling them in effect, as he managed to keep all of them in the air at once. He then got them to glide gently around the room in a line like a small flock of geese. As he brimmed with confidence he cockily tried to show off by stacking the books one upon the other whilst they rose high up to near the ceiling. The next part of his display was an attempt to get them to flutter their pages in mid-air but his mind went blank and he forgot the spell.

As his concentration lapsed the levitation spell collapsed and the books fell, stacked in a block, squarely onto the head of another novice. This flattened his fez and rendered the lad unconscious as he fell to the floor. The instructor rushed over to the scene of the little accident and spent some time to bring the novice round as Stumblebum picked up his books.

'Perhaps you should call it a day in here for now,' he advised Stumblebum 'you might like to continue your more complex levitation spells outside somewhere in the open.'

Stumblebum agreed as he made a feeble apology to the dazed novice with the flattened fez and gathered his books and other stuff and made a hasty exit. At least he had got the hang of some of it for now and he resolved he would continue that night on the beach. For the rest of his day at the academy he decided to practice some other spells in the main part of the spells lab, since he was in the vicinity.

In the spells lab Stumblebum seemed to improve some of his other magic skills, especially his use of his wand which until then had been rather hit and miss in terms of wand control and spell success. He felt that progress was made and he more or less had got the hang of these matters to a degree. As he left the academy that evening his self confidence in his ability to do magic successfully was at an all-time high.

When he got home he joined Auntie Maggie and Skipper in the kitchen and talked proudly about his progress at the academy that day. Auntie Maggie made comments of encouragement as she usually did before she told Stumblebum some news.

'I have had a letter from your mum and dad dear. They will be coming to stay with us at Christmas for a few days so you will have plenty to tell them about how you are doing at the academy. I bet you are looking forward to seeing them aren't you? It has been quite some time now.'

Stumblebum frowned at the thought. Of course he looked forward to their visit but Christmas was not too far away and he had to do something about his bald head before then. He remembered that Morris had offered to steal a wig for him from the theatre props so he made a mental note to remind Morris soon.

'What are you scowling about dear, I thought you would be pleased to see them again?' Auntie Maggie asked, seeing his reaction to her news.

'Oh, yes, I am Auntie, very much, it's just that I was worried that there would not be enough for them to do for entertainment here in Bilge on Sea, it's such a quiet place in the winter.'

'Why don't you take them to the theatre dear. Aren't some of your friends to perform in the pantomime around Christmas? It might be nice to take me and your mum and dad to see it with you. *Aladdin* isn't it?'

So it was agreed to visit the pantomime just after Christmas. He really looked forward to the pantomime as the girls would be in it and he was sure that they would look lovely in their exotic costumes. Perhaps Ramsbottom could advise him on some pagan love spells that he could have a go at. 'Might be worth a try!' he mused as he thought about the kisses he had been given the last time that he saw the two sisters. And he must remember to remind Morris to get him that wig before his parents' visit.

With much to think about Stumblebum relaxed for the evening before he retired to his room. He did not go to bed though as he intended to sneak out at midnight to do some levitation practice on the little beach behind Auntie's house, undisturbed by Violet Veronica and her endless pestering and questions. He could hardly wait until then as he was keen to perfect his levitation skills whilst the advice from the wizard instructor was still fresh in his mind.

* * * * * * *

Shortly before midnight Stumblebum crept down the stairs and outside to the little beach behind the house. It was a crisp, cold night and he had his cape firmly wrapped about him and his fez tightly pulled down to his ears. The sky was clear and starlit with a crescent moon on the ascent, which gave enough light for him to see the objects he was going to levitate.

He had not brought anything with him but looked on the beach for suitable items. He came back to the wall of the cottage just underneath his bedroom window carrying several things he had found lying on the beach, including a large piece of driftwood, a length of old rope and a couple of fairly large pebbles.

After Stumblebum placed the objects on the ground in front of him he looked around to make sure no one was about. 'Who would be out and about at this time of night unless they were up to no good?' He thought, clearly not including himself in this observation.

He spent a good ten minutes or so making the lump of driftwood levitate, doing a number of complex manoeuvres before he then successfully lowered it back to the ground. As he was about to levitate the piece of rope he heard what sounded like someone's hands clap several times and then again become silent. This startled Stumblebum and he peered in the direction of the sound, about halfway down the cobbled launching ramp close to the ledge below the groyne.

As his eyes tried to focus in the dim light he thought he could see something hover a few feet above the ledge. At first he thought it was a traffic cone suspended in the air before he realised it was in fact a grade one wizard's hat. Bewildered, he continued to stare at the unexpected manifestation and then was further startled when the person of Silas Suggs emerged from below the hat as he repeated his party trick from the upgrade ceremony.

Silas got up from where he had seated himself and planted his huge feet squarely on the cobbled ramp as he leered at Stumblebum whilst at the same time thumping his right fist into the palm of his left hand like the gesture he had threatened Mooning Mike with in the *Beverage Bliss* some time ago.

'Well, well, well! So you like to levitate things do you? How about yucca plants, can you make yucca plants fly then? It was you wasn't it, that time in the café?' Silas rhythmically thumped the palm of his hand as he spoke, a vicious look on his unpleasant face.'

Stumblebum was now a little frightened and did not know what to say.

'That wasn't me,' he lied, 'I was there at the time but it wasn't me. I didn't do it, I don't know who did, but it wasn't me.'

Silas sneered at Stumblebum and slowly nodded his head.

'We'll discuss that in a while, but the main reason I am here is that you have got something that I want, and you'd better hand it over or else...' Silas thumped his left palm again.

'I don't know what you mean, what have I supposed to have got that you want?' Stumblebum was nervous and beads of sweat trickled down his forehead despite the cold of the night.

'I've been watching you after a certain little birdie told me it might be of interest to me to do that. And I have asked some of the novices at the academy about you. It seems that you have spent a lot of time in the library recently and been seen to make copies of pages from a book on alchemy.'

Stumblebum's jaw dropped at this, shocked to learn that he had been the focus of Silas's scrutiny and that he knew about the book.

'Ah, I see you know what I am talking about. You've got the last chapter haven't you? What happened, you ran out of time or just got fed up with all of the copying? Never mind, just give me the pages and I might forget about the yucca plant, maybe.' Silas continued to thump his hand as he spoke.

'I'm sorry Silas but I have not got what you want. I did copy some of the book but the last chapter was already gone when I found it and now the entire book has vanished as well. Somebody else must have taken the pages but I haven't got them.'

Silas pulled his wand out from his jacket pocket and pointed it at Stumblebum who instinctively produced his own wand and pointed it back at Silas ready to do some defensive magic at this new threat.

A surge of magic energy shot from the older youth's wand and knocked Stumblebums arm up as it deflected his wand's stream of energy upwards and caused it to go high up in the sky, then wrenched the wand from his hand before it was hurled to the ground. This left Stumblebum without protection against Silas's magic so he tried to turn and run back to the house. He felt something grip him by the throat and squeeze him tighter and tighter until he was about to pass out.

Silas continued to point his wand at Stumblebum. It emitted a long tentacle of energy which wrapped around the novices throat like a large hand and slowly crushed his breath from him. Stumblebum could not move as he seemed to be paralysed by Silas's spell and unable to speak.

Silas put his wand away since the spell now had immobilised Stumblebum, who stood by the house, helpless and frozen on the spot by the magic spell. Silas thumped his hand again, his favourite gesture, and took a step forward.

'All reight then youth,[7] we shall do this the hard way then shall we?' He said with some menace.

It was at exactly this moment that Silas was suddenly struck on the head by a small wooden hulled fishing boat that had just fallen from the sky! The *Violet Veronica* arrived back on to *terra firma* with a sickening thud as it crushed Silas onto the hard cobbled ramp. The spell that held Stumblebum in paralysis abruptly ceased and the young wizard slid down the wall to the ground barely able to believe what he had just witnessed.

Stumblebum sat there for a full ten minutes before he calmed down slightly and managed to get back up on to his feet, a little shakily. He hesitantly went over to the ramp and looked in disbelief at the *Violet Veronica* and cautiously looked underneath the boat, where all that could be seen of Silas were his arms and legs protruding from underneath the boat's hull, splayed out roughly forming a swastika shape and ominously devoid of movement.

---

[7] Translation from northern : All reight then youth = Fair enough young man.

The young novice wizard panicked and could hear his head buzz as it throbbed and glowed under his fez. Should he send for an ambulance or the police he wondered, but no, he might be blamed for the tragedy, so he decided against this course of action. He looked up and down to be sure that no one else had seen what had happened before he picked up his wand and skulked off back around the corner and crept back into the house and up the stairs to the sanctuary of his room.

Stumblebum left the light off in his bedroom as he sat and looked at the scene outside below his window on the cobbled ramp. He sat there for several hours in the dark and in something of a state of shock at what had happened out there.

He watched the waves gently lap against the boat as the tide came in and he noticed it rise a little in the water. By the time that the tide was fully up it had risen free of the ground and as the tide turned and ebbed away he watched the boat drift out into the harbour with the flattened corpse of Silas Suggs dragged along in its wake.

Stumblebum watched the *Violet Veronica* drift out beyond the harbour mouth and out to the open sea and watched Silas's body drift after it in its wake as his huge feet bobbed up and down in the water like sharks fins until the boat and the feet faded into the dark of the night and away from the harbour, to the great relief of Stumblebum.

It was a troubled Stumblebum who climbed wearily into bed that night and despite his tiredness could not sleep for a long time. He decided it would be best not to mention the events that had happened that night to anyone, not even Auntie Maggie, and he hoped that no one would ever guess what had happened, since the evidence had floated off into the night. If he kept his mouth shut about it he might not be blamed in any way, so, comforted by this thought, he finally fell into a fitful sleep.

Chapter Nineteen

The following morning Stumblebum missed breakfast as he got up late due to his late bedtime. He was still troubled by the events of the night before and did not feel up to facing anyone at the academy for a day or so. He told his auntie that he was not too well and would stay in his room until he was a bit better.

'Don't worry Auntie, I am just a bit tired that's all. I've overdone things at the academy this last few weeks and it has taken it out of me but I shall be fine after a restful couple of days at home.' He told her, not wanting her to question his motives too much.

'All right dear you have a nice rest and I shall bring you some lunch up on a tray later, just take it easy and get better. I am sure that the academy administration will understand.'

When he got back to his room he sat by the window and gazed out across the harbour for a long time, his mind on the sudden demise of Silas Suggs and his own involvement in it. The emphatic return of the *Violet Veronica* had actually saved him from Silas's attack, but even so, it seemed to be a bit drastic.

'Not to worry,' he thought at length, 'it could have been worse! The blasted boat could have fallen on me instead! And besides, Silas was going to harm me so I suppose it turned out for the best really, so long as no one ever finds out!' Stumblebum's sympathy for Silas faded as he thought about the nasty threats he had made.

'I wonder how he knew about the little book on alchemy and what could he want with the missing pages since they surely would be no good on their own?' Puzzled, he thought about it for a while then shrugged and gave up since there seemed to be no logical explanation.

As he thought about the events of the previous evening he absently emptied his pockets and placed the items on the table. He was surprised when he retrieved his wand and found it to be buzzing slightly and glowing with a silvery mysterious light. As he watched the wand then grew to about twice its original length and the tip transformed from the two little leaves to a sharp silver embossed point. The heel of the now polished wooden wand also had silver shrouding it and the letter S was engraved into it.

Stumblebum held it up and looked at it curiously as a surge of magic energy pulsed into his arm. A play of harmony between the young wizard and his wand ensued. Stumblebum now felt as if he could make strong magic through his application of the renewed wand. He wondered if the recent combat with Silas and his survival of his attack could have something to do with this development. He decided to quiz Ramsbottom, without letting on precise details, about possible empowerment after success in a magician dual.

He conducted a few small spells in his room with his new improved wand and found it to indeed be more potent and improved.

Eventually his mood got better and he relaxed by the window and read his book of spells in order to better commit them to his memory. As he studied the day wore on and Auntie Maggie brought him a meal up on a tray, which he heartily enjoyed since he had missed his breakfast and was by that time ready for a good substantial meal. After he had eaten he returned to his studies for a few hours before he spotted something happen in the harbour that made him feel a little uncomfortable.

As Stumblebum watched from his window he saw the coastguard boat enter the harbour and it pulled after it on a tow line the *Violet Veronica* and dragged it up to the cobbled ramp before several coastguards jumped out and secured the errant boat to an iron ring set into the side of the stone groyne. The coastguard crewmen knew the boat and its owner, which they had had reports of as it drifted out to sea and had retrieved it in order to return it to Salty Sammy.

As he continued to watch he saw the men from the coastguard go to the fishermen's cottage and inform Salty Sammy of its return. The little beach outside of Stumblebum's window now got quite noisy as the two old fishermen excitedly came to look at the return of their vessel accompanied by excited shouts and whoops of joy. The two now high spirited brothers dragged the *Violet Veronica* from the ramp and on to its usual place on the pebbles besides Barnacle Billy's own little boat as they hooted and roared like a couple of elderly hooligans.

Stumblebum watched all of this with interest but made sure not to be seen from the beach, not keen to encounter Salty Sammy just yet.

'At least the pressure is off for me to return the money I owe him since he doesn't need to buy another boat now.' he thought and wondered also what had become of Silas's body. Swept a long way away he hoped.

* * * * * * *

Stumblebum was not the only one interested in the whereabouts of Silas Suggs, although he was the only person so far to know of his tragic demise. After returning to the academy on the Friday of that week he heard someone mention that Silas had not been in also, though not many novices could care less if he stayed away indefinitely. Stumblebum tried to put the matter out of his mind as he got on with some defensive spell practice during most of the day.

As he left for home he failed to notice that Slippery Jack lurked about in a shop doorway and closely watched the wizards leave the academy for the day. Slippery continued his surveillance until the last wizard had left before he made his way back to Mordecai Manor deep in thought. He joined his mentor, the sorcerer Mordecai, in the study and discussed this mystery with him.

'It's a bit strange! I've spent the last couple of days watching the academy and there has been no sign of Silas. I reckon he has done a runner with our book but it won't do him any good without the last chapter. You just can't seem to trust some folks!'

'I had a visitor whilst you were out today.' Mordecai informed Slippery.

'The mayor came here to see if Silas had approached us at all. It would seem that the two of them had retrieved the book from the academy library and were going to attempt the alchemy themselves. Anyway, it looks as if Silas has taken off on his own for some reason, but strangely enough left the book behind with his uncle.' Slippery raised his eyebrows in surprise at this information as Mordecai continued.

'The upshot is that the mayor wants to cut a deal with us! He says he will bring the book to us if we will agree to help him to make some gold!' Mordecai gave an enigmatic smile.

Slippery laughed loudly at this, amused by the transparency of the grasping mayor.

'Well, this has worked out better than we had hoped for, so how shall we play this then?'

'I think our eminent mayor's own greed will be his downfall in this matter. Just leave him to make all of the moves and we shall lure him into our little trap! How about a goblet of wine Slippery, to celebrate?' Mordecai filled two goblets to the brim from a crystal decanter and handed one of them to Slippery as the two men continued to plot.

Several goblets of wine later and the conversation turned to the matter of the town coven witches, Mordecai's arch enemies and the focus of much of his skulduggery.

'So what have you heard of our sisters of the five covens recently Slippery, they seem to have been somewhat inactive since our intervention of their wicker man ceremony?'

'Not a lot' Slippery replied, 'but I shall keep my ear to the ground and find out what's what. The winter solstice is not far away and they usually do something to mark that occasion. I shall see what I can find out.'

'Good, good! We must keep them on their toes or they might start to believe they are immune to our little entertainments Slippery, and that will not do at all will it?'

Slippery sniggered at this as he sipped at his wine and wondered what new evil Mordecai might have in mind this time to surprise the witches with. Both sorcerers drank their wine and continued to plan and plot as the evening wore on, punctuated with many sniggers and much hearty laughter as details were worked out. The dark night wore on and dark deeds plotted.

* * * * * * *

On the following Sunday Stumblebum went up to the Ramsbottom's as usual for his lunch and spent an enjoyable afternoon as they chatted and listened to Roly's anecdotes and reminiscences as he puffed away on his pipe. At a break in the conversation he enquired as to how the sale of the parchment pages of pentagrams was progressing.

'Ah, I wondered when you would ask me about that.' Ramsbottom shot a sly glance at Freda and then gave Stumblebum a benevolent smile.

'We went down to the moot at the *Smugglers* earlier in the week and I told the others about your little treasure. We all had a whip round to pay for it you will be pleased to know. I've kept the money in a safe place for you. Freda will get it in a while.'

Ramsbottom blew several impressive smoke rings into the air above him as he went on with a smug, self-important expression on his face.

'Calvin Pendragon, the "King of the Witches" no less, is very interested in these ancient pentagrams and the instructions which accompany them. He has agreed to join forces with us and a good few others from our moot and combine our knowledge to make some enchanted gold for us to share.' Ramsbottom paused as he allowed this information to sink in whilst he also took a long draught on his pipe.

'Of course many factors have to be in place for operations of this nature to be successful.' he continued, as he adopted the mannerism of a great sage about to impart ancient wisdom.

'Fortunately our house here is located exactly on top of a powerful ley line, which is why it has survived the demolition onslaught by the corporation. This is a perfect place to attempt the transmutation magic, with the help of our pagan spirits and nature gods, so it has been decided to hold a moot here when the time is right for the ritual.' More smoke rings wafted through the air as Ramsbottom savoured the moment of revelation to his young tyro.

Stumblebum had a feeling that he had been done somewhere along the line but at least he had some money due out of the transaction.

'So when are you going to do it then? The transmutation I mean, will it be soon?'

Ramsbottom chuckled knowingly and glanced at Freda as he replied.

'This is where my years of expertise in these matters comes in lad. You can't just do magic like this at any old time you know. The planets must be in the correct alignment and have to correspond to the proper phase of the moon. Of course, with my expert knowledge of these matters I can work out when that will be with some accuracy. Once I have an accurate day worked out I shall arrange for the moot to gather here and we shall hold the ceremony in the back yard under the auspices of the moon.'

Ramsbottom leaned forward in his seat and tapped his spent pipe bowl out into the fireplace before he refilled it again.

'When will that be then, and can I come too?' Stumblebum pleaded.

'Of course you can join us dear boy, it will be an education for you to see how our old religion method differs from the more formal academy magic. It won't be for some time though, by my rough calculations. I will let you know when I have worked out exactly the best time for it to take place. You will enjoy being with us then, prepare to be amazed!'

Freda went in to the kitchen to make some tea for them all, and returned after a few minutes with the three mugs on a tray.

'Whilst you are on your feet Freda fetch the sacred cauldron over here to show to the lad, he won't have ever seen such a rare artefact as this before. Just take care when you pick it up though, it needs to be handled with reverence!'

Freda went over to a corner of the cluttered little room and gently lifted an old iron pot with a hinged handle on top and with three talon shaped feet on its base, the sort of vessel usually associated with the three witches in Shakespeare's *Macbeth*. She brought it over to her husband who took it from her with great care and showed it to Stumblebum.

'This…' he said with solemn emphasis, '… is the very cauldron that once belonged to Dr John Dee, soothsayer and astronomer to Queen Elizabeth the first. She never made a move unless she had consulted Dr Dee first!'

Stumblebum said 'Oh!' and looked a little bewildered.

'You've never heard of John Dee? A very famous alchemist and wizard who advised royalty across Europe. This was his sacred cauldron which was an ancient artefact even when he was alive. It is believed to have belonged originally to a Celtic wizard of antiquity, possibly the great Merlin himself, so it needs to be treated with great respect. If you look inside you will see that I have placed your parchment pages in there to absorb the holy energy of the vessel. Oh, and your money is in there look, take it out carefully now.'

Stumblebum carefully reached inside the cauldron and removed a wad of banknotes which he pocketed, spirits lifted at the successful outcome to his business with Ramsbottom.

'You must know a lot of spells that we don't learn at the academy?' he enquired as Ramsbottom fiddled about with his pipe and refilled it with fresh tobacco.

'Look about you my lad.' he swept his arm about the room as he vaguely indicated the bookshelves crammed with many books on the occult.

‘I have a spell for just about any occasion a person might wish for should the need arise. Why the interest, is there a particular spell that you might need to do in the near future? I can advise you on a whole range of ancient pagan spells which are very effective so you just let me know if you need advice on anything.’ He relit his pipe and blew more smoke rings over Stumblebum’s head.

‘Well, there was just one thing,’ Stumblebum blushed as he stammered a little.

‘I have heard that some love spells can be quite effective, you know, spells to attract someone you like to you without their knowledge.’

Now Ramsbottom blushed brightly as he gave a furtive glance in the direction of Freda, before he turned again to Stumblebum and teased the lad with some relish.

‘Oh aye, oh aye, do you hear that Freda, the lad is smitten in love. So who is it then, one of those pretty lasses who were in the play you took us to, I’ll bet it is hey?’

‘No, no, I was just curious that’s all. Mind you I wouldn’t mind a try at it, just as an experiment in how to do the spell, should I ever need to give advice to anyone you see, it would add to my skills a good deal.’ Stumblebum said, a little lamely.

Ramsbottom and Freda teased him mercilessly for a while before he was given a book of love spells to borrow, and they insisted he come back for advice if he needed to do the spell.’

‘It’s very potent stuff so take care with it.’ He was cautioned as he left for home with the book of love spells tucked tightly under his arm as he waved goodbye to the Ramsbottom’s and headed off down the hill back to the Old Town in anticipation a successful outcome for his spell making at last.

* * * * * * *

That same evening in the little theatre in the Old Town rehearsals were being discussed for the forthcoming pantomime season, and specifically the planned production of *Aladdin*. Teapot was in a bit of a fluster as he cleared out Winifred's wigs from the cupboard they were stored in, ready to be returned to her, as she had requested. Morris was quick to see a chance and offered to do the task whilst Teapot got on with the more important work of his organisation of the arrangements for the new play.

'Whilst you are about it lovey, could you take Winifred's star off the door of the main dressing room, since she is determined to leave our little family.' Teapot instructed.

Morris took charge of sorting the wigs into a large bundle and then went over to the dressing room, which had a large star attached to it with the initials W.C. emblazoned in the centre and removed it from the door. Before he wrapped the bundle into a parcel he remembered his promise to Stumblebum and he selected one of the better wigs then stashed it under his own cape, which he had folded and placed on a chair at the back of the stage.

After the wigs had been sorted out the cast rummaged through the costumes to choose what they would be wearing in their respective roles. It had been decided that Morris would play the eponymous role of *Aladdin* with Teapot in drag as Widow Twanky as it was his turn this year now that Winifred was no longer in the frame.

'So what are we going to do for wigs once these have all been returned to Winifred?' Morris asked.

'Well lovey, we'll have to manage for now. Quentin and I do have some of our own personal wigs for when we play the ugly sisters *etcetera*, but you are right, we shall have to acquire a good many more. As soon as Christmas is over and the pantomime finished I will apply to the corporation for a grant towards the wigs and other props we need.'

'God bless the giant nurturing tittie of corporation funding,' Quentin put in, 'that particular bottomless pit has served our little theatre very well over the years. Long may it continue to replenish our coffers!'

'And what part will you play in this production Quentin?' Teapot asked as he adopted his usual stage production manager pose with his right hand high up on his hip like a handle whist his other hand held his clipboard high in front of his face, as was his wont!

'Something nice and demanding that I can get my teeth into lovey. Leave the new kids to get used to the starring roles this time, the experience will be good for them.'

Quentin eventually decided to choose the role of the wicked sorcerer and Mooning Mike agreed to play both of the genii. Since neither of the spirits would be on stage at the same time in this production Mooning Mike decided upon a cunning ruse to wear different coloured turbans for each part, along with a change of face fungus, which would be sufficient to fill both parts and fool the audience in the absence of the availability of more male actors.

It was still to be decided which of the two sisters was to take the part of the princess since either would be perfect in their costumes. Teapot promised to make a decision on this before too long and organised other parts with other members of the little theatre's regular troupe. Scripts were handed out and a rough schedule for rehearsals worked out before the excited actors left. It was on this high note that the two young wizards walked the sisters to a bistro bar where they took refreshments and chatted excitedly about their parts in the play.

'Well, here we are, Christmas almost upon us again!' Morris said as he carried his drink to the table with the others. 'I must say the involvement with the pantomime is quite a nice bit of light relief after all of the recent stress at the academy, what with all of the swotting for our upgrades recently.' Mooning Mike nodded in agreement and absently stroked where his black eye had been.

'It must be so good to be a wizard. I wish they would let us girls join, I think I would be ever so good at magic spells and stuff.' Brigitte said and smiled wistfully at the two young wizards.

'Well it has its ups and downs but on the whole it is pretty alright.' Morris replied. He took his hat off and placed it on the table to show it off to the girls.

'It looks a bit like a traffic cone!' Mandy observed now it was not perched on Morris's head.

'Yes, well, I think they stole the design from us when they first made traffic cones, but these wizards hats go back a long time, very traditional.' Morris informed her a little indignantly.

Both girls giggled at Morris at this and Mooning Mike also joined in with the amusement before Morris hastily changed the subject.

'Wait until you see me in my costume as *Aladdin* when we put on the panto then, I might have a really snazzy turban on with my costume. I can't wait 'till the opening night so that I can strut my stuff on stage again. Should be great.' The girls giggled some more at this.

'Do you have plans to do some of your stage magic tricks during the play Morris?' Mooning Mike enquired as the girls ribbed Morris about his planned performance.

'Oh, I might just bring a little sparkle to the procedure, if Teapot will allow it that is.'

'What do you plan to do Morris, tell us, it sounds so exiting?' Mandy asked eagerly.

'Oh, I have a few tricks up my sleeve you know. I shall surprise you with them on the night.'

'It must be so good to be able to do magic. It's not fair that we can't join the academy and learn some magic for ourselves.' Mandy said, a little wistfully.

'I know, if it was left to me you could join tomorrow but the stuffy old wizards stick rigidly to tradition so that's that. Why don't you join one of the Old Town covens and become a witch? They will teach you some types of magic. It's not as good as the magic we academy wizards do mind you but it would be a start for you.' Morris advised.

'Oh no,' Mandy looked appalled 'those fierce old women frighten the life out of me, they are so humourless too. I wouldn't want to be involved with them anytime, would you Brigitte?'

Brigitte shook her head in agreement with her sister.

‘No fear, they take themselves far too seriously for my liking. I want to have a bit of fun and a laugh when I do stuff, like now and at the little theatre.’

‘Well we shall see to it that you have some fun then! Stick with me and I will guarantee a good time. Come on then girls, we’ll walk you to the end of the road and get you both home safely before those nasty witches turn up to spoil things!’ Morris joked as they finished their sodas and got up to leave.

It was a merry little group who bade each other ‘goodnight’ as they parted company near to the girl’s house as they all anticipated the success of the play over the imminent festive season, a time of year that was heartily celebrated in the little town of Bilge on Sea. Over the next few weeks several plans were hatched in various parts of the town to put on a number of other unusual events to bring this year to a close, which promised to end with quite a bang!

Chapter Twenty

During the following weeks the Women's Centre became a hive of activity. As well as the classes and 'workshops' bringing their activities to a close for the year, various generously funded presentations and displays were to round off each group's year of 'achievements'. The five covens were about to plan their winter solstice spectacle also and the details were to be kept strictly under wraps until the last possible moment, after the lesson from the wicker man disaster they had suffered earlier that year.

The problem with this strategy was that little was ever planned in the Women's Centre without it being discussed over tea between 'workshops'. Not a lot got past Winifred Closet's attention, skilful gossip and busybody that she was, and when she overheard the witches' plans she listened, noted and digested the information.

Since there is little point to gossip unless it is passed on, Winifred went about town and gleefully discussed the witches' secret arrangements with as many acquaintances as possible 'in confidence' until there was hardly anyone in the town who didn't know about them in fine detail.

It was whilst Winifred took tea along with one such friend in a little café that she was overheard as she told her friend, in a hushed tone of voice, of her recent intelligence on the witches next big project. Slippery Jack was seated at a table in a corner behind Winifred's and held a newspaper in front of him in order not to be recognised. He took in all that was said as a big grin spread across his face. After the two women got up and left he put down the newspaper before he took out his notebook and hastily scribbled into it before he too got up and left.

As Slippery set off down the street he gave a joyful little leap into the air and clicked his heels together before he made his way back to Mordecai Manor with a spring in his step.

* * * * * * *

Upon his return to Mordecai Manor Slippery was surprised to see the town's mayor and town crier pushing a large hand cart down the drive with some exertion. The two sweaty characters looked up at his approach.

'Give us a hand Slippery, we've been struggling for hours to get here with this lot!'

Slippery glanced at the laden cart and sniggered as he ignored the request and went up to the front door of the mansion and rapped on it with the iron knocker. When Mordecai opened the door he stepped out and surveyed the little scene on his driveway and grinned at Slippery before he spoke.

'What's all this then Mr Mayor? I am not running a rag and bone yard you know.'

'Its lead, for making into gold. I can't keep it in my shed for much longer I thought perhaps that you could store it here until we turn it in to gold.'

Mordecai shook his head solemnly as he looked at the contents of the cart.

'That's a lot of lead, how much gold did you want to make?'

'As much as possible, you can do it can't you? I have got the book you want here with me.' The mayor held up the ancient tome and offered it to Mordecai who eagerly took it from him as he exchanged a quick glance with Slippery.

‘The deal I made was with Silas as you know. He said he would get this book for me in return for my making gold for him. Where is Silas, by the way, hasn’t he turned up yet?’ Mordecai was curious.

‘He seems to have cleared off for some reason, nobody has seen him for ages. That’s why I decided to close the deal with you since he had left the book with me.’ The mayor replied.

‘O.K, I’ll show you were you can stash the lead for now, in the cellars, but you will need some other ingredients for this alchemy, it is a very precise science.’ Mordecai set his trap!

‘I thought you just needed the lead! What else shall we have to get then and how soon can we get on with making the gold?’ The mayor was beside himself with impatience.

‘As soon as you can get the other ingredients.’ Mordecai replied.

‘Well can’t you get them, after all I have provided the lead.’ The mayor complained.

‘The deal was that I would make your gold for you and you would get the stuff for it but if you don’t want to go ahead…’ Mordecai trailed off as he pocketed the little book.

‘No, no, you tell me what’s needed and I will get it. Are you sure you can make the gold for me?’

‘Oh yes, but you have to get some special items for it. You will need some sulphur, some mercury, some saffron and a few other spices and some platinum. They will have to be in specific proportions to the lead and we can go ahead with it after Christmas when you have brought it all to me. We can do the alchemy in my cellars where you can take the lead now. Slippery will point out how you can get there and I will go and work out the quantities of the other ingredients we need for you before you leave.’

Slippery led the way to the door to the cellars and left the two to hump the lead down there on their own. They took a number of trips before they finally emerged, hot, sweaty and panting as Mordecai gave them a list of items and their quantities and weights as needed for the alchemy.

'Just bring it all up here when you have it and we shall turn it into gold for you.' Mordecai said as they left with the list and he then turned towards Slippery and gave a little smirk before they went back indoors.

'Game, set and match I think Slippery. Let's go and have some wine to celebrate shall we?' Both men laughed deliriously as soon as the door was closed and headed for Mordecai's study and the goblets of wine.

* * * * * * *

One of the last 'workshops' to take place at the Women's Centre before the Christmas break was a health and beauty seminar which offered advice to women 'of a certain age' on how best to deal with the ravages of time. Winifred made an appearance in order to 'pass on some tips to acquaintances less fortunate than me regarding their looks.'

Several speakers took turns to offer advice on which fillers would be the most effective for wrinkles and how best to disguise saggy bosoms and other extremities. Another speaker talked at length about hair care and explained how years of dyes, perms and other follicle enhancing strategies would often leave a woman's hair limp, lifeless and without body.

'Most ladies hair by the time that they have reached a more mature phase of their life has usually had damage inflicted which is beyond repair!' She advised.

'It is a good idea to give up the long hairstyles of our youth and adopt a much shorter, easily managed style of hair more befitting of the older lady.' She went on as Winifred squirmed uncomfortably on her chair.

It was a disappointed Winifred who left the 'workshop' and discussed how 'some women fare very badly over the years with regards their looks, poor things.' over tea as she chatted with some of the witches from another 'workshop' being held in the Women's Centre at the same time.

'That's one of the advantages of being in our covens. We don't tend to age the same way as ordinary folk do. Look at Meryl our high priestess! No one would guess the age she was at all but of course we all take part in certain rituals which guarantee our appearance remains youthful well into late middle age.' One of the witches told her.

Winifred's eyebrows arched upwards as she took in this information and remained arched for some time as she mulled over the implications this could have for her situation.

'You know, I have always been interested in witchcraft but have been too busy with other projects to ever get involved with the covens. Now that I have more time on my hands since I gave up my theatrical career recently I wouldn't mind joining one of the covens. Is that possible do you think?'

'We are always happy to welcome new sisters to our cause. You would have to go through an initiation ceremony though first. If you make an approach soon and apply to join you might just make it for the "Fountain of Youth" ritual and be able to be initiated then.'

'The Fountain of Youth ritual?' Winifred's eyebrows arched even higher at this.

'Yes, you must have heard us talk about the winter solstice ceremony we shall have on the beach this year, only keep it under your hat. It shall be devoted to our ancient "Fountain of Youth" ritual this year since we shall be on the beach by the sea which is ideal for both events. If you are lucky you will be able to take part and be initiated then. Go and have a word with Meryl, I am sure she will agree to it.'

Winifred, driven by her own misplaced vanity, did indeed seek out Meryl, the high priestess, and enquired if she could join one of the town covens before Christmas.

'We shall have a ceremony on the beach soon, if you can make it, where we can accept new initiates. We shall all meet in the evening here in the Women's Centre before we go down to the edge of the sea beyond the beach under the cliffs. You must not breathe a word of this to anyone you understand? It is a closely guarded secret.' Meryl cautioned, little knowing that Winifred had already broadcast the minutiae of the event all over the town.

Winifred got home that night pleased with this outcome and she looked forward to her initiation into the sisterhood of witches since this was yet another platform where she could become the centre of attention and hopefully soon be in a position of influence.

If the 'Fountain of Youth' ritual was all that it seemed to be cracked up to be then she would also soon be able to return to the little theatre in triumph to reclaim her rightful place from the new upstart girls Quentin had brought in. No longer would she have to rely on her wigs to get the lead roles in the plays as her newfound healthy locks of hair would astound Teapot and Quentin who would beg her to return to the *Little Theatre*. Her position as the leading star of the theatrical society would be justly restored.

* * * * * * *

Around this time, shortly before the night of the solstice, Stumblebum had several visitors call in on him at home. The first was Morris who brought him the wig he had filched from Winifred's pile at the theatre and took it up to Stumblebum in his room after having a brief chat with Auntie Maggie in the kitchen over a cup of tea and some cakes. The wig was black and long, with a fringe, having been used in a past production of *Anthony and Cleopatra*. Stumblebum scrutinised it and complained it was far too long.

'Not a problem, we'll just have to trim it down with some scissors. Have you got any?' Morris said.

'Yes there's a pair in the bathroom. I'll go and get them.'

Stumblebum returned with the scissors and the two lads went about the procedure to shorten the wig. After a good deal of snipping and clipping the two of them eventually got it as good as they could and Stumblebum tried it on. It wasn't a bad fit and Morris remarked that it made him look like Richard the Third which Stumblebum took as a compliment. He then carefully stored it where Skipper would not be able to find it, after he remembered the disaster with his other wig.

A short time after Morris had left Auntie Maggie called up the stairs to tell her nephew that Violet Veronica was at the front door asking to see him. It was with a little apprehension on hearing this message that he went down to see what the wretched child wanted, though he had an idea what it might be about.

Sure enough, after he found Violet Veronica waiting impatiently on the doorstep, he was informed that she had been sent round by Salty Sammy to ask for the return of his deposit for the curse removal fee.

'Well his boat has returned to him you know and is now curse free thanks to me.' He said.

'I know it came back and that was so awesome how it was found but Uncle Sammy says that he has lost a lot of time when he could have been out fishing so you should return the money and he will leave it at that.' Violet Veronica was very persistent so Stumblebum went back upstairs and got the money from where he had stashed it and reluctantly handed it over.

'Awesome! Now he might stop moaning about you all the time.' She said brightly as she skipped off with the money and took it back to Salty Sammy.

Despite this little setback, as Stumblebum had hoped to keep most of the money which Ramsbottom had recently given to him, he was nonetheless in a fairly good mood after Violet Veronica had left. His wig had arrived as promised and in time for his parents Christmas visit so he now could focus on a more pressing matter.

He had been studying the book of love spells and potions that Ramsbottom had lent him and had selected a spell which he thought would suffice in his attempt to become the object of Brigitte's affections.

The spell had to be done under specific conditions and the imminent winter solstice was an ideal time to perform this spell as the celestial configurations would be perfect for a good outcome. The charm would then take about a month or so to manifest a result as he would have to chant a short spell every night at midnight for forty nights in order for it to work. He now made his preparations for this pagan love magic with optimism and hope.

* * * * * * *

The much awaited winter solstice arrived several days before Christmas and two events were about to take place on two different beaches in Bilge on Sea at around the same time. A more sinister event was also under way in the gloomy cellars of Mordecai Manor as the sorcerer and his acolyte, Slippery Jack, conducted an evil black magic ceremony.

The pre-Christmas excitement also permeated the rest of the town as little gatherings got under way such as the hearty group of merry fishermen in *The Captain Barnaby*, all of whom swilled ale and cider like there was no tomorrow, and the moot of pagans, freelance witches, wiccans and their ilk celebrated the winter solstice with their king, Calvin Pendragon, by drinking enormous volumes of alcohol in *The Smugglers Rest*.

On the quiet little beach outside Stumblebum's house under the silver light of the crisp winter moon the young wizard lit four green candles positioned in the pebbles on the beach before he invoked his love spell and chanted for the spirits to '*guide my beloved to me soon and with passion*' as the book from Ramsbottom had instructed. He continued with the spell for some time, repeating the chant to the night sky in the hope that it would bring success in his attempt to attract the lovely Brigitte to him.

As this private little ceremony took place another much larger, also secret, ceremony got under way on the beach at the far end of the Old Town beyond the fishing beach. The witches of the five covens, along with their newest initiate, Winifred Closet, had removed their clothes and had waded in to the cold winter sea up to their waists as they too chanted secret incantations.

This was the Fountain of Youth ceremony, combined with the winter solstice ritual and Winifred's inauguration into one of the covens. As the witches chanted their magic spell the choppy cold waves rose up several metres high in a column and cascaded like a fountain of spray over the half immersed witches.

Two witches led Winifred by her hands into the sea in front of Meryl, their high priestess, as she commanded the spirits of the sea to purify the new initiate and allow her entry into the sisterhood of covens. As she said the words Winifred was immersed fully under the waves in front of the Fountain of Youth. Winifred stayed under for as long as she could in the hope of maximising the beautifying effects of the magic fountain. When she could not hold her breath any longer she pushed up to the surface gasping for breath and looked around for her sisters of the covens.

Unfortunately, whilst Winifred had prolonged her baptismal immersion under the waves, events on the surface had gone somewhat awry. The plume of seawater forming the magic Fountain of Youth suddenly boiled, hissed and steamed, to the bewilderment of the witches. The fire demon Groth stepped out from its centre spewing steam from his mouth, his entire body both smoking and steaming as the enraged demon stepped forward and cursed Mordecai for making him get wet and appear in his least favourite firmament.

As Groth shook the drops of water from his hissing, steaming body and wings he suddenly burst into a furnace of flames and the terrified witches, in a repeat of the wicker man incident, screamed, wailed and ran across the pebbles towards the tarmac road leaving Winifred to fend for herself as she surfaced, oblivious to this development. As she wondered as to why everyone had run away something made her slowly turn around. Groth looked down angrily at Winifred and gave a deep rumbling snarl followed by pouthers of black smoke from his cavernous mouth as she almost fainted with shock.

A minute later she furiously raced across the pebbled beach after the witches and screamed frantically. Groth watched her flat shapeless old bottom as it retreated across the beach and shook his head in disbelief before belching a long plume of flames to singe it out of pure demonic spite. Winifred screamed wildly as she caught up with the others. They all thundered past the terrace of the *Captain Barnaby* and once again headed towards the Old Town in all of their naked glory.

The half-drunk fishermen all fell silent as they watched the naked witches yet again streak past the pub, and yet again old Salty Sammy had to go and have a lie down.

Meanwhile, back on the little beach Stumblebum put out the candles and gathered them up, feeling very satisfied with the spell before going back around the corner to go back indoors. As he walked away from the beach he failed to hear the small voice utter something as Violet Veronica stepped from out of her uncle's boat where she had quietly observed Stumblebum, unnoticed, as he did his love spell.

'Awesome!'

As he was about to open the door to his Auntie's house a strange yet somehow familiar noise assaulted his ears. When he turned to look for the source of the sound for the second time in that year he watched helplessly as the onslaught of naked witches barrelled into him and sent him and his candles flying into the air. After he eventually picked himself up from where he had landed on the cobbles he then sat shakily on his auntie's doorstep for a long time and again gibbered and babbled incoherently before he calmed down enough to go in and, like Salty Sammy, felt the need to have a good lie down.

Back in the cellars at Mordecai Manor the fire demon Groth complained bitterly to Mordecai about being sent to be manifest in the middle of a sea fountain and he was so miffed about this recent outrage he considered the withdrawal of his services on a permanent basis.

Mordecai eventually pacified the monster slightly with a promise to do some sorcery to bestow greater powers on Groth and also swore to never again send him anywhere near water. This settled him down a little before the now subdued but still rather disgruntled fire demon returned to his layer secreted somewhere deep inside of the earth.

Mordecai and Slippery stepped from the protective circle after Groth had departed and took off their ceremonial robes, tidied up the items they had placed inside the pentagram and went up to the study in order to gloat about their latest mischief and to drink many goblets of wine, in the spirit of the seasonal festivities which Bilge on Sea was currently in the grip of.

Chapter Twenty One

Shortly before Christmas, just after the solstice and a day or so before Stumblebum's parents were due to arrive for their visit, he was invited to a moot at *The Smugglers Rest* by Ramsbottom, before they were to attempt the pagan gold-magic at the Ramsbottom's house later that evening.

Stumblebum had looked forward to this event and now was keen to 'watch and learn', in the hope that he might reproduce the magic for himself in private. Although he had been paid for the pages he still felt that he had been cheated somewhere along the line so intended to remember the pagan's spells and make lots of gold for himself after Christmas.

He made his way to *The Smugglers Rest* with some anticipation early in the evening and upon his arrival was greeted by a hearty scene of pagans and other revellers in high spirits as they drank, joked and laughed in a merry party atmosphere. Stumblebum elbowed his way through the happy throng of drinkers to the group of pagans holding their moot at the tables near to the pub's log fire which was blazing merrily away in harmony with the occasion.

Ramsbottom called him over to sit at his table and Freda went to get a coke for the lad from the bar. He soon became caught up in the merriment as the moot collectively drank to their hearts content, until Ramsbottom reminded them of the business due to be undertaken in his backyard that night.

It was a boisterous group of pagans, witches and wiccans who clinked together numerous bottles of wine and staggered up the hill to Ramsbottom's little terraced house along with Stumblebum. They all gathered in the yard as Ramsbottom and Freda went upstairs to don their magicians' robes and hats in a theatrical display of importance.

Before it was time to bring out the parchment pages and the sacred cauldron from the living room, to be filled with faery gold, they all saluted the pagan gods and nature spirits as they tipped the first few drops of wine from the bottles on to the ground as a libation for the earth spirits. They passed the bottles around for each to make a toast in honour of the said spirits and then took a large swig before the bottle was passed on. The little yard was soon cluttered with empty wine bottles and the ceremony was no further from its commencement.

'We need to make more libations and the wine has run out! What are we to do now?' Calvin Pendragon asked with an emotional tremor of panic in his voice.

Ramsbottom gave one of his knowing chuckles.

'Don't worry Calvin I have everything taken care of, all is in hand, trust me. If you look in my shed you will find enough bottles of the latest batch of my special rhubarb wine which will do the job!'

Several pagans rushed to the shed and rummaged about inside it before whoops of joy emerged from within and they passed the bottles of wine out to the others.

'Hey man, what are all these big flagons on the top shelf full of? Are they booze as well?' Someone called out.

'Go very careful with those they are a special ancient recipe called Druids Delight. Very powerful and to be treated with great respect. Leave them there and we can have the odd sip if the rhubarb wine runs out.' Ramsbottom informed them as the pagans uncorked the bottles of rhubarb wine and passed them round for more libations to be made.

As the night wore on the gold making ceremony never really progressed any further than the libation-giving phase. The problem arose when the rhubarb wine also ran out and they started on the Druids Delight. Events quickly became extremely confused and hazy from then on.

As dawn arrived a scene of utter chaos could be seen in the Ramsbottom's backyard. Empty bottles and flagons littered the yard. Several pagans who were asleep amongst the debris lay there and shivered in the winter cold. The back door to the kitchen had been left wide open and indoors the scene of chaotic mayhem continued to be in evidence.

More pagans and empty bottles were laid about on the floor and the sounds of rasping snores, loud posterior eruptions and feeble groans indicated their various conditions as a result of the debauchery of the previous night. In the living room Ramsbottom was laid back asleep in his armchair with his mouth open and a chicken perched on his head. Having found the kitchen door open all of the chickens had come inside from the cold and most of them had roosted amongst the books on the bookshelves.

Stumblebum awoke in the other armchair, took in this strange scenario and looked around, a little foggy-headed. He observed the chaos and wondered for a moment where he was and what he was doing there.

At this moment the king of the witches, who had sprawled his large frame face down onto the sofa, attempted to roll onto his back in his sleep and rolled off the sofa completely and fell to the floor with a heavy whump. This caused Ramsbottom to jump in his armchair as he too opened his eyes and emerged from his drunken slumbers.

Ramsbottom blearily watched as Calvin got onto all fours and crawled along the floor. He watched him with a blurred, detached interest as Calvin's large body convulsed and shook, as if in a dream and none of this was actually to do with him. When he observed where Calvin was headed as he crawled along the carpet he suddenly snapped out of his trance and called out urgently as Calvin heaved and gypped violently and crawled onwards.

'No, no Calvin, not the sacred cauldron! Be careful, go outside if you want to be sick mate, don't do it in there, it's sacred!'

Ramsbottom's pleas fell on deaf ears as Calvin thrust his head inside the sacred object. A moment later loud retching sounds emerged from within, amplified by the acoustics of the vessel, followed by the unmistakable sound of a torrent of vomit as it splashed onto the contents of the sacred cauldron, the parchment pages, accompanied by pitiful groans.

'Oh no! No! No!' Ramsbottom wailed as the king of the witches continued to desecrate the ancient sacred artefact.

The already thick pungent atmosphere of the room was soon also permeated by the acid stench of second hand vomit which caused Stumblebum to also retch and gag. He put his hand over his mouth and staggered to the kitchen door which was still wide open and spewed the contents of his stomach outside and over the sleeping pagan who was laid across the doorway with an empty flagon clutched tightly to his bosom.

Since the unfortunate pagan continued to sleep Stumblebum felt that this would be a good time to make his way home so he wiped his mouth on the back of his sleeve and crept down the little hallway, retrieved his cape from its peg and sneaked out of the house without a goodbye or farewell to his host, who in any case was preoccupied with his attempt to extract the king of the witches' head from Merlin's sacred cauldron, without much success.

Stumblebum groggily made his way home in the early hours of that winter morning and noticed very little of his surroundings as he staggered through the Old Town. He failed to notice altogether the furtive character who dived into a shop doorway in order to avoid detection and who remained there until Stumblebum had passed by.

Had Stumblebum indeed noticed the furtive character he might also have observed that he attempted to hide a large object under his coat, with some difficulty. The object in question was the solid platinum mace of the corporation's official regalia, taken from its glass display case in the Town Hall by the mayor to be temporarily hidden in his shed before he could get it to Mordecai Manor, as it was the last of the 'ingredients' required by the sorcerer to make the gold he had promised to the mayor.

The now empty glass case in the Town Hall contained a note hastily scribbled by the mayor explaining that the mace had gone away to be cleaned and would be back in place after the Town Hall reopened after the long Christmas recess.

It would in any case be several weeks before the Town Hall reopened its doors after its prolonged seasonal holiday and Percival Suggs planned to have a replica made and replaced before then, paid for from out of the pile of gold he was due to come in to with the help of the sorcerers alchemy, so no one would be any the wiser.

He rubbed his hands together with satisfaction as he stashed the precious item in his shed after he had arrived home, unseen by anyone, before going indoors to dream about how he would spend his imminent riches on himself. Percival earnestly hoped that Silas would remain absent for enough time for him to have the gold safely in his own keeping.

'Silas will have to whistle for it if he thinks I am going to share my gold with him when he shows up!' the mayor thought, unaware that his nephew was no longer in a position to demand his share of the gold or anything else for that matter due to his recent sudden and violent end.

* * * * * * *

As Christmas loomed the day of Stumblebum's parents visit arrived. Stumblebum took great pains to fix his wig in place under his fez after which he asked his auntie not to reveal to his parents that it was in fact a wig.

'Well as you know dear I don't like to tell lies, particularly to my sister, but if the matter doesn't come up then I won't mention it. With luck they might not notice.' She reassured him.

Shortly after this conversation Stumblebum's mum and dad did arrive and as soon as the warm greetings were concluded his dad looked at him and fell about laughing.

‘What’s the lad done with his hair now? He looks just like Richard the Third!’

‘Oh don’t tease the boy. At least he has got some hair!’ his wife admonished, unaware of the inaccuracy of her statement.

Stumblebum’s dad had started to go bald around the time that the boy was born and attempted to conceal his follicular deficit by the removal of any hair he had left on his head by way of that strange strategy peculiar to most balding Englishmen, that of attempting to conceal their baldness by becoming even balder! The thinking seemed to be that if they shaved off any hair that remained no one would ever notice that they were in fact bald!

He also displayed a remarkable lack of good taste in his manner of dress. Like Stumblebum, he like to wear ridiculous baggy three-quarter length cargo pants, even in winter, with shapeless patch pockets everywhere, along with sandals worn with argyle socks and an oversized tee shirt which came to well below his waist. This gave him the strange appearance of having an unusually long torso above short bandy legs.

Christmas Day arrived and Auntie Maggie put on a sumptuous dinner which they all enjoyed and presents were exchanged as they sat around the table. Stumblebum was also quizzed by his mum and dad in detail about his progress at the academy.

‘We’re all very proud of you son. You are the first one in our family to ever go to college you know. We all tended to take whatever work was around at the time when I left school. I never thought we would have an accomplished wizard in the family.’

Stumblebum took this as a cue to boast about his powers and achievements, which he did at some length although he declined to demonstrate any magic for them as he adopted an air of mystery and importance.

‘We are not allowed to use our magic unless absolutely necessary.’ He told them with a look of authority on his face. ‘They are closely guarded secret skills and not to be used lightly.’

'And have you made any friends here in Bilge on Sea since you came to stay with Auntie Maggie? You never seemed to have many friends before. Your dad and I used to worry about that a lot.' His mum enquired.

'Oh yes, I've got tons of friends, some of them from the academy. A couple of them will be in the panto we're going to tomorrow, *Aladdin*, you will really enjoy it.' Stumblebum boasted.

'And how about girls! Have you got a girlfriend yet? Only your mum and I used to be worried about that side of things too. You were always such a loner and lasses didn't seem to like you. Come to think of it nobody seemed to like you as I remember.' His dad commented, much to Stumblebum's annoyance.

'Well I know lots of pretty girls, really beautiful girls, don't I Auntie? Tell them about Brigitte and Mandy and how lovely they are. They will be in the panto as well so you don't have to take my word for it, you'll see yourselves.'

'Oh yes, he has got some lovely friends now and they are all very nice, all politely mannered kids, you will like them if we get to meet them. How about some Christmas pudding anyone, there's plenty?'

Auntie Maggie skilfully changed the subject as Stumblebum's annoyance mounted at his father's comments and she wanted to keep the happy atmosphere alive. The pudding was served and even Skipper had a large portion put in his little dish which he scoffed with relish and everyone left the table full and contented, seasonal harmony successfully restored.

* * * * * * *

On Boxing Day Auntie Maggie, Stumblebum and his mum and dad set off to go to the little theatre to see the production of *Aladdin* as planned. Both Stumblebum and his dad reluctantly wore the knitted jumpers that his mum had made for them after some heated resistance. Stumblebum's jumper had a Santa emblazoned across the chest and his dad had a reindeer with a bright red nose, unintentionally mirroring his own bulbous facial feature.

Despite this humiliation Stumblebum nonetheless looked forward to the panto and to see his friends perform, particularly Brigitte and Mandy, whom he hoped would wear some exotic and alluring costumes for the occasion. He would not be disappointed!

After they had arrived at the theatre his little party found seats near to the front with a good view of the stage. Teapot walked on and introduced the pantomime to the audience and invited them to join in when appropriate to shout things like 'he's behind you!' and 'oh no it isn't!' and other traditional standard panto heckles.

Stumblebum's dad shouted 'Get on with it then!' in the spirit of the moment which caused Teapot to mince off stage and exit into the wings in something of a huff.

'Do behave dear,' his wife said, 'act your age!'

Stumblebum's dad fell into a deep sulk at this and remained moodily silent as the play got under way. He was now determined not to enjoy himself after his wife's admonishment and stubbornly remained in a massive huff.

The play was quite a success, enhanced by Morris's special magic effects, particularly when he repeated his flying carpet routine from his upgrade ceremony. Not only did he float about above the stage but just had to show off and do a couple of circuits around the auditorium, to the astonishment of the audience, who gasped at the obvious lack of supporting cables usual for this sort of theatrical display.

The little group were in fairly high spirits apart from Stumblebum's dad, who still stubbornly sulked, as they wended their way back to the house. Once inside they sat in the kitchen with a light supper as they discussed the evening's entertainment.

'I didn't see that dreadful Winifred Closet in the play dear, which is unusual, as she always used to hog the best roles for herself.' Auntie Maggie said to her nephew as she cleared the table. Stumblebum gave a faint disinterested grunt as a reply.

‘At least the kids put on a good show, particularly Morris with his magic carpet, and he looked so handsome in his Aladdin costume don’t you think?’ Stumblebum’s mum agreed with her sister as a big smile lit up her face.

‘Yes, I thought he looked quite a dish! If only I was twenty years younger!’ Both women chuckled at this whilst her husband and son both groaned.

‘Who is this Winifred whatsit then, is she a friend?’

‘Oh good grief no! She is a dreadful woman who used to attend my séances regularly. Until I sent her packing with a flea in her ear, that is.’

‘Good old Maggie you never change do you? You have never suffered fools or put up with any nonsense even when we were kids. Anyway, it has been an enjoyable evening and a lovely pantomime, with or without this Winifred person.’

* * * * * * *

Winifred Closet had not left her house at all since her traumatic experience on the beach with the witches and Groth. Nor did she intend to leave the security of her bungalow for a long, long time. Although she missed all of her previous activities in the town she now found her only outlet for gossip and recreation was when one of her friends and her husband came round some evenings and joined Winifred and Walter for a game of bridge.

It was on one such evening just after Christmas and whilst playing cards that the conversation turned to Stumblebum’s Auntie Maggie and her séances.

‘I haven’t seen you at any of Mystical Maggie’s séances recently. You used to attend quite regularly didn’t you? Don’t you believe in spiritualism anymore? She is very good at summoning spirits from the other side you know. At the last one we attended we had a manifestation of an American Chief who gave advice on several important matters. He kept repeating that if a pledge or promise was made it was the height of dishonour not to keep to it!'

'Oh no I can't be bothered with that woman anymore. We never really saw eye to eye on these matters. Personally I think she is highly overrated. I could probably make a better medium myself and hold much better séances!' Winifred replied with a certain amount of vitriol as she embellished her supposed skills, as she always did, in her misplaced belief in her own talents.

'Ok well why don't we then. We could have a go after the bridge is finished. It should be easy to set up. All we need is some paper and pens and an upturned tumbler on the table and the four of us will be enough to do it.' Winifred's friend suggested, goading her on to take centre stage yet again.

Before long the table was cleared of playing cards and replaced with scraps of paper with each of the letters of the alphabet written on them and also the numbers nought to nine. These were laid out in a circle along with a 'yes' and a 'no' indicator and a small glass tumbler placed in the centre.

The two couples sat around after the lights had been dimmed and placed their forefinger tips on the bottom of the upturned glass and concentrated for what seemed to be a very long time. Nothing happened.

'Perhaps one of us ought to ask a question first to see if there are any spirits about.' Winifred suggested.

'Good idea!' her friend replied before she addressed the upturned glass.

'Is there anybody there?' She asked. Nothing.

'Is there anybody there?' She repeated. Nothing.

'Keep trying.' Winifred urged, not wanting to appear foolish.

After a couple more requests the glass slowly glided across the table and indicated 'yes', as Winifred slyly pushed the glass, unnoticed by her friends.

She would have got away with it had Walter not decided to push the glass also in a mischievous attempt to teach his wife a lesson. The glass resisted Winifred's efforts to move it to where she wanted it to go and it seemed to her to take on its own life. It moved willy-nilly about the polished table and spelt out rude words, much to her embarrassment, in front of her friends.

'We seem to have attracted a malevolent spirit!' She exclaimed. 'We had better call a halt for tonight but we can try it again another night. I am sure that I could summon a more important spirit next time.' Her belief in her own competence as a medium was growing rapidly as she could see that here was another area where she could display her own perceived importance and an opportunity to show off in a central role.

As her friends left to go home she insisted that they should hold a séance regularly after they had played their games of bridge. She assured them that she would surprise them with her newfound skills as a medium and conjure up an important manifestation for advice from the 'other side'. Winifred's head was filling with delusions of grandeur yet again and she spent much time afterwards convincing herself of her special 'gift' for the occult.

Chapter Twenty Two

At Mordecai Manor the real occultists Tiberius Mordecai and Slippery Jack made preparations for the transmutation of the mayor's lead into gold prior to the due arrival of that scoundrel and his sidekick. As well as their usual symbolic items which they used in their rituals they had also placed a large screen covered in tinfoil inside the silver magic circle and pentagram which was embossed into the floor of the enormous cellars.

As they set this up the sound of several loud thuds resonated around the old mansion as the two visitors rapped impatiently on the solid oaken door with its heavy iron knocker.

Slippery went up and let them in and escorted them down to the cellars to where the mayor and the town crier had previously brought their lead. The lead and other 'ingredients' were where they had stored them in a corner away from the pentagram and near to a stone pillar. Mordecai called over to his two guests and urged them to enter the pentagram with him and Slippery for their protection during the ritual.

'I don't need to stand in your silly circle to be safe from your mumbo-jumbo. Just get on with the procedure and we can be done with it.' The mayor sneered irreverently.

'Suit yourselves.' Mordecai replied as he began his ceremony.

After some time a smoky whirlwind appeared near to the stone pillar and as it slowed its revolutions the huge fire demon Groth emerged and billowed smoke and flames, and as usual growled and snarled at the sight of Mordecai.

The town crier and mayor scurried into the circle and hid behind Mordecai as he sealed the circle off as protection from the demon. He then urged the others who were inside of the circle to stand behind the screen as a shield from the heat of the flames due to be made by Groth. From behind Groth there also stepped a grotesque squat muscular hobgoblin whom Groth introduced as Gungewort and explained he was his new assistant and would help with the transmutation.

Behind these two denizens of hell the billow of dark smoke cleared slightly to reveal an enormous crucible on a pivotal frame and stand like a huge inverted church bell with a handle either side of the pivot.

Groth and Gungewort made short work of filling the crucible with the lead and other items before Gungewort stepped back a few paces as Groth breathed a long plume of fire in the direction of the crucible and held it there steadily until the crucible glowed a dull red. The contents of the crucible boiled and bubbled and a metallic smell permeated the fetid air of the cellars whilst Mordecai chanted the mysterious incantations from Silas's book.

Groth ceased to breathe fire and stood to one side as Gungewort sprinkled sand on the floor so that the liquid gold would not stick to it and then both demon and hobgoblin took hold of a handle each and slowly tipped the contents of the huge crucible onto the stone floor.

The two sorcerers and their two guests stood silently inside the pentagram and watched as the procedure unfolded. As Groth and his assistant turned the crucible mouth towards the stone floor a surge of steam hissed and spat out before it dispersed as the others watched in anticipation.

Groth gave the crucible a sharp knock with his fist and a small gleaming nugget of gold about the size of a gobstopper tinkled out and clattered to a halt on the floor. The mayor looked at this for a long minute before he scrutinised the upturned crucible in expectation of more. No more gold emerged and the crucible clearly appeared to be empty.

'What's going on here Mordecai? Where's my gold then?' The mayor demanded.

Both sorcerers pointed at the little nugget by way of a reply.

'That's no good! What happened to all of that lead and the mace and all of the other stuff?'

'None of it was without a lot of cost you know. There must be more gold than that piddling little piece.' The mayor was now extremely enraged.

'Well Mr Mayor this sometimes happens. The point of alchemy is to show that scientific procedures can cause base metals to transmute into gold. The molecular structure of the metals involved sometimes change their volume due to the manner of the sub-atomic particles' interaction. On the whole this experiment is a major success. We have made gold from other stuff!'

'You mean you knew this might happen and you went ahead anyway? You have ruined me! I'll finish you for this outrage Mordecai, just see if I don't.'

'I told you I could make gold for you and I have. We never discussed quantities at all.'

The mayor took a step towards Mordecai with a look of menace in his eyes.

'Why don't you take it up with Groth over there? After all it was he who conducted the procedure.' Mordecai nodded towards the snarling demon.

This subdued the mayor who waited moodily until the demon and his hobgoblin helper had left before he stomped over to the gold nugget and picked it up with a look of disgust on his face. He then immediately left Mordecai manor without saying anything further, followed by the town crier. They both sat on the doorstep of the big house as the mayor turned the small gold nugget over and over in his fingers.

'Damn that Mordecai! We are in big trouble now over this, what with the lead from the roof and the mace, and the funds I had to dip into to get the other stuff. If I had known the price of mercury and saffron in the first place I wouldn't have bothered.' The mayor complained to his companion.

'What "we" is that then Percy? There is no "we" as far as I can see. YOU are on your own with this one buddy, leave me out of it. If anyone asks, I know nothing!' The town crier got up and walked off swiftly down the driveway to the gate with the mayor left sat on the doorstep as he fumed angrily. His mind tried in vain to work out the best course of action in order to avoid ruin but he could not think of a way out of this one other than perhaps to do a runner.

'Damn Silas for ever mentioning that blasted book! Damn him to hell!'

Indoors Mordecai and Slippery were in the study drinking goblets of wine as they gloated over what for them had been a very successful outcome. They raised their goblets and toasted the recklessness of the mayor for trusting them and his stupidity to expect a good outcome from them over this, or for that matter, over anything to do with Tiberius Mordecai and Slippery Jack.

* * * * * * *

Several days after the alchemy at Mordecai Manor the remains of Silas Suggs were recovered having washed up a long way down the coast and it took the police some time to identify him. At about this same time the mayor, Percival Suggs, disappeared, so the police put two and two together and decided that foul play had been afoot in Bilge on Sea.

Stumblebum went into town to buy some more candles so that he could conclude the last of his forty-night love spells and it was whilst out shopping that he called into the *Beverage Bliss* for a coke. He was delighted to see Brigitte and Mandy in there having refreshments as well so he joined them at their table.

As Stumblebum approached the sisters Brigitte hastily stuffed an envelope into her handbag before he could read what she had written on it.

‘Hi girls. What have you got there Brigitte?’ He asked brightly.

Both girls giggled and exchanged cheeky glances with each other.

‘It’s a valentine card but no one is supposed to know who sent it. They are supposed to be anonymous so the intended has to guess who it’s from.’ Mandy explained. ‘It might be for someone you know so we mustn’t let you see it.’

‘Oh, go on, let’s have a look!’ Stumblebum was intrigued.

‘No!’ both girls were adamant and Brigitte pulled her bag closer to her.

‘We were on our way to the post office to get a stamp for it but it’s forecast rain this afternoon and by the looks of that sky we had better get home soon instead or we will be caught up in it. I shall have to deliver it by hand tomorrow.’ Brigitte observed as she and her sister got up to leave, and as usual each girl gave Stumblebum an affectionate farewell kiss on his cheek.

Stumblebum sat there and finished his coke with a light fluttering heart before he also glanced out of the window at the sky and decided he ought to get home too before the heavens opened, so off he went as he wondered if the valentine was for him. After all, she often kissed him these days.

‘I bet it is for me!’ he mused.

Stumblebum had just got home himself when the sky did indeed discharge its rain heavily until it became a deluge. It had not rained like this since well before Christmas and now it was as if the sky could hold on to its burden of precipitation no longer, so it rained and rained and rained, well into the night.

* * * * * * *

In the grand debating chamber of the Town Hall an extraordinary emergency meeting of the corporation’s finance committee took place. In the street outside of the Town Hall as the meeting began it rained with a vengeance. The rain poured down in bucket loads and splashed off the cobbled road as it fell to earth like a monsoon.

Inside the grand debating chamber it also rained with a vengeance! Some of the councillors who had brought umbrellas hastily raised them despite the superstitious advice against such action indoors and those without umbrellas sat dejectedly as rain teemed down over their heads and made the notepads on the table in front of them become soggy.

The corporation's treasurer Albert Trough apologised to the assembled councillors for the haste in convening the meeting. He also apologised for the damp conditions in the chamber. He then went on to declare the meeting open.

'I have called you all here because a crisis has come to light which requires our urgent attention. Our honourable mayor seems to have disappeared, and in suspicious circumstances.' A gasp of disbelief went around the room.

'It first came to my attention when I had a visit from the police enquiring as to the whereabouts of our leading citizen. It would seem that the police would like to talk to him concerning the violent death and disappearance of his nephew who's body turned up recently, washed up below the cliffs several miles away.'

A further gasp went around the chamber.

'They believe that foul play was afoot and that since the mayor has suddenly disappeared he might be implicated in some way.' The faces around the table all appeared to be shocked at this revelation.

'And it gets worse, far worse! After the police had gone I took it upon myself to check the state of the corporation's finances and was shocked to find huge discrepancies in them.' The treasurer paused before he delivered the death blow.

'In particular monies placed in an account to cover out of pocket expenses and the estimated cost of the planned working party visit to Rio de Janeiro had been withdrawn along with a substantial amount of other monies from other funds. And it all points to the mayor as the culprit. And I have to tell you that we have no option other than to cancel the said working party visit to Brazil.' A stunned silence followed this news.

A cry of 'No, not the trip to Rio! No! No! It can't be!' and cries of similar sentiments went up around the chamber. Some councillors broke down and sobbed loudly and uncontrollably as the implications sank in.

'Furthermore,' the Treasurer continued, 'the town is close to bankruptcy and some extreme measures will have to be made if we are to survive this storm. Severe cutbacks will need to be made to all but the most essential services. All local arts grants and financial support for local 'creative workshops' will have to be cut back entirely and any local organisations will have to look elsewhere for their financial support.'

One councillor asked if there could be some other explanation than the mayor's involvement in the absence of the funds.

'It all points to Percival Suggs. He removed the priceless mace on the pretext of having it cleaned, without committee approval I might add, and upon enquiries I made with all of the firms who specialise in this kind of cleaning I drew a blank. It looks more like Suggs has taken off with the mace for himself.'

'Perhaps there is another explanation, surely?' Someone asked hopefully.

'No, I am afraid not. After I had enquired about the mace I then attempted to get a refund on the air tickets that had been booked for our working party to Rio and found to my horror that the money for all but one of the tickets had been refunded into the account of Percival Suggs and the only ticket not refunded was Percival's own ticket!' He paused here for the information to sink in.

'After further checks with the airline it would appear that he has already flown to Rio, presumably along with the corporation's' money, including that from the refunded tickets. The police have been notified of this development I regret to inform you.'

'We have to now make a decision as to whether or not the funding for the printing and distribution of the 'Community Regeneration Arts

Project Press' magazine is to be withdrawn. Bear in mind before we put it to the vote that C.R.A.P.P. is a valuable 'unofficial' propaganda organ for the corporation and might be worth the expense of keeping, especially in these difficult times.'

And so it came to pass that the committee decided that all applications for grants in the near future were to be cancelled, with the exception of C.R.A.P.P., the covert unofficial mouthpiece of the Bilge on Sea Corporation.

* * * * * * *

Harry Grubdyke was riding the crest of a wave. His latest revue of the pantomime *Aladdin* had been so well received by the editorial board of the community arts magazine that they had decided to mention his article and use a photograph of the play on the front cover.

The picture showed Morris as Aladdin on stage with Brigitte, Mandy and Quentin in glorious colour. Both girls glowed in the picture and Mandy's long golden hair looked sumptuous as it gleamed in the stage lighting.

A copy found its way onto the doormat of Winifred Closet's bungalow and she seethed with envy as she picked it up and glanced at the image of the youthful girls in the picture. This put her in a foul mood for the rest of the day as she could not get the image of youth and beauty from her mind, a stark reminder to her of her own advanced years and fading of what little in the way of looks she had had in her own youth, and it was this loss of youth that rankled her the most.

'Why do you men pander to these young un's all the time, only I wouldn't mind there is nothing to them, not in the sense of the classic beauty that accompanies that natural poise of the more mature lady.' She complained to Walter as he gazed wistfully at the photograph of the two lovely girls.

Her mood became even worse when she read the Grubdyke column inside the paper where he lavished great praise on the skill of Teapot in casting such a pair of young beauties in the play. In particular Grubdyke banged on at some length about the young girls 'natural shiny bouncy hair making a refreshing change from jaded old women in dull lifeless wigs', an obvious dig at Winifred.

'She should have given me some biscuits!' He had thought as he had written the piece, enjoying the power that the pen endowed him with.

Winifred was livid after she had read the article and when her friends arrived for bridge later that evening she insisted that they got straight on with the séance in her hope that she might find some supernatural remedy for her loss of youth.

This time she actually managed to contact the 'other side' and with some style. As the tumbler moved around spelling what she thought at first to be nonsense a vapour of ectoplasm manifest above the small group around the table and slowly materialised into not one but two spirits.

Both couples were momentarily startled and astonished by this unexpected development and Winifred was the first to pull herself together.

'Welcome to our circle oh spirits, guide us with your wisdom.' She intoned theatrically.

The two spirits, identical Chinese gentlemen in ancient looking garments bowed together with beaming smiles on their ethereal faces.

'Your wish is our command. We are the Ho brothers, Ho-Ho and Yo-Ho, specialists in ancient herbal remedies lost in time from ancient China, and also experts in animal husbandry. How may we be of service?' They both beamed.

'Oh, did you say you were specialists in herbal remedies?' They both nodded.

'I don't suppose you know of any remedies that would restore a lady's former beauty, particularly to grow a lush, springy healthy head of hair, for instance?'

Winifred was driven by her desire to be the star of the little theatre again to the point of obsession.

The two spectres glanced at each other before they smiled widely and spoke to Winifred simultaneously.

'Funny you should say that ...'

* * * * * * *

The next day Stumblebum returned home to his auntie's after a rewarding day at the academy. He finally felt that he was getting somewhere with his studies and practice. Upon arriving home he found that there were two letters for him and his heart skipped a beat. One of the envelopes clearly contained a card and he felt sure that this must be the valentine card from Brigitte, particularly as it had been posted by hand as she said she would do the day before in the café.

As he was too embarrassed to open his card in front of Auntie Maggie he left both letters unopened until after tea before he took them up to his room with some trepidation. Although the heavy rain had eased during the previous night and the air had a winter freshness to it the sky outside Stumblebum's bedroom window had again become dark and gloomy and he was glad to be in the comfort of his warm cosy room.

He placed the hand delivered envelope on his windowsill as he opened the other and took out an official letter. It was from the academy to say that due to the recommendations of some of his tutors his name had been put forward to be included for the next upgrade ceremony subject to him passing some exams.

The letter went on to explain that the Academy Scribe in particular had noticed how much time Stumblebum had spent over his studies and taking notes in the library during the latter part of the year and the other senior wizards had accepted this commendation.

This was indeed an unexpected development and Stumblebum proudly took the parchment sign from his door and wrote on it '(grade 1- pending)' underneath 'Wizard' before he pinned it back onto his door. He then picked up his recently improved and empowered wand and waved it about in the air with a flourish. This sent sparks of golden magic energy everywhere and illuminated the ceiling. He then brought the mirror from the bathroom and posed in front of it with his wand and with his cloak and fez as he tried to look as important a wizard as he thought he had become. Self-belief is a wonderful thing!

As he removed his cloak and fez after he admired himself in the mirror the young wizard then took stock of his situation. He had come a long way since he had first enrolled at the academy and although he had suffered a few mishaps along the way, nonetheless he felt that he had arrived at a good level of proficiency as a wizard and his personal life now was on the up.

His thoughts turned to his desire for the lovely Brigitte and how friendly she was towards him these days. It would be wonderful if the love spell he had cast had worked as it ought to and she became besotted with him.

'A good catch for any girl.' he thought. 'Good old Ramsbottom and his book of pagan magic!' Eventually he remembered the valentine card and snapped out of his reverie and picked up the unopened envelope which he was sure was sent to him by his beloved Brigitte.

His excitement mounted as he opened the valentine card after he took it from its envelope in hope and expectation. His head now hummed slightly and pulsated as a green glow emitted at short intervals which cast an eerie light onto the beach below. Had he looked out of his window he would have seen Skipper illuminated as he busied himself on the floor of Salty Sammy's boat and ate some fish heads that the old sailor had left under the rear seat.

As expected, there was no signature on the card. Just a large heart drawn freehand with an arrow piercing it. At one side of the arrow was the initial 'S' whereas on the other side only a question mark. Just as Brigitte had hinted at! Stumblebum was cock-a-hoop and his head glowed and oscillated even faster.

Across the town Morris was also cock-a-hoop as he opened his valentine card and placed it in pride of place on his mantelpiece as he had a good idea as to whom his secret admirer was.

Back on the little beach, inside Salty Sammy's boat, Skipper regurgitated the contents of his stomach all over the rear seat of the *Violet Veronica* as he felt a bit queasy since the fish heads he had just gorged himself on seemed to be distinctly off.

He then washed his face before he jumped out of the boat and marched off along the beach and to some other nefarious secret feline mission. Had Stumblebum glanced out of his window at that moment he would have noticed Skipper, illuminated by the glow from Stumblebum's head, pick his way across a patch of exposed damp sand amongst the pebbles near to the water's edge. The cat left some paw prints across the large heart someone had drawn in the sand. An arrow pierced the centre of the heart with the initial S drawn at one end of the arrow and initials VV at the other end.

Had he looked closely he would have seen the waves gently lap over an inscription etched in the sand below the heart before they obliterated it as the waves washed back over it and ebbed away.

He would have seen briefly an inscription in large capital letters.

AWESOME.

The end.

Printed in Great Britain
by Amazon

81929533R10142